A Time For Memories

A Time For Memories

LYN BURGESS NEE LANGHORN

Library of Congress Control Number: 2014916941
ISBN: Hardcover   978-1-4990-8986-8
               Softcover   978-1-4990-8987-5
               eBook   978-1-4990-8988-2

This book was printed in the United States of America.

Rev. date: 09/19/2014

To order additional copies of this book, contact:
Xlibris LLC
0-800-056-3182
www.xlibrispublishing.co.uk
Orders@xlibrispublishing.co.uk
635324

Dedication

Hello, my name, as you know, is Lyn. I'm fifty-eight years old and a single mum of four. This is my first go at writing a book, or anything else. This has taken a good four years to write. I still live in Essex with my three dogs. I had spent a lot of my time with my aunt while growing up; hence, I would like to dedicate this in memory of her, Erica Wyeth, who was my mainstay as I grew up. She encouraged me in everything I had done, even writing this, even though she did not like romance novels (LOL). Sadly, she died in 2012, before I had finished writing this book. Just a week before she died, she asked me about my 'soppy book' as she called it, and I told her that it will come together soon. 'That's good. You know what, your mum (that would be June who had died twenty-two years earlier) would have loved it,' she said with a smile. June and Erica were sisters, very close sisters. I have decided to add June (my mum) to the dedication. I loved my mum dearly when I was growing up, but she passed away twenty-two years ago.

I miss you both very, very much. With all my love.
—Lyn

****

This book has come completely from
my head, heart, and soul.

One

It was a lovely day; the sun was bright and warm. Rosy was making her way to her job as a nurse at the local hospital where they had just promoted her to post of nursing sister, and with that came more responsibility. Suddenly, there was an all too familiar noise, breaking the wonderful peace of the day. A noise Rosy, her family, and everyone else had gotten used to, even though they dreaded that sound and what it stood for, and as a result, they hated it. The fear was written all over their faces. Although everyone tried to keep their morale up, it was the hand they had been dealt. It was no good panicking. Everyone just pulled together, coping with it the best they could. Although they expected it, it was for their own safety. Everyone realised that. It was World War II, and that noise was the air raid sirens. Rosy made her way to the nearest air raid shelter, hoping it would not make her late for work. As there was somewhere, to go first, it was the railway station she wasn't going to meet anyone in particular. Sadly though, it was to meet yet another Red Cross troop train; it was a task Rosy did not look forward to very much though it was a part of her job. These trains were came in three, four, sometimes five, times a week, carrying our men, who, very bravely, went to fight, in the hope of protecting us. They were all injured, or worse (the smell was always overwhelming). These men were shot down in their planes, torpedoed from their ships, or shot in action. Arriving at the shelter, Rosy found a seat and sat down to wait out the raid. Looking at her watch, Rosy realised it was a bit too early to get to the station, and her being there early wouldn't change anything. Sitting there, her thoughts started to wander back, as to why she took the decision to become a nurse. Yes, of course, it was to help sick and injured people, but mainly though because of one thing or, should I say, one person. His name was Derek. He signed up, before the beginning of the war, when he had finished his training, and he was stationed near her home town. Since then, Rosy had only seen him once. Rosy's mind went back to the day they met. With a bit of spare time, Rosy had decided to go for a walk in the park and feed the ducks with a little bit of stale bread her mum had kept for her. It was a Sunday, so there was no work. At that time, she worked in a clothes shop. It was so pleasant to be out in the open. The day was so like today, but not, if you know what I mean. It was warm and peaceful. That Sunday, Rosy was walking along, on the grass, admiring the beautiful flowers, which were so lovely. While she stepped off the grass and onto the path, her foot missed the edge. Poor Rosy went tumbling down and twisted her ankle. As Rosy sat there feeling rather embarrassed, not to say silly, and trying to compose herself, she heard someone's voice behind her. Rosy looked up and her heart skipped a beat. There, standing above her, looking down at her, was the most gorgeous pair of blue eyes Rosy had ever seen (Rosy was only eighteen then and there had not been that many). He was in uniform. Rosy then realised he was speaking to her; Rosy tried to rally herself. He was asking if she was OK or if he could help. Rosy was about to say, 'I think I'm OK. Just embarrassed.' But before she could say anything, a pair of strong arms lifted her off the ground easily and placed her onto the nearest bench, to where Rosy had been making her way to before falling.

He introduced himself. 'My name is Derek.' While he took a look at her ankle, he told her he was on a two-week leave from the RAF. Rosy said, 'Thank you' and placed her foot back to the ground gently. It was not too bad. 'My name is Rosy. I'm very pleased to meet you, Derek.'

'Well, I'm also very pleased to meet you too, lovely Rosy,' returned Derek.

They smiled shyly at each other. Rosy told Derek why she was in the park. She asked him if he would like to sit, joining her, on the bench.

'Thank you. I would love to as long as I'm not intruding. You see, I don't live locally. I've been stationed near here, since the war broke out. What makes things harder is that I don't make friends very easy.' Rosy smiled, 'That's funny. I don't either. I just have one friend. I also do have my family, Derek.'

'I do have one friend. We went to flight school together,' he said, quietly bowing his head. 'His name is Gilbert. He prefers to be called Gil.'

As they were talking, he pulled out a photograph from his wallet and handed it to her. It was of Derek; Rosy guessed the other young man leaning against an aeroplane was Gil.

As Rosy looked up at him, he whispered, 'Oh, but I do miss my family so, so much. Also, now I have just found out Gil is missing.' Rosy's feeling for him intensified, and feeling bold, she decided to tell him about the dance that was to be held that night, and she said, 'I wonder, Derek, if you would like to come with me.' Rosy stared at the ground. Derek lifted her chin; he could see her, and the poor little thing was blushing. Derek smiled, and then happily accepted. They sat talking for a while. When Rosy realised it was getting late, she said, 'Oh dear, I'd better get home. My parents were expecting me in time for dinner.' Then a thought occurred to her (she hoped he wouldn't think she was too forward, especially after inviting him to the dance). 'Would you like to join us for dinner, if of course you have nowhere else you need to be?' Derek again accepted gratefully; he worriedly asked if her parents would mind the extra mouth to feed, with all the shortages. Rosy replied that they would love to have a young man to spoil again, even if was for a short time, as her two brothers were away at war. 'It will make my parents very happy. I'm just their little girl,' she laughed and then continued, 'I don't make up for two very large boys. Oh, by the way, Derek, my parents' names are Eleanor and Albert.' They smiled at each other before setting off happily on their way to her home.

TWO

At home in Holly Mews, Rosy's mother was preparing dinner. While her father was sat reading the Sunday paper, like he always did, with his pipe in his mouth, enjoying it, he was trying to get used to fewer pipes a day now with the tobacco rationing. He said to his wife, 'Oh my, there has been quite a few boys missing, injured, or killed again this week, all nationalities, according to the paper.'

'Thank God, as long as it's not our Bert or Duncan,' came the relieved answer.

'Well, at least this time. Even though Duncan is missing, it doesn't mean he is one of the poor, unfortunate dead.' Eleanor sensed her husband was getting upset and decided it was time for a change of subject. 'I wonder where our Rosy has gone to.'

'Oh yes,' Albert said, 'it has been longer than she said.' Meanwhile, Rosy and Derek were still making their way home, still chatting. They slowed down a bit as Rosy's ankle was still quite sore and tender. Derek was telling her about his family – Mum Elizabeth, Dad James, Sister Frances, and Brother Jonathan. His sister, who was seventeen, was still in school, a private school, in her last term. Jonathan was in the Royal Navy, on an aircraft carrier somewhere in the Pacific Ocean. The family lived on a large country estate called Willow Farm that they had been left by James's parents. 'As both boys had joined up, our parents have their staff. They found they could also use army girls. That has helped a lot. They helped with all sorts of chores around the farm, mainly the more heavy work.' Finally, they arrived at the house. Rosy let them in with her key, and they made their way through, to the kitchen, where her parents were bound to be. Her mum called, 'Is that you, Rosy dear?'

'Yes, Mum, who else would it be?' she said, smiling.

'I have bought someone to meet you both.' They looked at each other, smiling. Rosy introduced them to Derek.

'Mum, is it all right if he stays for dinner?'

Both her parents spoke at once. 'Yes, of course, dear. That would be wonderful.'

Derek thanked them. 'Are you really sure it is all right, that it isn't putting you out?'

'No. We would love the company of a young man again. Bring this house to life a bit.'

Derek looked at Rosy, smiling, as that is exactly what Rosy had said they would say. Rosy went on to tell them how they met. That, of course, sent Eleanor into her mother-hen routine – making Rosy sit down and looking at her ankle to see if it may need a bandage just to support it a bit. Later on that afternoon, after the meal had been eaten, the clearing away, washing up, all done, Eleanor, told Albert to show them into the best room (the one Rosy's mother kept for special company). 'I'll make some tea for us all,' she said. After he had shown them into parlour, Rosy's after said, 'I'm just going to help your mother with the tray.'

'OK, Dad.'

They entered the room and sat down on the sofa to wait for her parents. They smiled shyly at each other, as they returned to the room. Her father gave a good loud cough. 'Oh, Albert, really?' Eleanor said, laughing as they went in. 'What an earth did you think they would be doing?'

When they looked at the couple sitting, one on each end of the sofa, Mum said, 'No, look, you have embarrassed them both.'

'Oh, Mum, that's fine. And no, Dad, well enough.' They all laughed together. Poor Albert! He felt really silly. Subject changed. Albert remarked on Derek's RAF uniform and asked him what he flew. 'Well, sir, I fly one of our big boys, a Lancaster. I have the honour of being a captain of the lovely lady. The crew have nicknamed her *Hope and Glory*. I am lucky, also to have a great crew of men. We all have nicknames. Mine is Rook. Gil's is Fish.' They laughed at that one.

'Rob is Gangly. Another is Winko,' Eleanor said. 'I have to ask why on earth, Winko.' Albert was laughing.

'I bet I know why he winks at all the girls.'

'Exactly right, Albert.'

'Good you called me Albert at last.'

'Then we have Bigfoot.'

'Why?'

'Because his feet are twice the size as anyone else's. Also there's Coffin.'

'Oh my goodness! How did the poor lad get that one?' Rosy asked.

'That's because his dad makes coffins,' Derek told them, laughing.

'Oh, there are so many different ones. Some funny, some weird.'

Anyway Albert, served the tea, and then said, 'I'm plying Mum today.'

'Oh, Dad that is awful and old,' Rosy said, looking at him and giggling.

Eleanor looked at Derek seriously and then said, 'Your family must be so proud of you, Derek.'

He replied, 'Yes, they are.'

Albert then told him about Rosy's brothers. Bert and Duncan. Bert was in the Middle East, fighting the Germans as a tank commander. He also slowly told him about Duncan, who was an army commando. 'He has gone missing out in the jungles of Malaysia. We found out he was missing back in November. It's June now. We still haven't heard anything more so far. That's the reason we are so glad to meet you.'

Derek went on to tell them about his brother, who was on an aircraft carrier in the Pacific somewhere. He then told them about the rest of his family. After a couple of hours of chatting, they asked, 'Where are you staying, Derek, while you're on leave?' Eleanor enquired.

He replied politely that he was staying in a hotel. Eleanor looked at Albert, 'He could stay here, couldn't he, Albert?'

'Yes, of course, my dear.'

He was so pleased that his wife had someone to spoil again even if it was only for a short time. He secretly hoped it would help keep her mind off their boys. Rosy was so pleased to see her parents smiling again.

'Mum, whose room should Derek stay in?' Rosy asked.

'Oh Duncan's, of course, my love. It is the biggest, darling.'

'OK, I will go air it, make up the bed, and put clean towels out.'

'It's OK, Rosy. I'd like to do it.'

'Are you sure?'

'Oh, yes.'

With that Eleanor excitedly hurried off, but just before she left the room, Rosy called, 'Mum, we are going to a dance tonight. At the local Red Cross hall. I am going to get ready as you are seeing to the room.'

'OK, Rosy. That's fine.'

'Is there enough water, Mum, for me to have bath and also wash my hair at the same time?'

'Yes, love, there should be plenty.'

With that, Eleanor disappeared before Rosy could thank her. Derek decided to take his leave. He stood, saying that he would use the time to go and fetch his belongings from the hotel. He wanted to be very sure that they didn't mind him staying, as they didn't really know him that well.

They said, 'Of course, we don't mind. We just hope that if it was one of our sons, someone would do the same for them.' They assured him again, saying they were looking forward to it. Off he went, with a smile, saying he would be back at six o'clock. After Derek left, Rosy went upstairs to wash her hair and then lay back, enjoying her bath. Her whole body was tingling and it dawned on her. *I think I maybe falling in love.* She just lay there thinking how lovely he was. Before Rosy knew it, it was five o'clock. She hurried out of the bath and then went back to her room to get dressed. Her ankle was still sore, so Rosy decided to strap it up again, hoping it would hold up for the evening. The decision on what to wear was already made – her favourite powder blue dress with white sandals. She also decided to put her beautiful, long flaxen hair up in her favourite style with a ribbon weaving through it so that it was at its best. Suddenly, Rosy heard her mother coming in. Rosy asked her, 'What do you think of Derek?'

Her mother replied, 'Both of us think he is a very handsome.' They smiled at each other. Rosy was blushing. 'Oh, Mum, although I do agree.' They smiled again.

'Your father and I also found him nice, kind, and, on top of that, polite. Do you think he is a bit homesick, Rosy? I'd say also a bit lonely.' Rosy said, 'Yes, he is. He has not made many friends yet as he has only been stationed down here for a short time. He flies Lancasters. His family lives too far away for him to be living there at the moment. Yes, of course, he is terribly homesick.' Rosy went on to tell her mother about his family and the estate. Her mother being very astute (like most mothers when it comes to their children) said to her daughter, 'You really like him, don't you, Rosy, my dear?' Rosy replied, still blushing, 'Mum, really, you are terrible. I have only just met him.'

'Well', her mother replied, 'that doesn't matter these days if you like him. You enjoy with him and then see what happens. With all that's going on in the world at the moment, you have to grab happiness where you can. Even a blind man can see that you're happy. Both of you will have our blessings because your father is happy as long as you're happy, you know that.'

All too soon it was six o'clock; as promised, Derek arrived right on time. Albert let him in, helped him with his things, and then showed him to his room that had been aired and the bed made up. When Rosy finally came downstairs, Derek was talking with her parents, 'Oh, Rosy love, you do look lovely,' her father said. Her mum agreed.

Derek just stood there with his mouth open, unable to speak; when he did find his voice, he said, 'Your parents are right, Rosy. You look beautiful.'

'You look very nice yourself, Derek,' she replied.

They said goodbye to her parents, saying they wouldn't be late and not to not to wait up for them.

'I've got my key, Mum,' said Rosy.

'All right, love. I'll leave some sandwiches with cocoa out for you both. We will say goodnight now,' her parents said.

'Shall we make a move?' Rosy asked Derek.

'OK, well, enjoy yourselves, you two.'

After kissing both off her parents on the cheek, Rosy and Derek left hand in hand, leaving her parents with big smiles on their faces, they were also holding hands.

Three

They had enjoyed the dance very much. Rosy had introduced Derek to her best friend Susan. Susan had said to Rosy, 'He is lovely. You are so lucky.'

There was lots of dancing, and there was even some American music playing. Rosy's ankle held up very well, surprisingly, with all the bouncing and jumping around they did. Then there was the slow romantic dancing, where he held her so tight it was a wonder she could breath. The walk home was good too; Derek offered to walk Susan home, as they had to pass by her home to get back to theirs, although it did mean going down a different street. Rosy didn't mind as it meant more time with him. Smiling to herself, as they were walking, Susan whispered, 'You don't mind, do you, Rosy?'

'No, Susan, much the opposite. It means I get longer time with him tonight.' They both giggled.

Derek who was walking slightly in front, turned, smiling, 'OK, you two, what's so funny?'

'Oh nothing you would be interested in.'

'OK, I believe you, but thousands wouldn't.' They all laughed at that, and the girls moved to him. Taking an arm each, they carried on, talking, laughing, and giggling. Fifteen minutes, or so, later, they arrived at Susan's home. After saying their goodbyes, Susan gave Derek a kiss on the cheek to say thank you for escorting her home.

'OK, bye for now, Susan.'

'Bye-bye, you two,' she said, leaning to over to Rosy to kiss her cheek, whispering in her ear, 'Enjoy, Rosy, enjoy.'

'You're as bad as my mum,' Rosy said, laughing.

'Now go, you two, and please be careful,' said Susan.

With that, they took their leave. Forty minutes later, they arrived home, and they went straight into the kitchen. There, as promised, was a plateful of sandwiches and a pan of cocoa, ready to heat up. They sat eating slowly, both enjoying each other's company so much that neither of them wanted the evening to end. All too soon, it was well past midnight, and they decided it was time to go up to bed. As they got up to go, Derek stopped, taking Rosy's face gently into his hands, and kissing her gently on the lips. It felt so right, even though they had only met a few hours ago. After the kiss, he asked her how her ankle was.

'It's hurting now,' she replied.

'Right, Miss Rosy, I want no arguments. What? Why? What? Oh no, put me down,' whispered Derek. They were laughing.

'Rosy, please stop wriggling. You don't want me to drop you, my dear, do you?'

'Oh, all right. I surrender to you, my dear.'

He got her into his arms, making certain she couldn't slip. Then he climbed the stairs as quietly as he could; the trouble was they were still giggling. As they reached her door, he pushed it open with his foot, walked in, and then carried her over to the bed. After Rosy had flicked the light on, he placed her gently down on to the bed. After he made sure Rosy was settled, he kissed her on the forehead, whispered, 'Good night, sweetheart.'

'Goodnight to you too, Derek, my love.'

The next morning, Derek was already up, eating his breakfast, when, finally, Rosy came into the kitchen. Her mother greeted her with a kiss. Albert had already left for work. Rosy and Derek greeted each other with a peck on the cheek. Eleanor had her back to them, but she was grinning widely.

Her mother asked, 'Well, you two love birds, what are you up today?' Rosy replied, 'I have to work, half day. Derek's has got a briefing this morning. I will be free about one o'clock.'

Derek suggested that he meet her from work, and then maybe they could go to the cinema.

Turning to Eleanor, he said, 'You are very welcome to join us if you would like.'

'Oh, Derek, that is a lovely gesture. To be honest, I don't think you two youngsters want an old fuddy-duddy, playing gooseberry.' They all laughed at that.

'OK, the invitation is still there if you change your mind.'

'Thank you, but I don't think I will.'

All too soon, the fortnight was coming to an end. Rosy felt so miserable, at the thought. On the last evening, Derek took her for a romantic meal at one of the best restaurants. Rosy took extra time on her appearance. When they arrived at the restaurant, the waiter had seated them and taken their order. Derek asked the waiter, whispering to him so Rosy couldn't hear, for a bottle of champagne, if they had any, and if not, the best wine they do have.

After the waiter left, he turned to Rosy. 'Now, darling Rosy, I'm all yours. I have something to ask you,' he went on. 'I know we haven't known each other very long, but with the war and all that's going on, I believe in living for the moment. Time is very precious, and it could also be short.' Rosy started to cry, and Derek looked at her, suddenly realising what Rosy might have been thinking. He stood, moved round to her, and pulled her into his arms. 'Oh, Rosy, my darling, please don't cry, Rosy,' he said tentatively, his head buried in her hair. 'I love you.'

She pushed him off her. He thought that he was going to be told to get lost. Rosy was shocked; she looked up into his lovely blue eyes and asked, 'Could you please repeat what you said?'

He was so relieved the built up tears rolled unchecked down his cheeks. 'Oh no, Derek, I'll never tell you to get lost.'

'Well, here goes,' he said, holding her hand. Derek, still holding her hand, knelt and looked up at her. 'I said I love you.'

'Oh, Derek', she cried, flinging her arms around his neck, 'oh, I love you too.'

'While you were at work, I went shopping,' said Derek. She sat back, listening to him, searching around in his pocket. 'I found this lovely quaint antique shop,' he continued. Now he had it in his hand, still in his pocket. 'I saw this, and I fell in love with it. I hope you love it as much as I do.' He gently placed the bag into her hand. Rosy took the small, red velvet drawstring bag, and when she looked inside, there she found an equally red box with gold writing on it. She pulled it out and proceeded to open it. There, inside it, Rosy found the most beautiful diamond and sapphire ring.

Derek went on, 'I hope you don't mind I talked to your parents this afternoon. Now I will ask you. Rosy, would you do me the honour of becoming my wife? Please marry me.' Rosy was silent for the longest time. Then she finally said, 'Oh, Derek, I love you too. The ring is wonderful. Yes, of course, I will marry you.'

'Oh, thank goodness. When you went so quiet, I thought you were going to say no,' Derek said.

Everyone in the restaurant cheered, many coming over to congratulate them. When the waiter bought the champagne, the manager was with him, and first, he congratulated them and he then said, 'The champagne is on the house. I have bought you two bottles.' Neither Rosy nor Derek knew what to say.

When Rosy found her voice, she said, 'We would like everyone here to celebrate with a glass of champagne.'

When everyone had a glass, they all toasted to the happy couple. When it calmed down, they sat talking as they ate their meal. They decided to get married during his next leave, which would be his last one before going into action. That was about eight weeks away, in early September. Her parents were over the moon for them.

Four

After Derek had left, Rosy and her mother started making plans. There was so much to do, in such a short time and there were many shortages. Although there was one thing shortages could touch and that was the one thing Eleanor took great pleasure in giving Rosy – her wedding gown. One morning, Eleanor grabbed Rosy's hand and said, 'You come with me, young lady.'

'What? Where are we going?' Rosy asked, looking at her dad.

'No good looking at me, honey. I'd say one of two things, Rosy. Either your mother has gone stark raving bonkers or there is something she desperately wants to show you. I do hope it's the second.' They both laughed just as Rosy was pulled around the corner.

Albert lifted his paper up again, exclaiming, with a smile, 'Women! I don't think I'll ever understand them. Not sure I want to.'

'Mum, Mum, slow down a moment. Where are you dragging me to?' Rosy asked her mum.

'You just wait and see.' They went upstairs and then headed into her parents' room, not a room Rosy got to go into very often in order to give her parents some privacy. Anyway, there they were in the inner sanctum, and Rosy thought with a giggle, *OK, Mrs mysterious, now what?*

Eleanor looked at her daughter, giving her the brightest and clearest smile Rosy had ever seen her mum give. Even her eyes lit up. 'OK, miss smarty pants, why would you say we are here?'

'I really don't know, Mum.' They both giggled.

'Oh, my darling daughter, what we are doing or I'm doing is the one thing I and only I alone can do for my beautiful daughter. Now,

Rosy, go open the cupboard.' Rosy did exactly what her mum asked her to. Rosy knew the door opened to a walk-in cupboard.

Then her mum said, 'Put the light on, honey.' Again, Rosy did as mum said. When the light came on, what Rosy saw really surprised her. There, in front of her, was a spiral staircase. They both climbed up, and when they got to top, it opened into a room.

'Rosy, my love, see that chest over there. Go open it.' Rosy went over, tentatively opening it. There, wrapped in pretty tissue paper was what looked like a dress. Rosy, very gently, pulled it out of the tissue; it was pretty with lots of lace, a beaded bodice and three-quarter satin sleeves with pure white fur around the ends. Also there was fur around the slightly plunging neckline. It also had a wonderfully long train with a full veil. The veil and the dress had little handmade flowers on it. The tiara that was to hold the veil was not too fancy. It had no jewels, just fur; it was more like a headband. There was also, if needed, a little white fur bolero. 'Oh, Mum, it's the most beautiful dress I have ever seen. I couldn't have chosen better. I'll be really proud to wear such a beautiful dress, Mum. If you're sure, I'll also be proud if you wear it, Mum. Can I ask you something?'

Absent-mindedly, Eleanor said, 'Yes, dear, anything you know that.'

'Why are you so eager for me to wear this wonderful dress? Don't get me wrong, Mum. I can't wait. Don't give me all the shortages. I get the feeling that's not all, and there is something more.'

'OK, honey, you see, Rosy, my darling, I was making this dress to wear at my wedding. I was about halfway to finishing right on time for my wedding on the Christmas Eve of that year.' Rosy sat for a moment, thinking. She was very confused. 'Oh, Mum, your anniversary has always been 5 November. OK, right, what was the reason for bringing it that far forward? Oh, Mum, you wasn't . . .'

'Oh, Rosy, no, of course not. Really, Rosy, you know, I was pure on my wedding night as I hope you will be.'

'Oh, Mum', said Rosy, 'nice one, Mum, you got me right back.' They both laughed a lot for a few moments, both thinking, *This is nice. Having some time for just the two of us.* Rosy was the one to say it out loud, 'I was thinking exactly the same.' They hugged each other.

'No, nothing like that I'm sorry, but it's a bit sad,' Eleanor said, looking at Rosy.

'Oh, OK, I'd like to hear it as long as you're OK telling me. I say that, Mum, as you have never told me about it before. Does Dad know?'

'Yes, Rosy, your dad knows.'

'Well', Eleanor started again, 'well, as you pointed out, my wedding was on 5 November. It was supposed to have been on 24 December. The reason it was changed was because your grandad Percy got called to go fight.' No Eleanor had tears in her eyes. Rosy handed her mum her hanky. She then continued, 'My mum, Doris, kept her composure, keeping everyone together, although inside, she was falling apart. You could see it was tearing her apart. She put up a brave face for my younger brothers, your uncles, Danny and Sydney. Your father and I said we will postpone the wedding, but my father wouldn't hear of it.'

He had said, 'You will have it before I go, you two. I don't want any more arguments. Understood?' He was due to go on 8 December. Well, that's when we all decided on November the fifth. It wasn't until a bit later that I realised why they insisted on me marrying before he left. He wanted to give me away. They knew he may not come back. That's when my mind went to my wonderful dress hanging in my room, waiting for the final touches. I knew I could never get it finished in time. I didn't get upset about it. I planned to finish it when I could so that's where it hung. It was covered to stop dust and sun getting on it. Well, the day arrived. Oh, they also made sure we would still have a honeymoon. That way, I would not be there to see him off. We said our goodbyes after the reception. I had said all my goodbyes over the few days leading up to the wedding. I'd come to terms with him going, and off we went on our honeymoon he had planned for your father and me. We were away for a fortnight. It was wonderful. It must have cost him a lot.' Rosy just sat there, letting her mother carry on, without disturbing her. 'Anyway when we returned, we had arranged to stay at my parents for a couple of weeks until our home was ready for us to move in. When we arrived at the front door, we both knew something was very wrong. The house was in mourning with black ribbon hanging on the front door. I hurried in, leaving your poor dad to pay the taxi. Worst of all, there was the luggage. The only thing I could think about was hurrying inside. I flew into the kitchen, where I found your uncles with Mum sitting and eating supper. My first thought was *You're all safe*. The boys got up to hug me just as I realised that it was Dad. Not realising I was screaming, "Isn't it?" The boys couldn't console me. My mum got up, tried to calm me down. By then your dad was in the house. He heard me scream, and he just dropped our luggage and then ran into the kitchen and flew to me when he realised my brothers were holding me up. He grabbed me and picked me up. I just collapsed into his arms, letting him take charge. We climbed the stairs and entered what was now our bedroom. He laid me on the bed and stayed until I cried myself to sleep. He told me later on that he crept out of the room and headed downstairs to see what had happened. That was when he found out that my father, your grandad, had been sent overseas. He had been there about a week when he was shot and killed.'

'Oh, Mum,' Rosy said.

'Your dad always called them Mum and Dad,' said Eleanor.

'I'm so sorry to hear that.' No wonder Eleanor was in such a state.

'Well, Rosy, that's the tale behind the dress, apart from how it all got into this particular wooden trunk. Well, when we moved into our new home, we found the trunk in the bedroom. I had seen it before in Dad's shed. I just thought it was full of his tools. We sat on the bed together. The card said, "To my Eleanor, my prettiest Rosy of the bunch, and her new husband." Oh, Rosy, it was full of anything you could think of to knit our new home together.'

'Mum,' Rosy interrupted.

'Yes, Rosy, can I ask you something?'

'Of course, darling,' Eleanor replied with her back to Rosy, still fiddling with the dress. 'What is it?'

'Well, you said what was on the card is how I got my name.'

Turning with that said card in hand to Rosy, Eleanor said, 'You are very astute, Rosy dear. Yes, it is. You're OK with that aren't you, my love? You do at least like your name.'

'Oh, don't be silly. Of course, I do. I love it even more now that I know how you chose it. I feel, oh I don't know I feel very special,' said Rosy. Both Rosy and her mum were both crying now. They reached in and embraced for the next couple of moments in silence until they heard Albert calling.

'Hey, you two, you got lost up there?' he called, laughing.

'I'll go, Mum, and see what he wants.'

'No, my dear, I'll go. Look in the box if you like,' said Eleanor.

'OK, Mum. Mum?'

'Yes,' replied Eleanor with a smile, knowing what her daughter was about to ask. 'Yes, my love, you may try the dress on.'

With that, Eleanor disappeared. Rosy spent the next half an hour rummaging through the trunk. In there, she found a gold chain with a cross. She looked into a dusty old mirror, but the catch was old, and it wouldn't undo. *Oh, dear, that's such a shame*, Rosy thought about it and then an idea hit her. She put the chain over her head and then very gently pushed and rolled it over her hair carefully so as not to get it caught. Then she went to look in the mirror. *Oh that looks nice*, she thought. Then her concentration turned to the dress, tempting her. She gently took it off the hanger and laid it over the trunk. Then Rosy went ahead, got undressed, picked the dress up, and placed it gently over her head. When all the bits were in place, she thought of showing it to her parents before the day. Then Rosy decided not to, letting it remain as a bigger surprise for them as much as to Derek. After they were married, telling him the story that her mum had just told her would be nice.

Five

Everyone decided it would be nice to have Derek's younger sister Francis as the bridesmaid, who would have her dress made out of one of Rosy's unused evening gowns. The chosen gown was lilac. Susan would be wearing a beautiful cocktail dress, which was similar, although of a slightly different material. The shades of the two dresses complemented each other. Her mum offered to do the alterations on them where it was needed. They would all have daisies in their hair; the bride's bouquet would be made of white roses, large daises, and gypsophila. All the neighbours wanted to club in together to make a real wedding cake, even if it will only have one tier. There was also going to be sandwiches at the reception as well as lots of other lovely things. The wedding was to be at the little local church. They decided to have the choir at the church. Only family and very close friends would be in the church, but everyone was invited to the reception, which was to be in her parents' garden. It was its best at that time of year. It had a lovely array of beautiful, wonderfully scented flowers; among them were roses, gladiolas, irises, lilies of the valley, tulips, and plenty of others.

Six

On the morning of the wedding as Rosy woke up, she remembered Derek arrived home the previous day at lunchtime. She slowly climbed out of bed with a big smile on her face; today was going to be wonderful day. Derek had managed to get two weeks' leave. She stretched and walked to the window; she opened her blackout curtains. The sun was shining gloriously. Opening a window to breathe in the wonderful morning air, Rosy was very surprised to see that the garden had been decorated within an inch of its life with all sorts of decorations. She found out a bit later that Derek's parents, Elizabeth and James, had bought them from their country estate, where the staff had made them, handing them to Elizabeth and James just as they were leaving for the wedding. There was also lots of buntings that her father, as ARP warden, had managed to borrow. Even all the tables and chairs were decorated. They belonged to the local church hall, which was next to the church they were to be married in. She thought of everyone's kindness as they helped out in whatever way they could. Perhaps it's not so surprising because her parents are so popular, always ready to help anyone, even with their own problems. Oh what a wonderful day this would be. The only sad thought was that she knew for her, and her parents too, was that her brothers Bert and Duncan would not be there. With mixed feelings, Rosy prepared to take a bath, first step to being ready to become Mrs Rosy Rook-Leigh. She had to make her parents proud, and then next one is for them to be happy for her, hopefully even for just a few hours, they had to take their minds off their worries. Stepping out of the bath, Rosy slipped on her dressing gown. On her way across the landing, back to her bedroom, the front door bell chimed. Her father answered it; Rosy could hear it was Susan, her best friend, calling down, asking her father if he would send her up. Susan was also going to do everyone else's hair too before getting ready herself. They went straight to her room and instantly started chatting. They had been chatting for about ten minutes when there was a light tapping on the door. Rosy said, 'Come in' and in came her father with two very welcome cups of tea.

'Thank you, Dad. How is everything out there?' Rosy laughed.

'You may well laugh, young lady,' replied he father, also laughing. 'Your mother is downstairs in a real flap, running around, panicking. She's never been happier.' They all laughed. Her father turned to leave. Rosy asked him if he would send Francis up in about fifteen minutes.

He replied, 'Yes, of course, my dear.' With that, he went, closing the door gently. After he had gone, Susan, who was very astute when it came to her best friend because they were so close, asked, 'What is worrying you, Rosy (that's what Susan called her)?'

'I wish Duncan and Bert could be here for Mum and Dad as much as for me. Derek's brother Jonathan managed to get some leave for only a couple of days. Then he is going back into action the same as Derek will be. After our honeymoon, I know that's just the way things are. That doesn't help. Is that selfish, Susan?'

'No, Rosy, of course, it's not. It's just the way you feel.'

'You can't help how you feel,' said Susan.

'I'm trying to stay strong for Mum and Dad,' said Rosy.

'Well, this is yours and Derek's day, so please try to stop worrying and enjoy it. It's a lifetime memory.'

Talking of memories, Rosy went onto tell Susan what her mother had told her. She showed her the necklace that she still had on with her mother's blessing. Then, opening her wardrobe, there, hanging on the door, was the dress with everything that goes with it. 'Oh, Rosy, you really are such a lucky girl.'

'Oh, Susan, it will happen for you one day.'

'Yes, I know. It's just so hard, seeing you so happy. Oh don't get me wrong. I'm really, really happy for you. Anyway, come on, where are you going for honeymoon?' Susan asked excitedly.

'I think it's a little guest house in Southend-on-Sea. It's on the seafront, I think. We are going by car. That way, we can have stopovers while going or coming back, as well as look around while we are there. We are very lucky as family, also some friends, have helped with petrol. I can't wait to get him on his own. Just him and me, all on our own.' They giggled.

Susan said, 'Oh maybe, I didn't need to hear that. You also said it without blushing.' They giggled again.

'It really must be the real thing. Oh, Susan, of course, it's the real thing, my dearest friend. Seriously, there will never be anyone else. We feel when one is in trouble, and we finish each other's sentences. Now I'm about to find out if we are compatible in the last way,' she said, giggling once again.

'I want to hear all about it when you get back. Well, not all. Oh you know what I mean.'

'Oh, Susan, yes, I know what you mean.' They hugged. 'You're a perfect friend.'

'Yes, Rosy, you too.' They were still giggling when Francis came bounding in, jumping straight onto Rosy's bed.

'Hello, Rosy. Oh hello, Susan, how are you?'

'I'm OK, Francis. How are you?'

'I'm OK. Thank you. I'm ever so excited. Susan, are you going to do my hair all grown up like yours?'

'Yes, yes, if you calm down and if Rosy says it's OK.'

They both turned and looked at the bride-to-be, who smiled and nodded. Francis threw her arms around Rosy's neck and said, 'Oh thank you, Rosy.' That was that, and Susan got on and did everyone's hair. Later, Susan helped her friend into her very special dress. It took all their breaths away. Susan burst into tears; Francis just stood, and then said, 'You look like a princess.'

Through her tears, Susan agreed, 'That's exactly how I feel. Do you want the bolero on?'

'Yes, please, Susan, at least till Mum and Dad get to see.'

'You mean they haven't?'

'No, not yet. I want to surprise them especially Mum.'

'Oh, Rosy, my dear friend, take it from me. You will certainly do that. I just hope their systems can stand it. What do you say, Francis?'

'Yes, Susan, I agree with every word.' With that, they headed for the stairs.

Seven

Francis, with Susan, descended the stairs together, and when they reached the bottom, they then walked into the parlour. Rosy's parents greeted them. 'Oh, don't, you two, look beautiful, ladies!'

That really made Francis feel grown up. They all moved to the bottom of the stairs to await the bride. A couple of moments later, Rosy appeared at the top of the stairs and slowly came down. Her mother was in tears. When she reached the bottom, Rosy noticed that her dad was almost in tears. She approached her mum, who hugged her and then stood back, saying, 'Oh, my darling daughter, you look beautiful. I'm so glad I finished the dress all those years ago. It was well worth it to see what I'm seeing right now. I warn you, Rosy, love, your nan doesn't know you're going to be wearing it. You think you have seen tears, girls? You wait till your nan sees you.'

Everyone laughed and then her dad said, 'I hate to break this up. I think there just may be an anxious groom waiting.' With a smile, he said that it was time for Susan, Francis, and Eleanor to leave for the church. After they had left, Rosy and her father made their way to wait in the parlour for the transport to return. As they were waiting, Rosy looked out of the window. Her father walked over to her, then turning her around and holding her hands, he said, 'Oh, Rosy, my darling, you look like a princess, my darling daughter.' He kissed her on the cheek and then placed her veil carefully over her face.

'Dad, before we go, are you OK with this? You do know that the dress was meant for your wedding, and Mum was making it.'

'Yes, my darling, Rosy, I know. Yes, I'm fine. I didn't care what your mother wore just as long as we were married.'

'Dad, what did Mum wear? I presume she wore something.'

'Oh, Rosy, really,' he said, and they both laughed.

'Yes, Rosy, her father bought her a dress. Just a normal dress. It was a cream one.'

As he turned away, the transport arrived back. That's when Rosy saw for the first time it was a horse-drawn carriage. She was still expecting a car, and tears rolled unstoppable down her cheeks. Her parents had teased her, saying as it was such short notice, they couldn't get it. Looking out of the window, Rosy could see it was being pulled by two of the most fabulous dapple greys she had ever seen, in all their glory. As they went out before climbing into the carriage, Rosy just had to ask their names.

The driver replied, 'The one on the left is Nelson, and the one on the right is Shianne.'

'Thank you. You have two beautiful horses,' said Rosy.

With that, Rosy turned, and with the help of her father and the driver, Rosy got into the carriage with the long veil too. They settled into the carriage. 'Are you all right, Rosy?'

'Oh, Dad, I feel so guilty, celebrating while Duncan, Bert, and all those poor boys are prisoners, missing, wounded, or worse.'

'Listen, Rosy, I know it's sad. There is nothing you can do at the moment. Please stop worrying. One thing I do know is that your brothers would not want you to be sad on yours and Derek very special day, so I want you to put a smile on that pretty face of yours. Stop worrying for today. Agreed? And, my love, it's not fair on Derek.'

'Yes, agreed, Dad. I love you.'

'Right. Since that's settled, now let's get on with this. Once-in-a-lifetime day, you, young lady, are to enjoy yourself. You will soon be Mrs Rosy Rook-Leigh. Quite a mouthful, isn't it, honey?' Both of them giggled at that. Then he continued, 'That's better. You are smiling and all that comes with that.'

'Dad, can you just check if my makeup is OK?' she asked, lifting her veil.

'It fine, Rosy. All in order, all tickety-boo.'

'Dad, where did that pop up from?' Rosy asked, really smiling. 'You used to say that to us when we were children.'

'Yes, it always put a smile on your face.' Rosy hugged him tight. Rosy whispered in his ear, 'I love you, Dad. I love you so much.' They separated as they travelled up the hill path. They were nearly at church. Rosy had one last thought of her brothers and then promised herself that, that would be the last until after the wedding.

Eight

They arrived at the church door; there was a wonderful smell of newly cut grass and perfumed flowers. The church was called St Barnaby's; it was only a small church. It had wonderful-sounding bells, a tower with a spire, and an outstanding clock with a Roman face and gold-coloured numerals. The bell was ringing and echoing across the fields, into the valley below. As the church was on a hill, the view was beautiful. The driver had lowered the steps, and they both stepped down. There, waiting for them, was Susan and Francis. They each picked a side of the long train up, and then they all started to slowly walk up the church path towards the church door. Finally, on reaching the closed door, they heard the organ playing inside the church. The warden was there to open the door, and as the door opened, the organ music changed to the wedding march. Oh, what a lovely sound! They all stepped inside and walked behind the pews to the top of the aisle. She looked at her father and saw a funny look on his face. He had gone very pale; she whispered in his ear, 'Are you OK, Dad?'

He didn't answer, and she started to get concerned. She pulled back her veil to talk to him properly, and that's when she saw what he was looking at. His gaze was fixed at the people standing at the end of the aisle. Standing next to Derek was Jonathan who was in his navy uniform, and along with him were two very smart, thin soldiers. Her eyes turned to her father, whose eyes had welled up with tears. 'Susan said Rosy, are you and your father OK? Both of you look as though you've seen a ghost.' Rosy replied, 'No, Susan, not *a* ghost but two of the most fantastic ghosts in the world.'

Susan looked at her as if she had gone mad, and then she followed her line of sight and saw four uniformed men where she thought was only supposed to be two – one RAF and the other navy uniform. Then she noticed there were two other very smart army uniforms. She gave Rosy a puzzled look. Rosy, with tears running down her cheeks, sobbed, 'My brothers.' That was all she could manage. She was too choked up to say any more.

Susan whispered into Rosy's ear, 'You see, dear Rosy, some wishes do come true.' Slowly Rosy and her father pulled themselves together, and Susan lowered Rosy's veil for her after dabbing away the tears as she and her father were both shaking. He had also composed himself as the wedding march was about to be played for the third time. As it started, all four of them slowly started to walk down the aisle with tears in their eyes. The boys hadn't even turned round; slowly they made their way down the aisle, when really all Rosy and her father wanted to do was run to them, crying their names out. As they reached the last pew, they could see that Elizabeth was in the wrong pew on the wrong side of the aisle, sitting and comforting Eleanor, who was weeping into a lace handkerchief. The priest was there too, and as he saw the bridal party start down the aisle, he moved back to his place at the altar. The choir was all in tears because, since being a small community, they knew them. A lot of them grew up with the boys and with little Rosy, hence everyone knew what was going on. Finally, they covered the distance down the aisle, and it seemed to last forever. As they came to a halt, the boys finally turned around. All their eyes met, and all of them smiled at each other.

The priest started talking. He said, 'I know this is unusual. Before we start, I would like to say a prayer for the boys, who are still overseas and also for the safe return of Bert and Duncan, who are two of the many children I have watched grow up. I also had the pleasure of christening them and then their sister Rosy. I united their parents in holy matrimony, and now we're here to see little Rosy get married.' Every one spent a couple of minutes praying. At last the choir started to sing, and the ceremony started and Albert handed her over to her husband-to-be, Rosy turned around and handed Francis her bouquet. Susan had laid the train down, and it looked lovely as it hung over the two small steps. *Oh what a wonderful day!* Rosy thought. *My whole family, friends, and the man I love all together for the first time, and I hope it is not for the last time.* They said their 'I dos', and the ceremony was over. Derek slowly lifted her veil up and kissed her passionately on the lips for the first time since they had met. It made her feel all tingly with pleasure, the longing an all new feeling for her. They walked around the side and duly signing the register. They turned to start the walk back down the aisle, and they stepped down the two little steps. When they reached the front pew, they stopped. Rosy looked at her new husband; he knew what she was thinking and nodded his head. She looked behind her and whispered to the girls. They laid the train down again and then walked around to the pew. Each grabbed a hand of one of the boys, pulled them up, took them behind Rosy, picking up a corner each again, handing one to each brother. The whole church smiled, sighed, and even just sat with tears in their eyes, They were all so happy, to see the family together again at least for now. The organists started playing and the choir sang. They changed from what they were going to sing and instead started singing 'All Things Bright and Beautiful'. As they walked back down the aisle, out into the glorious sunshine, down the church path, passing a lovely aroma of honeysuckle, that made a wonderful arch, with lavender on either side of the arch, the butterflies, bees, and everything seemed vivid and alive. They stepped onto a beautiful lawn, purposefully kept for photos. It was wonderful with the whole family. All the in-laws were there for this wonderful occasion. For the next hour, they spent posing for photos. The best one would be of Rosy with her new husband and her brothers, one on either side of husband and wife. Slowly, they made their way to the carriage, whispering again to Derek, 'Would you mind if we broke tradition and let Bert and Duncan ride with us?'

Derek readily agreed. 'Listen, sweetheart, whatever makes you happy is fine. The point is, as long as my Rosy is happy, then I am too.'

'Oh, Derek, now I know there was a reason I love you as much as I do. Thank you, darling,' she said with a smile that lit up her beautiful face. Rosy called them over, and the coach man lowered the step. They all climbed into start the ride home for the reception. Lined along the road were the many well-wishers, waving and the children running around, laughing and playing with not a care in the world – the way it should be. It was nice for them to have something to be joyful about with so much misery around, with the war. The carriage drew closer to them, and they all saw Bert and Duncan sitting with the newly-weds. Everyone started to cheer, as everybody knew each other's business. That was the way things were at that time. They pulled up outside the house. Rosy could see the front door had been decorated and the tall red rosy bushes that lined the front path had white bows tied in them (on getting a closer look, she realised they were bits of an old torn sheet). It made lovely bows. As they stepped down from the carriage and made their way to the front gate, there, in front of them, was the garden path, covered in a long red hall rug. Rosy recognised it from their elderly neighbour's hall. She smiled, *Obviously the dear couldn't afford to buy a gift and wouldn't be seen arriving without doing or bringing something.* There were tears in Rosy's eyes. Her emotions were all over the place. The unusually long bridal party went through the house to greet the guests coming through the side gate, when she saw Millie the elderly neighbour, who provided the rug. Rosy bent over, whispering in her ear, 'Thank you so very much, Millie. I really felt like royalty.'

'That was the idea. I thought it would be a nice surprise for you.'

'Turned out to be even more special than I thought it would be.'

'Was that your brothers I saw come with you and Derek in the carriage?'

'Yes, my dear Millie, it was Bert and Duncan you saw. If you would like to meet them, they will be out in a moment. They are catching up with Mum and Dad. They will join us soon.' Rosy turned to Derek and said, 'Darling, would you escort Millie to her seat?'

Derek said, 'Millie, take my arm, my dear.'

They walked to her seat slowly as she was so frail.

Millie looked up at Derek. 'Rosy is such a lucky girl. You are very handsome.'

'Oh, Millie, stop. You're making me blush.'

'Oh, tish, tish', Millie smiled, 'that, my lad, was a compliment I don't give them out very often.' That made them both laugh.

He kissed her hand and then bowed. 'OK, I will see you later. Now you enjoy, Millie.'

The music was playing; it was a Glenn Miller tune. Two tunes later, the last of the guests came through the gates. Just as they rounded the corner into the garden, her mother and father, followed closely by Bert and Duncan, came down the kitchen steps into the garden. Derek called out three cheers, 'To my brother Jonathan and also to my new brothers-in-law, Bert and Duncan, who are home safely.' As they were cheering, he saw another face he hadn't seen for a very long time, not since the day they left flight school together. He had wondered what had happened to him or when he would ever see him again. That was his best friend Gilbert; he had wanted Gilbert as his best man when they were growing up, and as he was missing, Jonathan had stepped in at the last minute. Otherwise it would have been his dad. He almost took off, across the garden, to greet his best friend. Poor Rosy got the shock of her life, until looking to where her husband had run to. Then she smiled and said to herself, *I'm so happy for him. Oh what a wonderful day this had turned out to be. More than anyone could have imagined.* It was still early, and as the afternoon turned to evening, the climate was cooler. When dancing started, Derek Rosy from seat, taking his new bride's hand, and moved to where the dancing was to be. They started the first dance and then was joined by her best friend Susan with Gil, Derek's best friend. They were followed by the two sets of parents.

Derek leant over whispering into Rosy's ear, 'Rosy, look over there, darling.' He spun her around.

'Ooh, oh dear, there is Francis dancing with Duncan. I wonder if the parents know.' Both of them laughed. All too soon it was past ten o'clock, and although the party wasn't due to end until midnight, he newly-weds went to change and get ready to leave for their honeymoon. As they came out the front door, they were faced with the same smiling faces, but this time they were throwing rose petals. The wonderful fragrance filled the night air. Then Rosy turned and tossed her bouquet into the crowd; as it flew through the air, it parted and became two bouquets. Susan caught the larger one, and Francis caught the smaller one. Rosy turned and smiled; the look on their faces just finished the perfect day perfectly. She looked at her mum; they grinned at each other. Their little plan had worked. They guessed Susan would catch it, but they didn't want Francis to feel left out. The look on her pretty young face said it all. For the first time as a married couple, they climbed into the car, set off down the road; the noise coming from behind was so loud, and they knew exactly what it was. Both of them laughed. Rosy, thought then laughed again, just as well all the neighbours are at the party, they stopped when they were around the corner, to remove the cans, from the bumper as they didn't want to disappoint the guests. They pulled up at the kerb; Derek climbed out, removed the three trails of tin cans that had been neatly tied around the bumper. Derek got back into the car and they kissed. Then giggling, they carried on their way.

Nine

They arrived at the guest house a little before midnight; they could hear the sea lapping against the beach. It was full moon, and the stars were shining brightly in the sky, which, in normal times, would have been idyllic, but with the war, well, it made it easy for the Germans to see and that also worked for us, of course. They agreed, 'Let's try to forget while we're here.' They climbed the stone steps, to the front door, and rang the bell. A few moments passed and then they heard a light switch go on, rustling of a curtain being pulled back, and the door then opened. Inside stood the guest house owner, waiting to greet them. She was a lovely lady, a grandmother-type. She welcomed them with a hug as if they were old friends. 'Welcome! Come on in, dears so that I can replace the blackout curtain and then turn the light back on.' After that was all done, then they proceeded with the introductions. 'Hello, I'm Mrs June Wyeth. You are to call me June, dears. It's lovely to meet you.'

'We are pleased to meet you, June.' Rosy gave her a hug.

After the cuddle was done, June said, 'I have the kettle on. I bet you'd love a cup of tea after your drive. Sit down. I'll go make it and then bring it in here.' Rosy offered to help. 'No, no. I'll be fine. I'd rather you sit there with your lovely new husband,' June smiled at her. Rosy instantly blushed. 'Oh, my dear, I'm sorry to make you blush. Just an old lady teasing.' All three of them laughed. Rosy did as she was very politely told to do. She sat with Derek. When June came back in, Derek apologised for the late hour and then went onto explain about the surprise guests and the wedding.

June said, while pouring the tea, 'Oh, my dears, how wonderful for you both. I bet your parents are over the moon.'

'Yes', Rosy went on, 'it's taken the pressure of me. I can go ahead and enjoy my honeymoon, knowing my mum and dad are happy and that my brothers are safe and happy.'

'Yes', Derek agreed, 'it's great to know that my best friend is safe too. I think all in all it has been a fabulous day, June.'

'I lost my husband in the last war. His name was Peter. He died at Gallipoli. I do have children, two wonderful girls, one's a WAF and the other a WREN. I don't see them very often. I did have a boy in between the girls, but it was not to be though. He died at about nine months.'

'Oh, June, that's sad. I'm sorry.'

'Oh, Rosy, it was a long time ago.' They chatted for another half an hour.

'Rosy, my love, it's getting pretty late. Poor June is probably very tired. I know I am.'

'Well', June replied, 'I had better show you to your room.'

They got up and climbed the stairs. When they got to the top, they entered a room that Rosy realised must look over the seafront. When they entered inside, there was a four-poster bed. It was fabulous with pretty mauve bed covers on the bed. They couldn't see out because of the darkness. The light was switched on and they walked further inside. Behind them, there was a small alcove, a fantastic fireplace with a low smouldering fire, two-seater seat, and a little table sat to the side. On the table was a wonderful arrangement of really lovely flowers. When Rosy remarked how lovely they were, June replied, 'Yes, they're from my garden. The same as the vegetables that will be with your evening meals.'

This reminded Rosy of something. Turning to Derek and giving him a nudge, she said, 'Darling, have you got the ration books in your pocket?'

With all the rush, Rosy wasn't sure if they had left it behind. He smiled, putting her mind at rest. Then he put his hand in his inside pocket, still smiling at her. They all giggled; he then dutifully handed them to June, who then took her leave. Finally, they were on their own for the first time. The first thing Rosy did was put the lights out and open the curtains. What they hadn't realised was that there were double doors, and they opened onto a small balcony. She looked at Derek, and they took each other's hands and walked out on to it. They stood at the railing, looking at the moon; it was shining on the water, and the waves lapped onto the sand, making the reflection of the moon ripple. It was so wonderful that you could be forgiven for momentarily forgetting the horrors that were going on elsewhere. *Shut your eyes. Start dreaming of better times*, Rosy thought as she tried hard to. She just couldn't think of a time when she was happier. She moved closer to Derek, took hold of his hands, and lay her head on his shoulder. He gently pulled her around to face him, tentatively kissing her, starting on her lips and slowly moving to her neck and then her shoulders. He slipped her dress over her shoulders. Rosy was running her fingers through his wonderful thick curly hair. He was running his hands over her back, neck, and letting her hair free. Then slowly his hands moved lower and then back up again, feeling for the buttons of her dress. Slowly he lowered it, already off her shoulders. It dropped around her waist; his hands Rosy again, feeling for her bra's clasp. Rosy could feel him slowly undoing it, dropping it to the ground. Her skin was extra alive and sensitive, and the sound of her heartbeat was pounding in her ears as her heart raced. Now she had removed his jacket and tossed it onto the chair. What Rosy hadn't seen was that he had reached inside, and he'd pulled a blanket and cushion out and even managed somehow to lay it down. By then she had undone and removed his shirt and then tossed it into the room. She was now happily running her hands through his chest hair, and he was now kissing her neck. Again, he slowly lowered himself. He could then kiss her breasts; her fingers were running oh so slowly over his back gently. He then took her fully erect nipples into his mouth, and her hands started to clasp harder on his back, her nails digging into his perfectly clear skin, head tossed back, Rosy was getting stirring feelings that she had never felt before, making her moan loudly. His head slowly moved down, kissing her pearly skin; as he did, it was sending shivers up and down her body. Her legs weakened, and he very gently lowered her to the blanket, still kissing her and running his hands all over her body. Finally, his hands arrived to the inside of her thighs. As he touched Rosy, she arched her back in pure pleasure. He gently rubbed her thighs, and Rosy felt him kissing them and gently opening them. That sent her to heaven; he slowly came back to her face, and as he slid up to her face, her hand slid to her side. 'Oh,' she gasped, feeling his manhood; it slowly reached her hand, fully aroused. She took it into her hand, as he slid up her body. He could feel his manhood had been caught, and his Rosy was feeling and exploring it. Her hand slowly let him go. He looked into her eyes and asked if she was OK. She murmured into his neck, 'Yes, my love. I'm OK.'

Her hands were now on his back, and he put his hands between her legs. He entered her, and every time he moved deeper, he checked that it wasn't hurting and that she was OK. Every time he moved a little, her hands held a little tighter. He slowly, gently pushed, and Rosy felt him enter her. She moaned and then cried out a little as he took her virginity. As he looked at her concerned, his love was weeping, feeling bad, he went to get off her. 'Derek, darling,'

'No, sweetheart.'

'I'm OK. Honest.'

He wasn't sure; he took her at her word anyway, as he pushed gently. He fully entered her, and he watched her face. The smile told it all. He relaxed, and he slid in and out slowly. As he did, her back arched right up; the pain had obviously subsided, being replaced with feeling she had never felt before. Gently, he started to move up and down inside her, and their faces were buried deep in each other's necks. What she didn't know though was he was also a virgin. He was hurting a bit too. Slowly his pain passed too. When the pain was gone, the feelings changed, and they returned into urgent love-making. Their faces finally met, and they kissed completely, lost in each other. They were both moaning with passion, a new feeling neither had experienced before. Gradually, the movement became more and more urgent as they both came to their climaxes together. The relief for them, both of them, was so intense, and they were both crying, almost sobbing. As he slowly, gently rolled off her, they lay together under the moonlight, snuggled on the blanket. He reached back and pulled a second cushion and blanket out, and he put the cushion under his head and the blanket over them. Then they must have fallen asleep.

Ten

Derek stirred awake and realised that dawn was breaking. He gently picked Rosy up and placed her in the four-poster bed, covering her up and kissing her gently on her forehead. Then he quietly went out and retrieved the cushions with the blankets. He folded them and replaced them on the chair. The fire had burnt itself out. He went over to the bed, climbed in beside his gorgeous new bride and watched her sleep for a few moments. 'Oh, my darling, you really are beautiful,' he muttered. 'I'm so lucky.' With that, he too fell asleep. The next thing Derek knew, there was a knock at the door. As he opened his eyes, he realised Rosy was looking down at him and smiling. He smiled back. 'Morning, darling,' they said in unison. 'Rosy, don't you think we had better answer the door? Poor June is standing there with a tray.'

They hadn't even unpacked. Grabbing the blanket, he went and answered the door. There was June with a very large tray, full of breakfast things. June entered and placed it on the table, greeted them with a wonderful cheerful good morning, asking them if they slept well. They looked at each other, grinning, and then both said, 'Yes, thank you very much. Also thank you for the breakfast.'

After June left, Derek got back into bed with the tray. They found there was eggs, toast, tea, and all the normal breakfast things. 'Derek, how did June manage eggs?'

'I don't know, darling.'

'Well, never mind. I'm ravenous. I'm going to enjoy this.' They both ate heartily. When they had finished, the tray was placed on the floor. Derek turned to Rosy, and asked, with concern in his voice, 'How are you, sweetheart?' Rosy turned to him and said, 'I'm wonderful. Very happy and content.'

Then she asked him the same question, and he replied, 'I feel the same.'

They hugged and lay in each other's arms, chatting. Then Rosy turned to him, raising herself on one elbow and looking down at him. He raised his head a little, so they could kiss. Both of them giggled.

'We had better get up,' Rosy said as she went to get out of the bed.

He grabbed her, and she giggled, 'I feel like a naughty schoolgirl' as he pulled her back down on the bed and pulling the wrapped sheet off her. She landed on top of him, and they started to kiss again with her on top, as she lowered herself down onto his chest. The closer he had the warm scent emanating from her soft skin and the sight of her breasts beautiful, round with those lovely dark nipples, his for the taking, he very quickly got aroused. As Rosy lay on top of him, she could feel his manhood growing beneath her, allowing her hand to tentatively investigate, realising she also was feeling very aroused. Her hand went around his full manhood, led him to where, desperately pulling, the need for him was so intense that it was a bit scary. Although Rosy trusted Derek explicitly, Rosy felt totally safe with him. With her still on top, he entered her this time she took the lead, at how fast he entered. He entered with great ease. *There is no pain*, she thought. He was thinking the same because there was no pain, and their bodies seemed to take over and work together. The urgency for release started to overwhelm them, and he pulled her to him. Together they spun over so she was again underneath, where he was able to control himself to make sure she was satisfied; he bend down, kissing her neck and breasts. Rosy was lost in rapture; her fingers dug deeper, deeper into his back. She cried out as she climaxed. He felt her claw his back again; there were tears in her eyes. He was again forced on to his back, and Rosy was once again on top. The movement made him realise he was unable to hold back any longer, pulling her down tight to his chest, he cried out as he climaxed, holding her tight. As they parted, Rosy smiled in great contentment. They lay, cuddled for a while, and then suddenly Rosy jumped up without warning, got of off the bed before he could grab her again, going over to her suitcase, pulled out a dressing gown and her wash bag and then proceeded to leave the room, for the bathroom which was on at the end of the landing. While washing, Rosy took a look out of the small window that was open. She saw the back garden just as June told them. There were flowers, such beautiful colours, and a good array of vegetables; then right at the bottom, there was June, feeding some chickens. Smiling to herself, she thought, *That's how fresh eggs come.* When she finished, Rosy headed back to their room, where Derek was unpacking their cases, putting the clothes and things away. She got back to their room, and after thanking him, Rosy told Derek about what she had seen. While she was dressing, Derek went to use the bathroom. While he was running the water, he couldn't help it. He had to have a peek out of the window. He smiled to himself, as he could also see June at the bottom of the garden, just shutting the chicken run. After they were dressed, ready for their first day out as a married couple, Derek picked up the breakfast tray and then headed downstairs. Heading to the back of the house and finding a door marked Private, Rosy knocked, and then heard a familiar voice call, 'Come in, my dears.' They both entered, greeting each other, as if they had known each other forever. Derek and Rosy thanked her very much for the wonderful breakfast.

As Derek placed the tray down, June said, 'Oh my dears, you were hungry.' They smiled at each other.

'Yes,' they replied. 'It must be the wonderful sea air.' They were both blushing. They made their excuses and then left for the day. They went out the front door, descended the steps to the street, and they just stood for a minute, trying to decide what to do and where to go first. They climbed in the car, and as they drove a long, they saw a sign come to Old Leigh. They drove along the seafront, towards Old Leigh, where the little boats were. Little did they know, later in the war, they were to rescue many servicemen. They had a wonderful day eating seafood, drinking some beer, enjoying walking on the beach. He chased her around the beach, and they both collapsed on the sand, kissing tenderly. Then they just sat, watching the tide come in and listening to the seagulls calling, as the fishing boats came in full of fresh fish. 'Oh, Derek, it's so peaceful apart from the right sounds. Why does there have to be so much destruction, killing, and hate?'

'Oh, Rosy, my love, I honestly don't know or understand it either. You know what we said when we arrived?' Rosy looked up into his eyes. 'I'm sorry, no more. I promise.' The afternoon started to move on, and they knew they had to be back at the guest house for their evening meal by six. Slowly they got their things together, returned to the car, and made their way back. They returned to the guest house at four thirty. They went straight to their room to freshen themselves up before dinner, and when they got to their room, there was a small fire in the grate, as the evening had started to be a bit cooler. Rosy sat down on the floor in front of it. He stood there just watching her for a few moments. He said to himself, *Oh, Rosy, I can't believe your mine. You're so beautiful.* She let her deep, shiny flaxen hair down, as Rosy was deep in thought and didn't notice him watching her. He walked up behind her, placed his hands on her shoulders, and said, 'Penny for them, my darling.'

She tilted her head up to him, smiled, and replied, 'How lucky am I to have such a loving husband.'

He returned the smile, sat himself down beside her with his arm around her shoulder. They sat quietly for a while, and then they started talking about the wedding, 'Oh, what a fantastic day it had been! It was even better with the three surprise guests.'

Derek started to talk about Gilbert and about how they grew up together on his parents' estate. Gilbert was the son of the estate manager. They went to school together and spent every school holiday playing all over the estate. They would ride the horses and help with all the jobs. 'We had such fun. Oh, Rosy, will we ever have those carefree days again, being able to do or go where we want without worrying?' Rosy took his face in her hands, then kissed him, and pulled him closer to her. They buried their heads in each other's shoulders and just sat there, holding each other for a while. When they parted, Rosy looked into his eyes and could see he had tears in them. 'Oh, my darling, please don't worry. It will be OK in the end.'

He looked back at her. Just looking at her, he believed her. He smiled at her. 'Now I know why I married you? You always make me feel better.' They laughed together, started to fool about, giggling and playing. Finally exhausted, they ended up lying on the floor, holding hands. They turned to each other, and he pulled her hand to his face and kissed it. He gently pulled her to him, started to kiss her neck, lifting up her hair, so he could kiss her ears. Her hands were around his neck, pulling him closer to her. Rosy started to undress him as he removed her blouse. They were together in the most intimate way, kneeling up, hands on each other's shoulders and looking into each other's eyes, slowly taking in each other's nakedness, enjoying each other's body, touching, experimenting, and finding where each other's sensitive areas were and then pleasuring each other as they went on. Finally found each other and then locked together, although this time, it lasted a lot longer, much to both their pleasure and satisfaction. By the time they had finished. They just had time to get dressed for dinner, if they were not to be late. As they entered the dining room, the lights were out. There were candles lit on the table, where only two places were set, especially for them. They took their seats, and a few seconds later, dear June came in, yet again carrying a loaded tray. Derek got up. 'Oh, June, that looks heavy.' He relieved her of it, placing it on the table next to theirs. 'Wow, something smells good,' Derek remarked, returning to his seat.

June placed two soup bowls in front of them, proceeding to dish up some lovely looking soup.

Rosy said, 'I don't know how you do it, June. Wonderful eggs this morning and this soup.' Rosy asked, 'What is in the soup?'

June said, 'There are onions, potatoes, and lots of home-grown herbs. My secret is I grow all my own vegetables, and I have some chickens for eggs. Well, my dears, enjoy. I will be back when you have finished.'

As June left, Rosy and Derek smiled at each other as of course unbeknown to June, they already knew. As promised, fifteen minutes later, she returned with yet another large tray again. Derek took it from her, proceeded to remove the soup bowls, replacing them with dinner plates with a full roast dinner. June told them, 'So I don't need to disturb you.' The sweet was left on the next table for them to help themselves which was an apple and rhubarb crumble with wonderfully thick custard. They spent the next hour talking and enjoying the meal. There was a tap at the door, once again. June entered with two cups of coffee that she placed one in front of each of them. 'Well, my dears, is there anything else you would like?'

'Goodness, June, no thank you. We couldn't eat another morsel.' They told her that was a most wonderful meal. 'June, thank you so much. You really spoilt us.'

Rosy hugged her; they all laughed, and June said, 'It's so nice to have someone to spoil.'

With that, she removed all the crockery as she was leaving. Looking over her shoulder, she said, 'Well, I'll say goodnight, my dears. Please blow the candles out when you leave.'

'OK, June, goodnight,' they said together. Twenty minutes later, they blew the candles out and left the dining room to retire to their room. The time flew by – the way it tends to when you're enjoying yourself and having fun. Their time was spent in much the same way as the first couple of days, sightseeing, wonderful love making, and fantastic meals that June made – all too soon, it was the last day of their honeymoon. They spent the morning, walking along the seafront, and then they bought a gift for June to thank her for all that she had done to make their stay comfortable. She felt like one of the family. They had promised to have lunch with her, but instead Derek said, 'No.'

June looked upset. 'Oh, Derek, you meanie, tell poor June the rest.'

June looked puzzled. 'The rest?'

'You have done enough for us. We are taking you out for a meal.' As they were the only guests, they knew June would be able to go with them. They had a wonderful afternoon out. They got back at about five. After they had their last cup of tea together with June, they went to get their luggage that they had packed earlier. They were ready to leave for home. They promised June they will come to stay again when they could. With that and all the goodbyes done, they left for home.

Eleven

They drove in silence. Neither of them wanted to break the spell of the honeymoon with talking about what's about to happen in the next few days. They drove in silence, just looking at each other now and again. It started to get dark as they got nearer home. Derek could feel that Rosy was getting more and more tense with every mile he drove. When he saw a little pub, he pulled into the car park. Derek went around the car, trying to encourage Rosy to get out. He managed to get her to sit on a seat outside by a stream. Derek got them a drink when he returned.

He said, 'I think we should talk before we get home.' Rosy agreed and looked at him, trying to smile, as they sipped their drinks, neither wanting to start talking. In the end, Derek said, 'Look, darling, it won't be forever. I'll be home under your feet sooner than you think. Then you'll get fed up with me being around.' Both of them smiled. They had already agreed that Rosy will stay with her parents until the war was over. That way he wouldn't worry. At least she would have company. He thought to himself, *If anything should happen, she wouldn't be on her own* (but he didn't say anything). She was tearful enough. He said, 'You're not to worry.'

He knew it was a silly thing to say. It made them feel a bit better. He asked if there was something that was really worrying her more than anything else. Rosy replied, 'I'm going to do some sort of work not sure yet what.' Turning to him, she asked him how he felt about it. 'Whatever makes you happy, darling,' he said as he gave her a reassuring kiss.

'Well, are you ready to go home, sweetheart?'

The reply surprised him. She said, 'Would you mind very much if we didn't go home tonight?' She had seen that the pub had bed and breakfast rooms. He still had three days of leave before he had to leave, so he agreed that if they had a spare room, they could stay. He re-entered the pub. A little bit later, he returned with a key in hand. 'I had better ring home to let them know what's happening. They are expecting us, so they will worry, OK?'

'I'll ask if they have a telephone you can use, Rosy?' When he enquired, the pub landlord said that they did and then he showed them to it. 'Your room is at the back of the pub downstairs. It opens on to the garden. Is that OK?'

'Oh, yes', Rosy said, 'that will be lovely.' They made their phone call, and her father answered. They explained that they were fine. 'We have decided to spend a night, maybe a couple at a little country pub called the Haymaker, OK?'

'Rosy, that's fine.' He told her about her mother and brothers. 'They're still there. Bert for another few days, and Duncan a bit longer, so, honey, go and enjoy yourselves.'

'OK, Dad. Send our love to all. See you soon. Bye.'

'Bye, dear.'

While Derek went to fetch their bags, Rosy spoke to the landlord, asking if it would be possible to stay for three nights, if they wished to, as this was the end of their honeymoon. Rosy told him they had been staying in Southend and were on their way home. As they still had another couple of days more, they wanted to spend it with each other. She said, 'I'm not sure when we will see each other next.'

He said, 'The room is free.'

'I will let you know in the morning,' she said.

'OK, dear, that will be fine.' Also Rosy made an arrangement with the landlord who said his name was Jeff, to have breakfast in their room. He also added that they can talk some lovely walks through the woods on the other side of the stream.

She thanked him and then asked if there was any chance of some sandwiches and maybe some wine, if it was not too much trouble. 'I'm being a bit cheeky, asking as you must be busy.'

'Oh no, my dear, that will be fine.'

'Oh, thank you so much,' Rosy said. He said he would bring it to their room in about twenty minutes. Rosy thanked him again and went off to find Derek who was just coming back in, heading towards her she smiled at Jeff, putting her finger to her lips. He smiled as he walked back to the bar. Derek joined her, and they made their way to their room. It was downstairs three steps, next to the bar at the back of the pub opens straight on to a garden, it was yet another lovely room, with a view of the stream, the woods spreading out beyond. They couldn't see much, as it was getting dark. There was also a door that opened out to the garden. They sat on the window seat, watching the sun disappear behind the trees. They sat in silence, not needing to speak and each knowing what the other was thinking. As promised, about twenty minutes later, there was a knock on the door. Rosy said to Derek, 'That will be Jeff.'

He looked at her in confusion, and asked, 'Jeff?' Rosy replied, laughing, 'The landlord.' They both smiled, and he went across the room to answer the door. Just as Rosy said, there stood Jeff with a tray, a wine cooler, with ice in, with not wine, instead, a wonderful, what looked like, expensive bottle of champagne. They both looked confused, as Rosy was expecting just ordinary wine. They both looked at Jeff. He said, 'We have been saving this for a special occasion. My wife Kathy said she couldn't think of anything more special, and I agreed.'

Derek looked at Rosy. She said, 'While I was waiting for you to get the bags, I told Jeff that we are on our honeymoon. Also that you only have a couple of days left until you went away.'

Jeff asked, 'Should I stand here or would you like it in your room, on the table?' They all laughed. Derek moved aside so Jeff could set the tray on the table. On the tray was a selection of sandwiches and also other goodies. They said, 'Thank you, Jeff. Please thank your wife for us.'

After they were left alone, Derek opened the champagne and poured it into two wonderful cut crystal glasses. The bubbly was a wonderful surprise. They both giggled as the bubbles caught them unawares. They walked over to sit back on the window seat. A while later, they had turned the lights off. They decided to wander into the garden with their drink, sandwiches, and all the other goodies. It was such a lovely full moon. They sat down on the grass under a beautiful willow tree, the wonderful intoxicating aromas of honeysuckle, lavender, with all the other countryside aromas. They sat talking about what they hoped would be their future. God willing, as the champagne took hold, they started giggling and playing around Rosy jumped up, went behind him, jumping on him and then ran off. He got up and chased her all over, and then finally caught her. He pulled her down under the large willow tree, and they started to kiss passionately, and hands were all over each other. They were hidden under the willow fronds as it was old and very dense; they slowly removed each other's clothing, hands exploring each other body – every curve from top to bottom, hands, fingers, feet, even toes included. They missed nothing; they took their time. After all, they had all night. Not that they were thinking about time as his hands reached her thighs and then her special place, known only to him. He found her and his fingers entered, as his mouth found her breasts, while her hands had done some fondling of their own, finding his manhood, Rosy then realised he is forever hers. They both started teasing each other, bringing each other to the height of passion and then stopping, only to start and repeat it again. Neither had ever known such intense feelings. Both cried out for the other not to stop. Derek turned, lowering himself to her thighs and started kissing them. His face moved up, and he buried his face in her womanhood, while Rosy was still teasing his manhood with her fingers. After a few minutes, neither could stand it any longer. Rosy was crying real tears, desperate for him to enter her. He slowly looked up at her face, her back arching up and then down, and then he slid up her body kissing her all over, as he went. Rosy could feel his manhood between her legs. Her desperation took over, and she pushed him hard. He fell to her side, his manhood tall and erect, hers for the taking. *Take I will*, Rosy said to herself, placing her hand around him, slowly putting a lovely soft skinned leg over his thighs and letting go. Once in place, although his manhood was there, more than ready, Rosy needed to keep him wanting, not wanting him to flip her over, for what was in her mind, smiling at him, slowly lowering herself down a little bit, still not lowering on to it fully just the tip, of his manhood until he was crying for her, turning over now was the last thing on Derek's mind, he was just very desperate, for her to let him enter her. Still, she just let him enter enough to move a couple of times and then pulled of. He couldn't suppress the overwhelming feeling, he grabbed her and pulled her down. As he did, he raised his hips, pushing hard inside her and pulling her down. Now he was completely inside her. Rosy cried out in pure ecstasy. Both of them were out of control and couldn't stop themselves (even if they had wanted to). Suddenly Rosy cried, 'God, Derek, don't stop please. I love you, Derek.' As she said that, she climaxed fully and was satisfied. As she had finished, Rosy could feel he was about join her with a great loud cry. 'I love you too, Rosy.' He climaxed hard and warm inside her. It was the first time that had happened inside her. He hadn't withdrawn, and they were both too far out of control to think about it. He didn't know that was Rosy's plan. He was so upset as they lay there her on top of him, still locked together. He kept saying, 'I'm sorry, Rosy. I'm so sorry.'

He was weeping. She looked at him and kissed him and then put her fingers against his lips, reached for her jacket and pulled out a handkerchief. She wiped away his tears. 'You couldn't have withdrawn with me on top,' Rosy said; she was smiling very widely. He looked at her. 'Oh, Rosy, what have we done?'

'Derek, darling, I have a confession to make. It was all my idea. I deliberately teased you at the beginning.'

As she dismounted him, it was her turn to say sorry. She was now worried that he would be cross. Moments passed, and then finally he smiled. He pulled her close, and they lay there quietly, looking at the stars. As they lay close, so close, both of them spoke at once. 'Did you see that bright shooting star? Oh so beautiful.' They both wished upon it together and then smiled. Dawn was approaching all too soon, so they dressed. Giggling, she said, 'I feel like that naughty school child again.'

With that, they ran back to the room. It was about five in the morning; they undressed, climbed into bed, lay entwined with arms around each other. Sleep over took them, and the next thing, there was a loud knock on the door. Both awoke, and Derek got his dressing gown on, went over to open the door, as they thought it would be Jeff. Rosy slipped into her dressing gown, and when he opened the door, he was a bit taken aback when he saw it wasn't Jeff. Instead, standing there was obviously Kathy, with a wonderful tray of breakfast fare, very much as good as June's the morning before. They introduced themselves as Kathy placed the tray on the table. Kathy picked up the tray from the night before, and after a chat, Kathy asked if they would like evening meal, maybe a small picnic, to take with them, as they said they may go walking to explore. 'Oh, Kathy, that would be lovely. Are you sure it's not too much for both picnic and evening meal?' With that, Kathy left the room, saying the picnic would be ready when they were. They sat and enjoyed their breakfast enormously. Both washed and dressed. Rosy put on the same dress that had been worn on the first day, when they went to the dance – the powder blue one with white sandals. He picked up the empty tray, and they walked together along the corridor to the kitchen, where Kathy was washing up. Derek handed her the tray, saying, 'Thank you for the lovely breakfast.'

'Thank you, my dears. Here is your picnic basket. Hope you like what's in there.' She opened it to show them some of what was in it.

'Wow! That is wonderful, isn't it, Derek?'

'Yes, it's wonderful. We thank you so much. I think you and Jeff are spoiling us just a bit.'

That made them all smile, and when they turned to leave, Kathy called, 'Have a great day, my dears.'

'Oh, we will,' Rosy returned, with her wonderful smile. They moved along the corridor a bit more to where it met the bar. There, they found Jeff preparing the bar for opening. They thanked him for breakfast, also the tray from the night before, especially the champagne. Jeff said, 'That's OK.'

Kathy walked in with the some clean glasses. 'Oh, my dear, how pretty you look with the pretty blue dress and your long flaxen hair hanging freely down your back.'

'Thank you,' Rosy said. 'Jeff, is it still OK to stay for another night?'

'Yes, of course, pet.'

Derek gave her a quizzical look. She smiled at him and took him by the arm. Derek picked up the basket, and Kathy came up behind them. 'Rosy, oh sorry, may I call you Rosy?'

'Of course, Kathy. Yes, that is fine.'

'Well, I don't know if you have been outside today, but it's very windy.'

'Oh, dear, is it? Oh, Derek, I have nothing to put over my hair or my face.'

'Well, Rosy, I just went to find this,' handing Rosy a beautiful hairband and tie-back to match. 'Oh, I can't borrow that.'

'Well, it's just sitting on the dressing table.'

'There's no harm, my love. Go on, borrow it,' Derek coaxed.

'OK, thank you, Kathy.'

On the side, Derek saw a photo of Jeff and Kathy with a little girl and three boys. 'Is that your family?' He carefully picked up the picture to show it to Rosy who came over, hair all done.

'Yes', Jeff said, 'that's Michel, David, Joshua, and Violet.' They added that David and Joshua were still at school. Michel was also in the RAF, and Violet worked away from home. After chatting for a few more moments, they set off. 'Are you going to walk through the woods?' Jeff asked.

'Yes,' they replied.

He told them there is a lake in the middle. 'Do you like fishing, Derek?'

'I have never tried,' said Derek. Rosy surprised everyone, saying, 'I do.' They all laughed. She ignored the laughing and said, 'Well, when my brothers and I were younger, I used to feel left out, when my father always took the boys fishing, so one day, I asked him if I could go with them. "Of course, Rosy, if you would like to," said my dad, but my brothers both scoffed and giggled. "A girl fishing? We will easily catch more than her." My dad told them off, saying, "If your sister wants to come, you make her welcome, boys. Understood?" "Yes, Father," they replied together. That's how we always ended up spending our Saturdays. The boys always got upset, as nine out of ten times, I caught more than them,' Rosy explained, smiling. 'Even after the boys had gone to war, we sometimes went.' Derek smiled at her. Rosy politely took the rod that was being handed to her, thanking, Jeff. Derek did the same. 'Thank you, Jeff.' They finally said their goodbyes, picked up the basket, and the rest of the fishing bag. Of they went down the garden, over the stream, into the woods. As they entered the woods, they saw a fawn with his mother walk by. Derek took a photograph, trying not to scare them. Afterwards, Rosy remarked, 'Oh, thank you, oh, Derek, they're so beautiful.' He turned to her, held her shoulders, and made her look at him. 'Come, let's sit. Then we can watch them.' After about two or three moments, the pair wandered off into the trees. 'Rosy, my love, do you realise what last night could mean?'Rosy turned away. 'Yes, my love, of course, I do. I hope it has.' Thinking he may be a bit cross, Rosy got up and ran. When she finally stopped, she found herself at the lake. It was very large; the sun was shimmering off it. She sat down and cried a bit. When the tears subsided, she started making a daisy chain with all sorts of things going around in her head. A little while later, Derek came running up. 'Oh God, Rosy, please don't do that again. You scared me.' He dropped the stuff on the ground, and he sat down a little way away from her, in case she decided to fly again. 'Rosy, darling, look at me please.' Slowly, Rosy lifted her head and turned to face him, but with her lowered. 'Now, sweetheart, why did you run off like that? If it was about last night, did you think I would be cross?'

She slowly looked up at him. 'Well, I . . .' He stopped her by leaning over and kissing her hard on the lips. 'Well, does that put you mind at rest? Just let me say I could never get cross with you.' He pulled her towards him and held her tight in his arms. Rosy placed the daisy chain over his head and smiled. Rosy explained to him. 'Yes, darling, I do know what last night meant. With you going away, I just wanted a part of you here.'

'Well', putting his fingers to her lips, 'it's OK, darling. I understand we will just have to practise a lot before I go.'

Rosy blushed, 'Oh, Derek, what a thing to say.' They both laughed. They went onto have a wonderful day, fishing. Though he was just mucking around, Derek found he really enjoyed the fishing. They made their way back to the pub. They had dinner and then enjoyed a drink in the bar. The next day was again spent relaxing and exploring. They came across a farm with cows, sheep, a donkey, and there were even a couple of goats. The path went through the fields. There was a pair of collie dogs running around; they came running to greet them. The farmer was not far behind. Rosy loved fussing over the dogs, telling them all about the wedding. All of a sudden, the long grass next to them burst into life, as three pups came bounding out of it to join them.

'I'm Jed. Pleased to meet you.'

'Hi, this is Rosy. I'm Derek, Jed. You have made some friends there, Rosy, my dear.'

'Oh, I know I'd love to own a place like this and have animals wandering around.'

'Well, Rosy, we had better push on. Before you go, the three rogues are looking for homes.'

'Oh, are they really?' Rosy said. They chatted a bit longer then carried on with their walk. As they talked along the way, Derek said, 'Do you think your parents might like a puppy? I know my sister would. It would be something for your parents to dote on when you and your brothers are not around.'

After talking a bit more, they decided that they would get the pups. They made their way back to the farm. They found Jed getting the cows in for milking; they spoke for a little while to make arrangements to collect the pups. After it was all arranged, they planned to pick them up in the morning on their way home. They made their way back for dinner.

Twelve

The next morning, after breakfast, they went back to their room to pack and put the bags in the car. Then they went back to say settle their bill and then came the goodbyes. Jeff and Kathy both wished them all the best. They all hugged and promised to keep in touch. They set off to the farm down the lane. When they arrived, they were again greeted by twenty-two pairs of feet, five four-legged and one two-legged. When they looked up, coming across the farmyard was a short well-built lady, drying her hands on her apron. She greeted them with a cheerful, 'Hello, my dears, you must be the newly-weds. Now let me think, Rosy and Derek, right? How are you? Jed told me all about you.'

Jed said, 'This is my wonderful wife and best friend, Grace.'

'Newly married? How wonderful!' said Grace.

Derek replied, 'Yes, two weeks, three hours, and fourteen minutes.' Rosy blushed. 'Not that he is counting,' she smiled.

'Oh, that's nice,' Grace said and then added, 'We have been married forty-seven years. All happy ones.'

Jed pulled her close. 'Every day is like the first,' Jed said, looking down at his wife with adoring eyes.

She said, 'Jed, go on and find the pups. These newly-weds will want to be on their way home.'

Jed duly went of to round the little rascals up while Grace said, 'Come inside while you wait and have a cup of tea with a piece of home-made cake, my dears.'

'Oh, that sounds lovely,' Rosy smiled at Derek who said the same as they entered the lovely farmhouse kitchen with the smell of fresh baking. A little lamb wobbled over to greet them and then went to Grace, bleating. 'Well, that really is some greeting, isn't it, Rosy?' Grace had put the kettle on and then magically produced a baby bottle full of milk. The lamb got very excited. He knew it was for him. Rosy asked if the lamb would mind if she fed him. 'Oh, yes, deary, he won't care as long as he is fed.' They all laughed, Rosy sat in the big farmhouse chair by the nice warm range. The little lamb wobbled, following her. That made Derek smile. He watched as the lamb suckled on the bottle every now and again, giving it a shove and then back to drinking as he drained the bottle dry. Grace appeared with a lovely fruit cake to eat with their tea. Realising there was no more to be had, the lamb curled up in front of warm range and went to sleep. As they drank their tea and ate their cake, Rosy asked why the little mite was being hand reared. Grace told them that his mum had twins, and for some reason, she rejected him. 'Sometimes that happens. Secretly I don't mind. It gives me something to mother. Jed says I'm daft and as if I don't have enough to do,' she said smiling. As they finished their tea, there was a commotion, and then the door exploded open and in burst three little balls of fluff – one black-and-white, the second was white with black and brown blotches, and the third was a mix of its two siblings. He had a very dark brown patch right on its forehead. 'Oh, Derek, they're so cute,' Rosy said as they were pounced on by said balls of fluff. Everybody laughed as they all tried to scramble onto Rosy's lap. Jed said that the black-and-white one would make a working sheepdog if they wanted. Derek had said about his parents and where they lived. Derek replied said he had a feeling this pup would be taken on by his little sister Francis, as a pet, and she is capable of training him into a working dog. 'Our grandad took great pleasure in teaching her, as neither of us boys was interested. The last time I was at home, Francis had said that if she was allowed a dog, she would call it JD, after him and our brother.'

'Oh, that's really nice,' Rosy said. 'I wonder if my parents will try and do that. My brothers' names are Duncan and Bert. Well, I suppose DBR isn't too bad.' They all laughed. Rosy asked Jed, 'What will happen to the third puppy?' Jed replied that they will find a home for him as my two are young. 'I don't, at the moment, really need a third working dog.' Rosy looked at Derek. Above the bundles of fluff, he said, 'I know that look already. You would like to have him, wouldn't you, my love?'

'Yes, please, darling. At least, I'll have something to love, cuddle, and look after,' she said, smiling at him, and he knew what she meant.

'OK, Rosy, we will take the little monkey.'

'Oh, that's nice, isn't it, Jed?'

'Yes, my dear Grace.'

'OK, Rosy, what will you call yours? I think I'll call him Charm.'

'Oh, that's lovely, Rosy,' they all said.

Grace said, 'Have you got a box in the car to put them in?'

'Oh no, didn't think about it, did we, Rosy?' She didn't hear a word as she was too busy cuddling the lamb. Now the pups had found their way up. Grace smiled at Derek. 'Oh I think your wife has her hands full.' They laughed.

'Well, Grace, she is in her element.'

'Yes, she is, isn't she? Not to worry, we have a crate and an old blanket.' Grace rose to go and get the things. Derek got up and said he would help her. After they left the room, Jed said, 'That little fellow seems to have chosen you.' The one with the brown patch around his eye was lying in her arms and the other two little ones were on her knees. Jed was drinking his tea and eating his cake.

'Why the long face, lass? You look very sad. You worried about that man of yours, aren't you?'

She looked at him with tears in her eyes, saying, 'Oh yes, Jed, very worried. I manage to keep my chin up. I'm afraid it's getting harder the nearer the time comes.'

Jed replied, 'How long before he goes, lass?' Rosy said, 'Tomorrow evening. Oh, Jed, he will be OK, won't he?'

'He will be fine, lassy, you'll see.' She smiled, hoping he was right, and just then, the others came back. Rosy pulled herself together and said, 'Help.' They looked at her. The pups hadn't moved, and the lamb was now lying on her feet. Grace walked over, whispering, 'Lambikins'. That's what she called him. She heard laughter behind her. Grace hadn't realised that Jed had heard her. He threw his arms up and said, 'I give up on you, my dear', then, turning to the younger couple, he said, 'Ever since I've known her, my dear Gracy had to name every living thing. Even the chickens have names, and the dear old cockerel has a name too. He is proudly known as Corky.' They all laughed. Grace bent down, picked little Lambikins up and placed him back on the blanket in front of the range, where it was nice and warm. The two older sheepdogs had made themselves comfy in front of the fire. Then picking up the first pup, she handed it to Derek, the second went to her husband, who picked him up and placed him gently in the box. Grace picked the third off Rosy, and Rosy stood up. As soon as she did, the little pup, Grace had taken from her, cried for her. Hearing him cry, Rosy took him back gently. He snuggled deeply into her neck and hair. Grace whispered in her ear, 'Bless him. This little one senses that you're upset, dear, so you hang on tight to each other, OK?' Rosy gave a watery-eyed smile, and Grace placed a clean hanky into Rosy's hand so that Rosy could compose herself before the men could see. The men had already gone to the car. 'You take your time, deary.'

'Thank you, dear Grace. You and your husband are so kind. I also loved meeting the animals.' Rosy gave the lady a big hug. Rosy wiped the tears away, Grace said, 'If that hubby of yours asks why your eyes are red and watering, then you blame that little fellow and say his fur got in your eyes. That way, he won't worry.'

They looked at each other and gave a little chuckle together. 'You're so wise. Would it be OK if we come visit when Derek comes home?'

'Oh, my dear, you come any time. Bring charm and the babies with you. Now off you go.' Rosy didn't take in all that Grace had said. After they had settled the pups in the back of the car, they said their goodbyes and were on their way home. Oh and what a ride that was!

Thirteen

A s soon as the car started, the pups came to life, not wanting to be in their box, so they started to make a fuss. Rosy said to Derek, 'What have we let ourselves, and our families, in for?' Both of them laughed. After a while, one by one, the pups fell asleep. Most of the journey was spent in silence. Rosy was pleased the pups were there, not for the obvious reasons. They were a genuine reason not to talk too much, just in case they woke the pups. It meant she didn't have to make small talk. Rosy was scared. The tears wouldn't stay put. She didn't want to do that in front of Derek. A promise that Rosy had made to herself was that wouldn't happen, not wanting to upset Derek. After about fifteen minutes, Derek asked, 'Are you OK, Rosy, darling? You're very quiet.'

She whispered, 'I'm just trying not to make too much noise, in case we wake those three little rascals. It's better they stay asleep.' She turned to him, smiling, and then turned to look out the window again. Rosy hoped he hadn't seen her red-rimmed eyes. Soon, they would be pulling up outside her dear parents' home and then her tears can run freely. He will think it's because everyone was glad to have her home, being able to see her brothers before they went back to duty, with all the emotions women have. He said to her that he thought women are funny as they could cry at a drop of a hat. She smiled to herself. The sun was still high in the sky, as they pulled into her street. The street that just two weeks ago was a totally different sight. Slowly, they pulled up in front of her parents' home. There was also another car parked in the drive. She guessed that her father's was in the garage. 'I wonder whose car that is, Derek.'

'It's Gilbert's car, I think,' he said. 'I wonder what he is doing here.'

Rosy managed a smile, 'Well, you won't know until you ask him.' They both smiled. As they got out of the car, the front door flew open, and they were greeted by a lot of smiling faces. In front of them all was Francis, jumping straight into her brother's open arms. He swung her around. Derek whispered in her ear, 'I have a surprise in the car for you. Also for Rosy's mum and dad.'

'Where? Where?' asked Francis, jumping up and down with excitement.

'In a minute,' he said. 'Now calm down please. Let's get everyone inside.'

'OK, big brother.'

And then she promptly shouted out, 'OK, everyone inside for sandwiches and tea.'

Derek laughed and said to her, 'Well, I see. I'll have to watch you, Miss Francis. You're a proper little bossy boots.' They both burst out laughing. Anyway, everyone went inside. No one realised that there were two individuals missing. They were all chatting to Rosy, asking how the honeymoon was and what they saw, where they went, whether the weather was nice, the people they met and such. They wanted to know everything they saw or did, people they met. Rosy, who by now was smiling, all tears, red eyes gone, forgotten for now, taking a seat on the sofa, taking the cup of very much needed tea, knowing what Derek, with his partner in crime Francis were up to, made her smile to herself. Knowing her job was to keep everyone's attention, she looked around the room and saw Gilbert sitting in a chair. To her surprise, Susan was sitting on the arm, and they were holding hands tightly. Rosy said with a smile, 'I think some of you have news of your own.'

Susan blushed. 'No, Rosy, you first.'

Now they were all settled – her parents on the sofa with her and they were holding hands too, from the beginning. Outside, Derek and Francis went to the car, and he told her to open the door. Francis did as he told her. There were noises coming from a wooden crate on the back seat. She leant over to look after removing the jacket that covered the box. What happened next made her jump out of her skin, as three little heads popped up. Derek laughed at her. After giving him a well-deserved sisterly punch, she then promptly climbed over the front seat into the back seats. Before heading home, Rosy and he had agreed to let Francis choose a pup or a pup chose her. Secretly, Rosy hoped that wouldn't be her favourite. Sitting in the back of the car, Francis said, 'Oh, Derek, they are beautiful. Whose are they?'

'Well', Derek replied slowly, 'I wonder who do we know who would like a puppy of her own.' Looking at him with a big grin on her face, it slowly dawned on her that he meant her. 'Oh, Derek, do you really mean it?'

'Yes, one is for you for being a fantastic little sister.' Again he got a sisterly punch, less of the little please. 'Oh, Franny, you will always be my little sister.' That made them both laugh. 'I was about to say you are a great bridesmaid too.' Then he handed a pup to her and said, 'He is yours, on one condition you must look after him all the time, feed him, take him for walks and not expect Mum and Dad to look after him. They are too busy. One other thing, make sure he goes to the vet when he needs to. No getting bored with it as it's yours for life. A present from Rosy and me.'

'Which one is mine, Derek?'

'Well', he replied (keeping his fingers crossed, knowing how Rosy felt about one and hoping Francis wouldn't chose that one), 'which one do you like best?'

Straight away, Franny said, 'The one with the brown patch.' Derek's heart sank a little until he saw the one his sister was holding. It was the one without the brown eye. 'Is that the one you like, Francis?'

'Oh yes, Derek, very, very much. I love him. Is that OK if I have this one?' she asked, picking the one with a bit of brown on his head.

'Oh yes, Franny love (that was his nickname for her), that's all right. You see, Franny, Rosy has her heart set on', he delved in the box, pulling out the smallest pup, 'this one.'

His sister looked at him. 'You mean Rosy wanted me to have that one if I had chosen it?'

'Yes, Franny, she was.'

'Who is the other one for?'

He replied, 'For Eleanor and Albert.'

'Ooh, ooh!' Franny was jumping up and down again. 'Will you calm down? You will scare the pups. You're like a jack in the box.'

'Ooh, ooh but, Derek, please, please may I give him to them please.'

He laughed, 'Then will you calm down?'

'Yes, Derek, I'm sorry.'

'That's fine, honey. OK, you may give him to them. First though, I want you to take them all into the back garden. Very quietly, go through the back door and find a bowl. Let them have a drink. Let them run for a few minutes. When that's done, I want you to come in with Rosy's pup. I want you to walk over to her and hand him to her. If he will let you, I'd like you to gently tie this around his neck,' Derek said, handing her a ribbon the same colour as Rosy's best, also his favourite dress, fixed to the ribbon was a gift card Francis said I think he will. He pulled out a pen and wrote on the card, 'To my darling, beautiful Rosy, thank you for becoming my wife to share your life with me. I love you so much, Rosy. I always will. All my love, Derek.'

Francis said to him, 'How come you had the ribbon, Derek? I was going to get her a present and then attach this to it. Oh, Derek, you are the best brother anyone could have.'

'OK, I'm going in before someone realises I'm missing.'

'OK, Derek.'

Off they went their separate ways – Francis with the three little bundles of fur and Derek inside the house. Before parting, Franny called to him, 'Derek, guess what.'

'What, little sis?'

'I'm going to call my puppy JD'. Derek smiled, setting off to join the others. He entered the house and made his way to the lounge. Then he stood just inside the room. Duncan was standing in the doorway. 'Hi, Derek.'

'Good to see you, Duncan. You still having trouble being in a room, especially with lots of people?'

'Yes,' Duncan replied. Derek asked him if he would do something for him.

'OK,' he said, 'what would you like me to do?'

Derek explained about the pups. Derek asked him if he would mind going to help Francis and then look after the other two while Franny brings Rosy's pup in. With two, they are less likely to escape.

'OK, Derek. I'll be happy to help. That gives me the excuse to leave, to get outside.'

Derek wasn't quite convinced that was the only reason. Duncan liked Franny. He smiled. Off he went to find Francis; he found her in the garden.

'Hi there, Francis. Your brother asked me to come to help you. Right now, it looks like you could use another pair of hands,' he said, laughing as Franny was chasing the pups around.

'Oh yes, please. I thought I'd be able to manage. I forgot I have to get them a drink. I dare not leave them, in case they get through the fence or hedge.'

'OK', said Duncan, 'how about I go and get them some water?'

While he was gone, Francis saw the tables from the wedding reception in the corner. She pulled three out and put them up and then turned them on their sides and made a triangle with them. Just then Duncan returned and saw what she had done. 'Very clever,' he remarked promptly grabbing an escapee, giggling, between them put the pups were put, in the triangle, placing the water down inside the make shift pen. 'Francis, look I snaffled a bit of tomorrow's mince mum had boiled up to make shepherd's pie tomorrow.'

'Oh, Duncan. There's enough there for the three of them.'

They fed them. Also while he was inside, he found his mum's old shopping basket. He lined it with an old towel. Francis said, 'What a great idea, Duncan!' The pup was tired and sleepy, so he would lie there quietly. Franny placed him in, and they tied the ribbon, managing to make a lovely big bow.

'Well, how shall we do your parents' pup, Duncan?'

'I know,' he said. Off he rushed again, and he came back with a crate like they arrived in. It was not as big with lower sides. With a towel, they decided on a plan. She would enter with Rosy's pup first and then Duncan would enter with his parents' one, while her little fellow waited asleep in the kitchen on her cardigan. Rosy was just telling them about the fishing, when Rosy beckoned Derek to join her. He crossed the room, just managing to squeeze on the sofa between her and Albert.

'You OK, lad?' Albert asked.

'Yes, I am fine thank you. How are you?'

'Same thanks, lad.'

He turned to give Rosy a kiss and take hold of her hand. He looked over to the chair, where he saw his best mate with his wife's best mate, holding hands. He smiled. Rosy carried on, 'Jeff the landlord asked if Derek liked fishing. Before he could answer, I piped up that I love it. He handed me the rod.' Everybody laughed, especially her father as he was the one who had introduced her to fishing. They all looked up as the lounge door opened, and Francis entered with a basket in her hand. Derek looked at Francis and gave her a quizzical look. She smiled at him; he trusted her, so he just stayed quiet. Francis came over to where Rosy was sitting. Francis gently laid her parcel on Rosy's lap. Francis uncovered the gift card tied to the basket. Everyone wondered what was going on, as, at the angle that Francis was standing, no one could see the basket, let alone what was in it. Bending nearer to Rosy, she said, 'I think this is for you, dear sister.' And then she added, 'Thank you, Rosy.' Francis then stepped back so that everyone could see what was going on. Rosy undid the ribbon. After reading the card and before Rosy could say anything to anyone, even her husband, there was this little scratching. No one knew what was inside the basket. All were anxiously watching, with baited breath. The scratching continued, then little cry, and slowly a little head popped out the top. At first, Rosy was disappointed, and she looked at Derek. He turned to her, whispering, 'What's wrong, Rosy?'

When he looked at the little head, he realised what his wife was thinking. 'It's OK, love. Go on, let him out, go on, I promise it's OK really.' Rosy didn't get the chance to let him out, the furry ball jumped, scrabbling his way out, on to Rosy's lap. Everyone was surprised; there was silence. When the surprise had worn off, there were cheers and laughter. Rosy whispered to Derek, 'I thought Francis had chosen him.'

They hugged, and he whispered in her ear, 'I love you, Rosy.' As things quietened down again, the lounge door opened, and Duncan entered carrying what looked like just a pile of clean laundry off the washing line.

'Very convincing,' Eleanor said. 'It's a day for surprises. I don't think I have even seen either of my bo . . .' she was interrupted, and before she could finish, the bundle started moving and wriggling and then it started squeaking as he approached his mum. A little pink nose appeared, followed by an ear, and then eyes then the other ear, a little paw, and then all of a sudden, the laundry leapt out of Duncan's hands in one movement. Albert and Eleanor moved together, catching the wriggly laundry bundle of fluff in mid-air. They both looked at Derek, who then, with Rosy, went over to her parents.

Before they spoke, Bert said, 'Unwrap your laundry, Mum.' Everyone laughed at that. Albert helped his wife as the laundry was really squirming. As they untangled the poor little mite, the first part that showed light of day was a very tiny hairy backside. 'Oh look, Albert, a baby.'

'Yes, my love. I can see,' his mum said to Duncan, 'Whatever possessed you, Son to wrap him up? Oh, never mind. He's safe.'

Smiling, her parents looked up at Rosy, who said, 'We thought you might be able to give this little fellow a home. He will be great company for you both.'

Bert said, 'There you are, Mum. Your new baby will be the baby till grandbabies appear.'

'Oh, Bert, what a thing to say, apart from the fact you have made your sister blush.'

'It's OK, Mum,' he said, looking at Derek, smiling. Bert carried Mum's baby, then Dad's new project, to make the baby a bed. 'Hey, you two, we can't keep calling it "baby". It is a boy, isn't it, Rosy?'

'Yes, Dad.'

Albert discussed with his wife, for a few moments and then proudly looked up, saying, 'This little man, everyone, I'm proud to announce, is to be known as Badger.'

They both bent and kissed her parents on the cheeks. Everyone was milling around fussing the newcomers, oohing and aahing. 'Well, lass, what are you going to name yours?' his father asked.

'I'm going to name my little boy. . .', giving a smile as Rosy hadn't even told him, 'well, I gave this a lot of thought. Now I would like to introduce Charm.'

'Oh, Rosy, that is lovely,' Elizabeth said. As things quietened down again, there was a scrapping at the closed door. Francis ran to open it, scooping up yet another ball of fluff. Moving over to Rosy and Derek to thank them properly, she then hurried over to her parents, who were now in real shock, and introduced them to JD.

'Oh, Derek, Rosy,' they said in unison. Francis looked over at Derek, smiling; it was their little secret for now. Looking at his parents faces, particularly, his mum's, he said, 'It's OK, Mum. Francis and I have a deal. The only thing she'll come to you for is the vet. Everything else is down to her. If he is not looked after, I shall take him away.' They all spent the rest of the evening chatting and playing with the new additions to the 'now very extended' family.

Fourteen

After a good night's sleep, they all gathered for breakfast. Everyone was very quiet as it was the last day for Rosy and Derek to be together for a while. They had decided to spend it with Susan and Gilbert. As Gilbert had said he had something to tell Derek, after breakfast, Rosy went to get ready to meet them. As they were leaving, Bert said, 'Would you mind giving me a lift to the station. I'm off back to barracks.'

'Today?' Rosy cried. 'Why didn't you tell us last night?'

He said, 'I didn't want to spoil your evening.'

'Yes, we will drop you off,' they said, leaving Bert to say his goodbyes to their parents, a very tearful one as you can imagine. On their way to meet their friends, they dropped Bert at the station. 'Don't wait with me. Go and enjoy your last few hours, and Derek look after my little sister. She's the only one I've got.' The three of them laughed. Charm, who had been quiet until now, yapped from the back seat, so Bert said, 'Yes, to you too, Charm.' Off he went, disappearing into the station. None of them knew when they would see each other again. They drove onto Susan's home to pick their friends up for the day. They had decided to go for a picnic as Derek only had nine hours before he had to catch his train. They drove out to the countryside and found a place to park. They all climbed out of the car, including Charm. As the girls set out the picnic, Derek and Gilbert went for a walk with little Charm tagging along. As they wandered along, Derek said, 'Well, Gill, what is this news you've got for me. A good one, I hope.'

'Well', Gill said, 'depends how you look at it.' He gave a little laugh.

He said, 'You know you are a crew member short a navigator, am I right?'

Derek stood there, wondering how he knew that. Gill went on, 'Well, dear friend, you are looking at your new navigator.' He stepped back and threw his hands in the air.

'Hey, sir, you should see your face. It's a picture.' They both started laughing. As they were laughing, the girls came up behind them. 'Well, what's so funny?'

Gill told them as they walked back to where the lovely meal was set out; the rest of the afternoon went quickly as it does when you don't want it to. The men said, 'We had better get you girls back.' Derek felt a tug at the bottom of his trousers. 'Oh, I'm sorry, little sir. Yes, you too little man.' He picked him up, saying to him, 'You, my little fellow, I'm leaving in charge of our favourite person, your Mum Rosy.' The pup looked at him, whined and then licked his face as if to say, 'of course I will, Dad.'

Off they drove, dropping Susan with Gilbert off on the way, promising to meet at the station in an hour. They arrived home and gathered Derek's things. He said his goodbyes. Rosy spoke to her mother, 'Mum, do you think I could leave Charm with you while I see Derek off?' Her mother laughed, 'Charm? Where did you get that from?'

'He feels like a charm. He is the first thing that is ours, not his, not mine, ours.'

'Oh, OK, dear. That's fine. He can play with Badger now.'

It was Rosy's turn to smile, 'Badger? I really love that he is looks much like a badger.'

'Yes, that's nice.'

Off they set out to the station. Twenty minutes later, they arrived. Susan and Gilbert were already there, waiting. They made their way to the right platform, where the train was just pulling in. The men climbed aboard with lots of other servicemen, and after their goodbyes, the whistle blew and the train moved slowly out of the station. Finally lost in the smoke and steam, both of them silently wondered when they would see their men again. The girls turned and made their way back home . . .

Fifteen

Derek and Gilbert arrived at the barracks about ten o'clock that evening. They settled in and then went to the mess and had a drink. While there, they were told that there would be an early morning briefing about the next raid. They decided to turn in. At six o'clock, they were up, had breakfast, and now they were on their way to the briefing as ordered. As they arrived, they couldn't hear each other above the many, many voices, all trying to talk at once. It was deafening. They found seats and sat. All of a sudden, it was silent as the big boss man walked into the room, calling for silence. The briefing resulted in flying orders for that afternoon at 15.00 hours, so they had time to check all that needed checking, have some lunch, and maybe a quick nap. By 15.30 hours, they were well on their way, over the Channel to where they were to drop their bombs as the Germans did on their homeland. Derek and Gilbert were about to return the favour. With that first raid, he realised just how good a crew they really were and how in tune with each other they really were too. If someone said something, the others instantly knew what to do before he has finished talking. When it was over, they turned for home, flying through thick ach ach that was lighting up the skies at dusk. They soon landed back at the airfield, bringing *Hope and Glory* to a halt. They exited the plane and headed straight for debriefing. Then they headed for something to eat. This went on for over three months – briefing, raid, and debriefing. It was much the same routine. One evening, when Derek was outside the barracks, he saw the full moon. Derek's thoughts went to the last time he had seen a full moon. He was safe. This full moon could be fraught with dangers of an air raid. His thoughts went to Rosy, wondering what she was doing right now. She was hopefully cuddled up in bed with the fluff ball going in the guise of Charm. He laughed to himself, *I'm jealous of a puppy, oh dear.* He laughed again, *The name Charm, thinking about it, only my Rosy could come up with that. That means there's JD, Charm, and the last one being Badger. What a mixture of names!* He smiled again as his thoughts went back to the honeymoon, lying with Rosy in the moonlight and the warm sea air, blowing over them as they stroked each other, slowly his hands running over her soft silky thighs and listening to her breathing getting deeper as his hands wandered further towards . . . His thoughts were broken as Gill came running up to him. 'Hi, sir, emergency briefing now. Wow! That's some smile. Love to know what you were thinking. I'll never tell even under torture.' Both of them laughed. Derek was to remember those words he used in jest. Together they ran to the briefing room. They were told in the briefing that they had a special raid to undertake. It was a special mission with a specific target for them to bomb. Special mission with a specific target it might be, but they were not told why and what the real point was.

'Oh, well, it's down to us to do as we are told. That's right, mate. We do not question,' Gil said from behind. It wasn't going to be easy as it was further into the enemy territory than their other missions. No one apart from captains and navigators were to know the target. The rest were dismissed. After the briefing, Derek went to his room, started to write his letters home – first to his parents, Franny, and, of course, JD. He wrote, hoping they were all well. To Franny he wrote, 'Hope you looking after JD properly.' He closed that letter and sealed it. Then he started his most important letter. To Rosy, answering her last letter. He hoped Rosy wouldn't notice how long it had taken to answer. He stared at the blank page for what felt like forever. Finally, he started trying to keep it as normal as he could. He had been told he was not allowed to say what the mission was. He just wrote normal everyday things like what they had for lunch and what they had been doing. He asked how she was, how the fluff ball was, as he wrote. He smiled because she had scolded him good for calling Charm the fluff ball, saying he is growing into a fine dog. He added, 'Fluffy ball fine dog'. He knew that would make her smile. Then he got to the important bit. There had been one sentence that had stood out in her letter. 'Derek, darling, I've been to the doctors. That wonderful last encounter, under the willow (he chuckled to himself at the memory), well, it has had the outcome we expected.' *We?* he laughed. *Cheeky Rosy, I didn't know anything till it was done.* Her letter continued, 'I'm really happy. I hope you are too, Derek.'

He carried on with his letter, writing, 'Yes, my darling, you know I'm happy as long as you are.' He added, 'What about nursing?' After wishing everyone well, he said his goodbyes, gave hug for Charm. Once again, it was time to seal the envelope, so he added, 'PS: if it's a girl, may we call her Jessica?' Then he finally sealed it, kissed it, and then went to eat. Then he decided to get some sleep. They were to take off at 05.00 hours. He met Gill, and together they walked to the mess, talking small talk, both in their own little worlds. As they sat eating, they told each other about the letters they had had to write.

'Gill, I'm hoping Rosy thinks it's just another letter.'

Gill looked at him with a quizzical look. Derek smiled and said, 'She's pregnant. It was in her last letter.'

Gill shook his hand, saying, 'Congratulations, sir. That's wonderful. That must have been some honeymoon. Now I know what that look on your face was. You were reminiscing.'

Derek blushed. 'Oh yes, it was.'

After they had eaten, they posted their letters and then agreed to turn in for the night. They were up again at 03.30 hours, dressed and breakfasted, into the briefing room for the last briefing. Thirty minutes later, they were airborne . . .

Sixteen

Back at home, Rosy was busy with finishing her training, working. She looked after her best friend, whom Derek called, 'Fluff ball', which always made her smile. Now, that she was pregnant, her parents were pleased too. On one of her rare days off, she was sitting in the garden watching Charm and Badger play. Her father had just come home for lunch; he came and sat with her and handed her a letter. She knew straight away that it was from Derek. Excusing herself, she went to her room to read it. When read, she read it again, then again, taking in every word. No matter how hard he had tried to hide what was going on Rosy, instinctively knew something was different. There seemed to be an urgency in the letter, an urgency she just couldn't put her finger on. One sentence stood out. He had asked that if it's was girl they could call her Jessica after his favourite grandmother. Rosy liked that name very much. The answer will be a definite yes to his touching request. The name for a girl was decided Jessica Marie, Marie after one of her grandmothers. Rosy went back downstairs to tell her parents. They were pleased, and then she showed them the letter, wording her fears aloud to them. They tried to waylay her fears; they knew it was a waste of time as they knew that their daughter and Derek were like one. They seemed to know what each other was thinking still they tried. Then it hit her what was odd about the letter. They had a few months to go, and he had named the baby. Why so soon? Why the urgency? She looked at her parents, bursting into tears. When Charm heard her, he ran to her side and handed her his 'not so little' brown paw and then clambered up next to her. Her mum sat the other side, not quite knowing why her darling girl was crying so hard. She just held her. When Rosy had calmed down a bit, the explanation came. 'Why would he do that unless he thought he may be in danger, maybe never see me again?'

'Oh, darling,' her parents said. They knew it would be a waste of time. They just comforted her the best they could. Her mother said, 'I'll go make some tea.' It then was just her with her father. She looked at him like she did when she was a small child, knowing all he had to do was kiss her hurt, and it would magically disappear. He sat beside her. By now, Badger had joined them; he sat by her legs, looking up at her and whining. Charm was lying with his head on her tummy. Her father looked at her and said quite sensibly and calmly, 'Listen, my darling, please calm down. Think of the baby.' The sobs subsided slowly, and she slowly calmed down. She put her head on his shoulder, and he, in turn, put his arm around his beloved daughter's shoulders. Rosy started thinking about the night the baby was conceived. She thought about Derek's gentle touch and caressing and those wonderful kisses. Yes, those touches up and down her inner thighs and then feeling his lovely, warm, hard manhood as it slipped inside her, and as he carried on still touching her, she had managed to turn him over, teasing him. He really had no choice but to lose control inside her. They were both pleased with the result. Slowly she calmed down and fell asleep on his shoulder. A little later, Duncan walked into the room after hearing all the commotion, saw the scene, mouthed to his father, 'What's wrong?' He beckoned him over and explained, and then asked if he would take over slowly. Duncan slid his arm around his baby sister's shoulders. His father placed her head on his shoulder but still the two pups wouldn't leave her. Albert said, 'I'm going to help your mother in the kitchen.' Duncan knew he was really going to make sure she was OK. As Albert reached the kitchen, he could hear his dear wife weeping. He took her in his arms, saying, 'Now, now, my dear, we must be strong. Rosy needs us right now. With the baby getting closer, lucky she has her job, and the pups help.'

'I know she isn't working right now. She will go back after the baby,' Eleanor said. 'I know, Albert, the poor little mite. I feel so sorry for her at the moment. It is just a feeling. You know her and her feelings.'

'When it comes to Derek, yes I know my dear. Is that tea ready?' he smiled. Together they laid the tray with four cups, four saucers, and everything else they needed for that much-needed cup of tea. As they were pouring the water into the teapot, there was a knock on the back door. It was Susan who quite obviously had had a letter too.

'I hope you don't mind me coming over unannounced. I know what Derek and Rosy are like, and how she feels something's wrong before being told. I know she has had a letter as I got one this morning.'

Albert said, 'Yes, Susan, Rosy's in the front room with her brother. She is asleep on his shoulder.'

'OK, Mr Maye, I'll try not to wake her.' With that off she went while Eleanor and Albert added another cup and saucer to the tea tray. Albert carried it through into the lounge and placed it on the coffee table. Duncan was still holding Rosy; he also had dozed off. The three of them smiled, saying, 'Don't they look cute.' Duncan woke up, whispering less of the cute.

'Please, I'm a 6' twenty-one-year-old man.' Then he smiled back at them.

'OK,' he said. 'where's this cup of tea I was promised?' He laughed. A few minutes later, Rosy stirred and woke up. 'Oh, at last, Sis, my arm has gone to sleep.' He pulled his arm free, and as he did, she jumped. Charm looked shocked as he was very rudely awoken. Duncan thinking he had hurt her, said, 'Sis, you OK?'

'Oh yes, I'm fine. The baby kicked.'

'Oh, Rosy, can I feel it?' asked Duncan.

'Of course, Big Brother.'

Both of them laughed. 'Oh wow! That's incredible, Rosy.'

From the other side of the room, Susan said, 'Rosy, may I feel it, if you don't mind.'

'Oh, my dear friend, come here, sit with me.'

Susan sat down and placed her hand on her friend's swollen tummy. She said with a smile, 'Oh, that's fantastic.'

Her dad was looking a bit left out, a bit sad, so Rosy said, 'Would you like to feel your grandbaby moving?'

He smiled and looked at Eleanor. 'Go on, you silly old thing, it won't bite,' Duncan added, and everybody laughed. He went over and placed his hand on his daughter's tummy.

He smiled, 'Oh, darling, that's so beautiful. My Rosy, thank you very much for letting your old father feel his first grandbaby.'

Duncan and Susan emulated the same thing. Her mother, having already had the pleasure of feeling her grand-baby, carried on laying out the cups and saucers, ready to pour the much-needed cup of tea. They drank it in relative silence. When they finished, Rosy noticed Duncan was missing. Getting up, she said, 'I'm just going to let the pups into the garden.' Following her, the pups knew it meant garden. As Rosy walked out, following the pups, there was her big brother, sitting on the wall. She joined him and then asked, 'What's wrong, Duncan?'

For the longest time, he stayed silent, and when he finally looked at her, he said, 'When I felt your little one move, it suddenly dawned on me I may never be a dad.'

Rosy said, 'You listen to me. You will be a daddy one day. Not only that, you're going to be a good one, but for now, dear Brother, you'll have to put up with being an uncle, OK?'

'OK, Sis.' Rosy kissed him on the cheek, got up to go back inside. He turned to look at him and said, 'Hey, Big Brother, bring those scallywags in when you come.'

He replied with a smile, 'OK, Little Sis.' They both laughed. With that, Rosy went back indoors. Returning to the lounge where her parents and Susan were still sitting, she sat. Her father said, 'We are going out. Will you be OK?'

'Yes, Dad. Duncan and Susan are here now. Go, take mother out and have a nice walk.'

After they left, Rosy turned to Susan and said, 'Did you get a letter?'

'Yes, dear Rosy, I did. That's why I'm here. I know what you're like where that husband of yours is concerned.'

'Oh, Susan, there's more to that letter than he could say.'

'Why do you think that, honey?'

'Because, Susan, he named the baby.'

To take the tension out of the conversation a bit, Susan asked, 'What's the name then?' Rosy replied, with tears in her eyes, 'Jessica Marie. Jessica after his favourite grandma and Marie after mine.'

Seventeen

It was now 07.33 hours. They were nearing their target; they were met with plenty ach-ach, from ground guns with search lights, worse as the target grew ever nearer to what could potentially be their deaths. They were working closer together to get the best outcome; they could because they all now knew what the target was. They all knew they would be lucky to get out unscathed. That's why it was a dawn raid, simply because day or night, it was just as dangerous. The only difference was at least they could see well enough during daylight to hit the target. Twenty minutes later, they reached their target and started bombing the heart of very important German complex made up of what looked like factories, living accommodation for the workers, and that's when they knew that this must be very important to the Germans. It was well placed; it backed on to a mountain, the rest was trees. What Derek and his crew didn't know was that the trees were excluding from their sight the POWs who were obviously being used in whatever was going on in that factory. There could be a tunnel into the cliff. But what they did see was something none of them had ever seen. There was a huge sheet lying over the trees. As they looked harder, they saw that on the white sheet was three letters, just three. They were hard to digest – those three letters were POWs. All at once, there was a lot of noise over the radio as everyone said the same thing, 'POWs! They're our blokes.' The local resistance must have put the sheet or whatever it was over the trees during the night, just before they came, hoping we would see it, before we started bombing. That way, we could avoid bombing there. The sheet was to try to protect the POWs. This was another reason for the early-morning raid because they couldn't put that up during the day before, and it couldn't have been done the night before, in case the guards see or hear it flapping in the breeze. All this happened in seconds. That's the way war was – fast. They must have heard the planes coming, and then somehow got it up and spread out. Everything was done in split seconds in hope of being first. To continue to survive, you can't take your eye off the ball even for a second because it wasn't just you on that plane. You had many lives to think about. That's why Derek was so lucky to have a crew so in tune to each other, although Gill told him the other day, 'You wouldn't know they were great if you had seen them on leave, often fighting amongst themselves.' They had both laughed, agreeing it was good for them let off steam after a bombing run. As they pulled up to go around again to bomb for the second time, Derek radioed the other pilots in case they hadn't seen the warning, and as they went around the second time to drop their bombs, they heard a sudden bang coming from one of the engines.

'Oh, blast, that ach, ach did catch us.' They looked out, and the engine was on fire. Gradually, it was spreading to the wing. Derek pulled up hard after his bomb run. They couldn't extinguish the fire, so they started to head home. He radioed the other pilots, telling them what had happened and what he was doing. 'OK, Rook, good luck. See you at home.' As he started to fly away from the target, the plane was hit again, in fact, twice more. As they had been bombing, they hadn't been able to get higher enough for the crew to parachute out, so Derek decided to try to bring her down, if he could find somewhere. The other choice . . . well, he wouldn't let himself think about that. He managed to keep her going and then his co-pilot said, 'Hey, Rook, there is a large field down there. Also there are woods nearby.' Derek manoeuvred the plane as much as he could, under the circumstances, and he managed to get into an OK position and then shouted through the radio. 'OK, chaps, we are going down into a field. When we are down, I want you, no, I order you to run like hell to the woods.' As he started to take the plane down, a picture of Rosy flashed through his mind, a picture of her holding their baby, a beautiful little girl Jessica Marie with her mum's blue eyes and flaxen hair. He pulled his thoughts back to reality; they tried to lower the undercarriage. It didn't want to know. Worried about that, he once again shouted through the radio, 'OK, fellas, we are going down on our belly.' He heard them all gasp, but like the way Derek trusted them, they all trusted him as well, and they knew that he would do his best to make sure they were all safe. It seemed like forever before they hit ground; it had only been a couple of minutes. After the initial thump, there was grinding, groaning, and sliding across the ground before coming to a stop about twenty feet or so from the trees. As they had hit ground, the plane had ignited, but all of them escaped unhurt and ran to the trees. Derek found all his crew had survived with just minor cuts and bruising and abrasions. Gilbert had broken his arm, and Alan, their medic, splinted it as best he could and held it in position with a couple of tree branches wrapped around with a bandage to stabilise it. 'Will he be OK, Alan?'

'Well, sir, with a lot of hope and some painkillers, which we don't have much of.'

Derek said, 'Sorry, fellas.'

The whole crew, at once, said, 'Sir, it's not your fault.'

'Thanks, guys, but, I think we had better make ourselves scarce double quick, as any German around this area even with bifocals and half blind couldn't have missed the flames shooting from the dear *Hope and Glory.*' All of them had had grown so very fond of the plane; she was part of them.

All of them replied, 'Yes, sir.' Then they set off at double-pace.

Eighteen

Back at home, Easter and Christmas passed by hardly noticed, as just before Christmas, Rosy had a premonition that Derek was in trouble; she felt him calling for her. When it suddenly stopped, not faded out, just stopped dead, it convinced her that he was dead. That feeling doesn't just stop for any other reason, even when he is ill. It was there, and it didn't cross her mind to think of him losing his memory. A couple of days later, Rosy had received that all-too-dreaded telegram that read, 'Sorry to inform you, your husband is missing in action.' Rosy kept saying, 'I knew it. I knew it.'

Her parents couldn't console her and even Susan failed. Duncan, who was leave, was just about up and spoke to her, 'I won't pretend to know how you're feeling. I've never been that close to someone. Oh, dear Little Sis, please, please calm down. You keep this up, then you *will* lose that darling, that little life you are carrying, and you would never forgive yourself.'

'They say he is missing, sweetie.'

'I know you two seem to have a link that us mere mortals don't understand.'

Rosy, looked at him, smiling, 'Well, *when* he comes home, you want little Jessie to be with you to meet her daddy, don't you?'

Rosy thought for a minute. 'Oh yes, Duncan, more than anything.'

He said, 'So are you calming down?'

He held her in his arms, and slowly, the racking sobs turned into a smile with a few tears. After the episode, she had calmed down. Life carried on, and Duncan went back to his unit. Susan had heard through Gilbert's parents that he also was missing. When she wasn't working, she would go to keep Rosy company. In April, Rosy received a letter inviting her to go to Derek's parents' estate; her parents were also invited, as was Susan if work would allow. Staying for as long as they liked, the furry duo were also invited. Rosy wrote back, accepting for all. Susan would love to come as long as her employer will allow her the time off. Her employer, knowing the circumstances, allowed it. It was all arranged. It was now early June, and the baby was due any day. Everything, well, as much as possible was ready. Rosy had received a visit by Derek's squadron leader with the chaplain. They introduced themselves. 'I'm Jeffrey Avery.' Then looking at the chaplain, 'I, for my sins, my dear, am Dougle Winden.' They sat opposite her and then proceeded to inform her of what little they knew and that was, the plane had gone down in a field. It seemed they had escaped before it went up in flames. 'Sorry, we haven't heard anything more since. That was at the end of April.'

They took their leave, assuring her that they would let her know as soon as anything else was heard. The chaplain took her hands in his and, looking in the eyes, asked, 'How long have you got to go, Rosy?'

'Oh any time now, Chaplain.'

'Well, my dear, good luck. Would it be too much for you to let me know? I'd love to see the child.'

Smiling at him, she gave him a hug, 'Oh, Chaplain, I'd love that. I will let you know as soon as the baby comes.' With that, the two men took their leave.

Rosy woke a few days later and told Susan, 'It's a lovely late May morning, Susan. Let's have our breakfast and then go out for a while.' At least there was hope, although that's not what was really on her mind. The belief Derek was dead still stayed. Rosy knew it would help Susan. 'Come, best friend, shall we take Charm and Badger for a walk? Let's see if we can find Franny with JD. Then we can all go, OK?' Susan agreed.

Off they went to find Franny and JD, who were never far away from each other. They found them in the kitchen. Franny was washing up, and Rosy, looking around, saw JD under the table. Surprisingly, along with him there were the other two, sleeping with him. The three girls laughed.

Susan said, 'Well, at least, we don't need to look for them.' Rosy told Franny what they were doing and suggested that she too join them. Franny agreed. Then she looked at them and said softly, 'Watch this.'

They watched the dogs as Franny spoke, 'I wonder who would like to go for a walk.' As soon as the word *walk* was said, it was like a stampede. They reacted all at once and made a move, and the girls followed at a slower pace, laughing as they went. They had a great time, wandering the fields. Franny kept asking questions about Duncan. Rosy and Susan looked at each other. Smiling, Rosy, whispered, in Susan's ear, 'She is smitten.' Franny was over eighteen now; he was just twenty. Rosy answered all her questions happily. When she was satisfied, Franny ran off with the dogs. Susan said, 'Rosy, don't you think we should be heading back? You look a little pale. Do you feel OK?'

'Yes, I'm OK, Susan. Just a little tired. Haven't been sleeping to well with the baby, of course, and I keep worrying about not hearing anything about my darling Derek. Oh, Susan, I can't bear thinking what he is going through, if he isn't dead.' Then, suddenly thinking about Gilbert, she said, 'Oh, dear Susan, you must be just as worried about him.'

Susan said, 'That's fine, my dear friend. At least we can understand what each other are going through.' Susan was hiding the truth. Just before leaving to come to the farm, Gilbert's parents, who had just been told he was on his way home, after being helped by the resistance, to get on to a ship heading for England. The whole crew was with him, except Derek and Rob. Apparently, Rob is missing instead of Gilbert because he'd broken his arm. When Susan had arrived, before going to Rosy, after speaking to the others, it was decided for now because of her fragile state, not to tell Rosy until the baby was safely born. As they entered the gate, Rosy suddenly bent double, crying out. Susan grabbed her to stop her from falling to the ground. She helped her to a garden seat and sat her down. 'I'm going to get help. Now stay here, Rosy.'

Susan ran towards the house; on the way, she ran into James who was walking with Jonathan. He was on leave, and his ship was in dry dock after a torpedo hit them and nearly took them down. They were walking to the stables. Running up to them, she cried, 'Help! Quick, quick, it's Rosy, the baby. Oh, hurry.' She told them where she had left her. 'I'm going to ring the midwife.' Both of them ran to where Susan had left Rosy; they found Franny holding Rosy's hand and the three dogs sitting around them. Charm, as usual, had his head in her lap, looking up to her. In an instant, Jonathan lifted her up, whisking her indoors, straight up to her bedroom, where Susan, with both Mums, were waiting and getting the bed ready. Jonathan placed her gently on her bed.

'Susan said Evelyn, the midwife, is on her way.' About half an hour later, Evelyn the midwife appeared, shooing everyone out of the room so she could examine Rosy and talk to her. After all that was done and telling Rosy that it won't be long, she allowed the Grandmas back in. She also allowed Susan into keep Rosy calm. While they talked to Rosy, she got her things ready. There was a knock on the door. It was James with a tray of tea; he entered the room and placed it on the table near the window, and as he was leaving, he asked if there is anything else. Rosy said, 'Yes, could you bring me some water.' Everyone giggled because through all the rush and panic, they forgot to ask if there was anything she needed or wanted beside the obvious, of course, Derek.

He smiled, 'Yes, my dear.' Then off he went to fulfil Rosy's request. On his way back, he bumped into Albert. He asked him if he would like to take the tray. He replied, 'Yes, thank you.' As he reached the door, he smiled. There, sitting on his bed, was Charm, and his brothers had joined him. Albert wondered how his bed had appeared, and then bounding up the stairs came Franny with another bed, plonking herself down with the pups to wait. He said, 'You OK, dear?'

'Yes,' she said, 'I'll keep these fellows company.'

'OK,' he said. 'Do you need anything?'

'No' came the reply. 'Not at the moment. Thank you, Mr Maye.'

'Listen, Francis, I think you are mature enough to call me Albert.'

'Oh, thank you, Mr, oh I mean, Albert. In that case, you may call me Franny' came the reply in her best grown-up voice.

'OK then, Franny, that's a deal.' Albert approached the door where he knew his beloved little girl was about to have his first grandchild. He knocked but didn't enter. He waited until the door was answered, in case it wasn't a good time to enter. His darling wife opened the door. He said, 'Here is Rosy's water.' He went to hand the tray. Rosy, on hearing him, called, 'Father, is that you?'

'Yes' came the reply. 'Are you OK, dear?'

'Come to me, Dad.' He went to his darling girl and placed the tray on her beside cabinet. He poured some of the water in the glass and held it out to her. She took it and drank some and then handed it back saying, 'Thank you.'

He turned to leave, but she pulled him back, asking him to sit with her for a while. He agreed. He perched himself on the bed with her and took hold of her hand tighter as a labour pain made its appearance and then loosening as it slowly subsided. 'My goodness, my girl, that's quite a grip you have.' Rosy tried to laugh. 'Oh, Father, don't make me laugh.' He turned to the midwife. 'Is there time for my wife, Susan, and Elizabeth to have a break, maybe something to eat?'

Evelyn replied, 'Yes, we have time.' As they turned to go, Elizabeth asked if she would like anything while they were downstairs. Evelyn replied, 'Ooh, I'd love a cup of tea and perhaps one of your famous home-made cakes.'

Eleanor blushed. 'How did you know about my cakes?'

'Francis told me.'

'Oh yes. That's OK.'

Eleanor loved to bake, though she hadn't been able to do much lately due to the shortages. Being on the farm, things were a little more plentiful. She had been spending her time doing something she loved doing. Off they went. As they exited the door, they came across the door and guards. Franny said, 'Charm won't leave. The others won't either,' she laughed. 'I'll stay with them and make sure they don't get in the way.'

'OK,' her mother said. 'Do you want anything, sweetheart? Oh yes. Mummy, could I have a drink when you come back?'

'Yes, dear.' Off they went downstairs. An hour later, they returned with a cold drink for Franny with some biscuits, a bowl of water for the furry trio, and a bowl of doggy biscuits in case they wanted any. The three laughed Elizabeth said, 'Oh, dear, those three are funny.'

Her father held her hands, and he talked about everything except one. They stayed clear of that as Albert knew how much it would stress and upset her. It did make it a bit hard going as, of course, most subjects could go back to Derek. When the Mums came back into the room, he was most grateful. He bent over and gave Rosy a gentle hug and kiss on the cheek. He then got up and walked over to his wife and Elizabeth. As he kissed his wife on the cheek, he whispered, 'Be careful what you talk about. She is starting to get tired and bit weepy. I've tried to keep her talking about other things other than Derek. Every topic seems to lead back to Derek,' he laughed and said, 'It's hard going.' From behind him, they heard her cry out louder than before. Evelyn went over and examined her. 'Well, my dear, I think we're nearly there.'

Albert took that as his cue to leave the room. As he opened the door, Rosy cried out again. 'Very near now, darling,' her mother said. 'Oh, Mum, I wish Derek was here or, at least, I knew he was all right.'

'I know, darling. Right now what do you say we concentrate on this very large bump of yours for now?'

'What do you say, my dearest friend?' Susan, who was standing the other side, asked. Rosy tried to laugh but another pain gripped her. This carried on for a while. In between the pains, Rosy's mind would wander back to when she and her beloved husband were on their honeymoon. Rosy would see the balcony where they first discovered the wonderful pleasure of being close, feeling each other, remembering his gentle hands running over her body, down between her thighs and making her hips rise and her body shiver all over. Suddenly, Rosy was bought back to the present with another racking pain. As it started, Rosy called to Evelyn, 'I feel different.' So again Evelyn examined and saw that the baby was ready to make its entrance. The two Mums took their places, one on each side, holding her hands as she pushed their grandbaby into the very upset world. 'Derek, my dearest husband, this is for you.' A few moments later, there was a wonderful sound of a new life crying loudly for the whole world to hear, saying, 'I'm here, and I'm staying.'

Rosy raised her head, asking Evelyn, 'What is it?'

She wrapped the little mite up and handed Rosy the baby. 'Well, Rosy dear', Evelyn said, 'it's your much-wanted little girl.'

Ten minutes later Evelyn gently took the baby to start cleaning her up when Rosy said, 'Oh, I have another pain. What's happening?' Her mum took little Jessica Marie and placed her in the crib and rushed back to her side, asking Evelyn, 'What's happening? What's wrong with my girl?'

As Evelyn examined Rosy, she had a shock. Then she smiled. 'Are you ready for this, ladies? There is another head. Oh my goodness, you have another little one coming.' The mums both gasped, and Rosy started to cry. She was told to push as the head slipped into the world. Evelyn, suddenly and urgently (Rosy knew whatever Evelyn said, she must do it. No matter how hard she had to do it), without question, said, 'Stop pushing. Rosy, please, whatever you do, don't push, Rosy.' She quickly explained that the cord was wrapped around the little mite's neck. Rosy thought, *God, how on earth can I do that?* She let her mind wander to when Derek came home and the look on his face. He would be shocked; she started to smile at the thought of him holding her and the babies and whispering, 'Who's a clever girl? I'm so proud of you.'

In turn, she would say, 'Well, Daddy, you had a bit to do with it', and they would smile together.

All of a sudden, Evelyn's voice broke into her dream, 'OK, Rosy, now give me one last big push.' The baby was born as she cried this again, 'This is for you, my darling Derek, wherever you are.' With that their second baby was born.

'Is it OK, Evelyn?'

'Yes, both the babies are fine.' With that relief, Rosy just couldn't hold back her emotions any more. She lay there, just sobbing, and then suddenly turning to Evelyn, through her sobs, Rosy asked, 'What is the baby, Evelyn?'

'Well, my dear Rosy', as Evelyn leaned over, handing her the well-wrapped baby, 'here you are, Mummy, meet your new baby boy.'

'What, Evelyn, did you really say? Boy?'

'Yes, my love, I did. Rosy, you have your pigeon pair, one of each.' The Mums laughed, and Susan moved to her friend's head, kissing her. 'Congratulations, my dear friend.' All the emotions that had hung around not faced all through her pregnancy so as not to harm the babies then surfaced. She thought, *Oh my goodness, my two babies.* Again the tears rolled, and this time her mother-in-law took the little one and laid him next to his sister who was a full hour older than him. Exhausted, Rosy cried herself to sleep. Eleanor and Elizabeth asked Evelyn, 'Why didn't we know it was twins?'

'Well,' she replied, 'Rosy was not that big, and when we listened for the baby's heartbeat, we could only pick out one clearly. The other baby must have been lying behind the first one, towards the back, so when we felt the baby, we could only feel one.' Now as the shock was subsiding a bit, they decided to leave Rosy to sleep. Both the babies were fast asleep as well. As they turned to leave, Rosy stirred calling, 'Mum, I want to see Charm.'

'OK, darling, I'll find him for you.'

They opened the door, and as they did, they came face to face with the scene.

Once they were outside the door, Franny asked, 'Is everything OK?'

'Yes, my dear,' said Eleanor. Her mother said to her, 'Franny, have you been here all this time?'

'Yes, Mother, apart for ten minutes after the baby was born when I made the boys go into the garden. I guessed Rosy may want Charm with her.'

'Well, my dear, you're right about two parts of that sentence.' The Mums smiled at each other.

Francis asked, 'What's going on?'

'Well, my darling, you were right about taking the dogs to the garden as Rosy would want to see Charm but not about the baby.'

'What do you mean, Mother? You're scaring me. I don't understand.'

'Oh, I'm sorry. I didn't mean to scare you. It's all right. You did hear the baby, the first baby.'

Franny looked at them for a little while and then it dawned on her. She began shrieking, and they said, 'Shush!'

'Sorry,' Franny whispered, 'you mean twins?'

'Yes,' they replied, 'you are an auntie to two at once.'

They hugged. Then the door opened, and Evelyn poked her head out, and said, 'Sorry, to break up this happy scene, ladies. I wouldn't normally allow this, but I see that Rosy is getting very upset again asking for her very hairy friend.' Everyone laughed, but by then, it was too late anyway. Charm had gotten fed up with all this 'human whatever'. All he knew was Rosy wanted, needed, him. He could hear her calling his name in a funny voice. He pushed his way in, and the other two went with him. They were very good; they just sat next to the bed, watching Charm gently move closer to the top of the bed, sniffing, and then putting his front paws up, looking Rosy in the face. 'Hello, my darling, you come to see your mum. Make sure I'm OK.' He gave a little yap. 'OK, OK,' she said, moving herself back towards the other side of the bed. 'Come on, lad, we have to be quiet.' He jumped up and lay next to her. Rosy could see four more soulful eyes. 'Oh, come on.' Both of them leapt up and settled at her feet. Rosy put her arm around Charm, instantly falling asleep.

'Oh well,' said Evelyn, 'that settles that.' She smiled, turning to go back in, and the scene that greeted her was so lovely that she called the others to see. As they put their heads around the door, the scene that greeted them was so touching that it brought tears to their eyes. All the three pups were sleeping quietly with her. Eleanor could see Evelyn's face, the surprise on it. 'Oh, Evelyn, it's OK. The sheets can be changed before the babies need feeding.'

Evelyn said with a smile, 'OK, just pleased to see her relaxed.' Franny saw that Rosy had drifted off to sleep, so she asked Evelyn, 'Shall I see if I can get the pups out? I'm not sure Charm will follow without Rosy telling him.'

'That's OK, my dear. Leave them. One or three doesn't make any difference.' Both of them laughed.

'Tell you what, Franny. Come back in about an hour and a half, and if I need you before that, I'll come find you, OK?'

'Yes, Nurse, that's fine. I'll go and prepare their dinner.' With that, off she went to prepare their dinner.

Nineteen

Meanwhile what might as well have been a million miles away, Derek and his crew were hiding in the trees, getting themselves together to move on and working out how to avoid the German soldiers who had obviously seen the plane come down. There were truckloads of them, covering and searching the area. They moved slowly, in silence, through the thick trees and undergrowth; then they came to a railway line. Gilbert looked at his map and worked out that one way headed towards Germany. Very sensibly, they started to walk the opposite way, keeping themselves within the treeline. They walked for what seemed like hours, and they were exhausted. They saw a small barn just ahead, but not quite in the woods. They had to take the risk of crossing a bit of open ground. Derek knew his men couldn't go on without rest; they were so tired and so was he. He also knew that was when mistakes happened, so he decided the barn it will be. As they approached, Rob said, 'Sir, the far side of the barn is in the shade. It would be the safer way to enter it.'

Derek agreed, and they approached cautiously, moving one step, one man at a time. Derek went first, and then he signalled for the next man to follow. The last one to enter was Rob, who had been covering their backs. Derek told them to rest for a while and said that he was going to see what was ahead. Rob offered to go with him as Gilbert was too badly injured. It was settled that Gilbert was to stay back and be in charge of the others. It was decided they would hide out here until nightfall. At 14.00 hours, with everything sorted, Derek and Rob set off into the unknown. Before he left, Derek gave one last order. 'If we are not back by 20.00 hours, move out.'

Everyone spoke at once, 'But, sir . . .'

Derek said, 'Men, that is an order. Is that understood?'

The men weren't happy, although they all agreed reluctantly.

Gilbert said, 'Sir, I . . .'

Derek interrupted him, 'That means, you too, airman.'

'OK, sir.'

He wished them well, and the two men set off . . . The rest of the crew stayed, and they settled down. Between them a rota was set for keeping watch. All of them were doing different things, some sleeping, others eating, and some even writing; all in all, they were just relaxing in the best way each man felt happiest. Time passed by uneventful. It was now Gilbert who was standing guard, and when his replacement came, he re-entered the barn. It was now 19.10 hours. Gilbert sat, ate something, and had a drink as he had slept earlier. After eating, he went outside for a cigarette. As he lit up, he looked again at the time. It was now 19.30 hours. He was starting to worry, but he hadn't let on to the others. Alan appeared and said, 'Time for some more painkiller, sir? You're worried about them, aren't you?'

He replied, 'Yes, Alan, I am very worried. I won't take that dose of painkiller. It looks like I'm going to need a clear head. I have a feeling we're on our own.'

Meanwhile, a mile or so a way, Derek and Rob had found a town, and they decided to stay hidden, until it started to get a bit darker and then do a quick scout about. They were sitting there at about 18.10 hours when they heard a noise behind them and then to their left. They cocked their weapons and then from the left, a rabbit hopped past them. That put them into a false sense of security – a silly thing to do! They relaxed too soon, putting it out of their minds. Then they heard another noise from behind them. By the time they remembered and took a fighting stance, they were surrounded by German soldiers. They were told to put their weapons down and put their hands up by a soldier who seemed to be in charge and who spoke in English. They were told to march, and a guard was assigned to each one of them. While marching towards the town, the soldier in charge said, 'We know you come from the aeroplane that crashed two days ago. We will be questioning you both. It would be a mistake to lie to us. We will make you talk one way or the other. I'm telling you this now so that you will have time to think.' The rest of the march was done in an eerie tension-filled, cool air. Even though it was a warm night, it felt like walking in icy air, without the snow, like it moved with them as they moved. They were marched across the town square to what looked like a building that maybe used to be the town hall. Now hanging above it was a very large flag with a swastika on it. If they hadn't realised before, they did now. With that slapped in their faces, they were in the hands of some 'not very happy or polite' Germans. They were marched up a couple of dozen steps into a very large entrance hall and told to halt. The two guards that had been guarding them all the way were left to watch them, while their commander went into a side room. About fifteen minutes later, he returned, still as sullen and poker-faced as he was when he left. Derek looked around, and he managed to see into that office from where the soldier returned. From where he was standing, he could see clearly the inside of the room. He saw what he had only heard about. There they were, larger than life, a couple of SS officers. He looked at Rob and rolled his eyes. Rob looked over and then back at Derek. Derek could see he had been told the same, by the look of fear in his eyes. Ordinary German military were bad enough, but these were a whole new level; these were a lot worse. They had real reason to be worried and scared. The commander marched them across to where there was a door, one of the many, many doors in the entrance hall. A soldier guarded it, and when he saw them coming, he opened it. It wasn't into a room; it descended down a spiral stairs.

Rob whispered to Derek, 'I don't like the look or feel of this. It seems to be over the top even for the Germans.'

Derek agreed.

'What the hell were we bombing that warranted all this?'

'I don't know, Rob. We weren't told. We were told just were to bomb and not what the target was.'

'What you mean no one knew what we were bombing?'

'That's right,' said Derek. When the guards heard them talking, they thrust the butt of their guns into the prisoners' backs, telling them in no uncertain terms, to be quiet. He managed to remind Rob to say the name, rank, serial number only as they were pushed down the stairs. When the reached the bottom, Rob looked at Derek, and he in turn nodded to let him know he understood. Then the commander spoke to the guards in German; it wasn't hard to understand, that they were to be taken to separate rooms. This turned out to be cells with a small window with bars, of course. One guard marched Derek to one end of the corridor, and the second marched Rob to the other end. Derek thought, *They are going through a lot of trouble to keep us separate.* He wasn't sure why, but that worried him. They were shoved roughly into their cells. Derek went to the tiny window with bars. Outside were the guards walking with the dogs. A courtyard had a fountain and lovely flowerbeds in bloom. His thoughts went to Rosy. *Oh, how his Rosy would have loved it.* When he looked further back, there was a pole. He wasn't sure why. It made him feel very uncomfortable. He would very soon find out. He turned around and saw there was a bed in the corner. There was a chair, a bucket, for the obvious, a drop-down flap on the large thick, wooden door, where he guessed there was a guard fully armed. On the other side, up until now, he thought now they were prisoners of war, in full uniforms; he honestly didn't think they had anything to much to worry about. As prisoners of war, with the Geneva Convention in place, he was thinking like a true Englishman; he was very naive as it turned out. What he and Rob were about to face wouldn't even have crossed his mind in his worse nightmare. He couldn't believe the fact that one human being could do what they would do to him, another human being. The hatch he guessed was for food or talking, that way they didn't need to open the cell. What he couldn't work out was why there was such bright light, but he was to find out soon. At the other end of the corridor, Rob was having the same thoughts, but it was a different scene outside his window. There was the street they had crossed to get here, a few French people were going about their daily chores, shopping, working, or just walking before the curfew was actioned, like it was every night. He had heard the guards talking to each other about the curfew. There were plenty of Germans marching up and down – some in pairs, others with dogs, some guarding and marching up and down, with their heels clicking loudly on the cobblestones.

Their dogs barked now and again just to let everyone know they were still around, an uneasy peace between the few people on the street. You could feel the tension in the air; it was that thick you could cut with a knife. Suddenly, there was a commotion that broke the thick air. Two German armed vehicles came to a screeching halt and half a dozen soldiers jumped out of each, surrounding the German staff car that had pulled up; the car had screeched to a halt in between the trucks. It had left tyre marks on the street. The car had some sort of ensign emblazoned on its front wings. Two men exited the car, and Rob could just about see them in the fast-approaching dusk. One was in the same uniform as the officer that had caught them and marched them here, but the other wasn't in uniform. He had a long black overcoat. They proceeded to climb the steps as they entered the building. He lost sight of them halfway up the many steps. Then all went silent, not the normal silence, an eerie silence you feel perhaps when you walk around a graveyard at night or when something was going to happen. Along the other end of the corridor, Derek was sitting on his bunk, not particularly worried, as he had been told in training that as long as they were in uniform, they would be treated OK, better than being without uniform. Then they would have been shot as spies. When he heard the clicking of boots on the stone floor, getting closer, he just thought, *OK, name, rank, serial number, and then prisoner of war camp. Maybe for the duration. Well, it is better than being dead.* He smiled as he allowed his thoughts to wander back to the wedding. Yes, the duration, not life as the marriage vows say, that for life or until death . . . He could see Rosy's face looking up at him, and that order, he had taken willingly, with great pleasure to have that wonderful smile the first thing he sees as wakes in the morning, and then last thing he sees as he falls asleep at night. Suddenly, he was bought back to reality as the cell door slammed back as the guard pushed it open. He stood, as two officers walked into the cell; they spoke. One spoke in perfect English and he recognised him as the soldier who had captured them. 'Come with us.'

Derek asked, 'Where is my comrade? Is he OK?'

He was told to be quiet. 'That does not concern you.' For his efforts, he was slammed in the back with the butt of a soldier's gun.

He fell to his knees now, and he started to feel uneasy. This didn't feel right. When he started to protest, he was rewarded with the gun again, this time to his legs. Again he fell to the ground, and again he was told to get up. He struggled to his feet. The officer said, 'You, English, are so inferior. You never learn.' Derek was told to march to the stairs.

Derek very foolishly tried again, 'I demand to be treated as an officer under the Geneva Convention.'

The guard laughed, and the officer said, 'We don't abide by that.' Derek still wasn't sure who the other man was until he turned and saw his lapels. Then he saw the double 'S' and realised just how serious this was. He was dressed in black and stood face to face with Derek. In broken English, he said, 'You bombed far into our Fatherland. Why?'

Derek again repeated his name, rank, and serial number as he was trained to do. For that, he was hit again. They kept marching until they arrived in another room. Along the corridor, he was pushed into a dark room and onto a chair and told to keep quiet until spoken to. He sat, as best he could, on the seat, finding it difficult, as the last blow from the young soldier with the rifle had broken his leg. He was also bleeding pretty badly from his head. His ribs and kidney area hurt pretty bad too. He sat there for what seemed like forever, but in reality, it was only a few seconds. He heard a light switch go, and a very bright light lit up the room. The German officer crossed the room in two strides. The SS man right behind the door open it, and in walked two more SS men to join them. The officer said, 'Well, Captain Derek Rook-Leigh, you resisted our *questioning*. I will reluctantly hand you over to my more-ruthless colleague. Now your co-pilot could have made this easy on yourselves, just by cooperating with us.' He looked at the German officer and asked, 'Where is Rob?' The officer looked puzzled. 'Rob Mackie, my co-pilot, what have you done to him?'

'Oh,' the officer replied, 'he was also very reluctant to talk. Then after my comrade here had finished with him, we now know that he knew nothing of your mission. Only what you did, not why. Only, you, my dear captain, he said knows. Now here we are.'

Derek said, 'How did you find out he really didn't know anything? What the hell did you animals do to him?'

The officer said, 'You will have the pleasure of finding out a bit later, wouldn't you?'

With that, the two young privates dragged him back to his cell, threw him on his cot and left, locking the cell as they went. He must have drifted off into a fitful sleep. When he awoke, his head was sore, although it had stopped bleeding for now. His leg was hurting and swollen; he tried to get up but must have passed out as the next thing he knew, he was being dragged out again. This time, he was dragged down the corridor and then down another flight of stairs to a very dank damp area where the lights were already on. He then realised his eye was stuck shut and very swollen from the wound across his temple, but out of his good eye, he could see a chair. They dumped him on it. Against the wall he saw what looked like a hospital trolley, and from what he could make out on it, there was what looked like a syringe, a small bottle with 'god knows what' inside. He tried to get up but got punched again. The one he thought to be SS started beating with a heavy walking stick. He seemed to like heads, so he told the soldiers to step back. 'You dare to defy our orders, I'll teach you.' He lay into him with this stick, and he used the top end, where it had a very large knob on it, beating him again on the head. Before he could sit, he passed out. Just before he lost full consciousness, he heard the commander say, 'You, fool, give me that stick. While you're with me in here, you don't need it.' This time when he came around, he was tied to the chair. As he came fully around, something was really wrong. He didn't know where he was; all he knew was that he was tied to a chair, in a room of German SS. He was in what was left of a RAF uniform. To say he was scared was an understatement. Before he could think any more, someone had come from behind him on his blind side, and he realised he couldn't see. His leg hurt like hell, but his head hurt the most. There was blood everywhere. Then he felt a sharp sting in his arm. Of course, he couldn't do anything as he was tied. Slowly, he became woozy, his head swimming even more than it was as he drifted. There were no memories this time. His head and mind were very, very empty. All of a sudden, he was jerked to consciousness, and a bright light was directed to his one good eye. Every bone was hurting, and every muscle felt like it was being torn apart and on fire. He didn't know why he wasn't sure if he was shaking from pain or fear. He was so groggy his captives were shouting at him and asking him questions, but of course, he couldn't answer as he didn't know what the hell they were talking about. That just made them angrier. He got beaten some more, and the SS officer kept saying, 'Give him more. He will answer.'

The other officer said, 'You give any more, you're going to kill him.'

'That doesn't matter. Just do it.'

'I will not.' The officer stormed out the room to go and tell his superior what was going on. 'Leave them for a couple of hours and then go back, and find out whether he has got what he wanted or put a stop to it. If he gives you trouble, send someone to get me.'

'Oh no, you didn't leave the drug in the room, did you?'

'No, sir, it's here.' He handed it over.

'Good. You may leave.' They saluted each other and he left. After the said couple of hours, he dreaded going back into the room, as he had expected the prisoner to be dead. The officer went back into the room, saw the state Derek was in, called for a halt, and ordered the SS officer to get out. Before he could argue, he turned to the young soldiers, 'Get him back to his cell.' They obeyed without question, and as they left, he heard the officer shouting at the other men, even though it was in German he knew by the tone of his voice that he was very angry. He was yet again dragged back to his cell and again thrown on his cot and locked in again, which seemed silly. He couldn't have crawled, let alone walk or run anywhere. Left half and half off the cot again, he drifted into unconsciousness. Many hours passed. He was awoken by a lot of noise from outside. He painfully got up off the cot and went to the little window, managing to see out. His view was blocked by a big wet nose with a drooling tongue. One of the dogs was looking at him, trying to sniff him. As they moved away, he could see out for what was sort of like the first time. He saw it was about midday by the position of the sun. He had already met the dogs up close and personal. There were lots of flowers and a very

large pole. Again it went through his mind, *What's that for?* He slid
to the floor, unable to stand any longer on one leg. The hustle and
bustle went on for a while and then it seemed to go eerily quiet. His
inquisitiveness got the better of him. He struggled to his feet again
and looked out. He saw two guards dragging, what looked like, a
half-dead man across the yard, tying him to the pole. Then a group
of soldiers appeared, marched to the centre of the yard, and there an
officer with them. He recognised the officer as the one who tried to
put a stop to the other men from hurting him. Then time seemed to
stand still. The officer raised his hand, and the soldiers all shot at
once, killing the English serviceman to death. Shocked, he again fell
to the floor. *That poor fellow! I wonder why he was shot.* He was in
uniform, and he hadn't recognised the poor fellow as Rob, his co-
pilot and good friend. He didn't understand what was going on. All
he knew was something was really wrong, and that man had an RAF
uniform on, just like what he was wearing, the same uniform. He was
sitting on the cot when he heard the cell door open slowly, quietly
this time, not like earlier when the soldiers opened it. He couldn't do
anything but just sit and wait. In what seemed ages, when in reality
was just a few seconds, two men came up to him carrying guns. He
thought, *They don't look like the soldiers who knocked him about.
Who were those other men? Oh that's right – the SS.* A few seconds
later, half a dozen other men ran in, one stayed in the doorway,
keeping watch. One of the men he had recognised as a cleaner. He
had seen him in the corridor and hadn't thought much of it. *He must
be the leader of these brave, or stupid, men*, he thought. We are here
to rescue you, sir.'

'But I can't walk.'

'That's OK. We will carry you out. I knew you were hurt. That's
why we're risking extra men.'

'Why you risking your lives for me?'

'I have my orders to get you out, no matter what you say.'

'We know you're the one that did the latest bombing. What's your
name, sir?'

Derek replied, 'I don't know.'

'Don't worry. That's fine. You're going home. I'll just call you *sir*,' that made everyone smile. 'You coming? Or do you want some more SS hospitality or the firing squad perhaps?'

The look on his face must have told the rescuer that he didn't know what the hell he was talking about. Looking quickly at Derek's wounds, he realised that he had two severe head wounds. They were the visible ones. He ordered his comrades to get him out as fast as they could, trying not to jolt him around any more than absolutely necessary. Three men grabbed him up, exited the cell as fast as they could, and shut cell door after themselves. They had just started along the corridor when Derek heard soldiers marching down the stairs. His rescuers flew behind a large concrete post with a filing cabinet next to it. There was also a desk with a chair. Derek was trying his hardest not to cry out; one of the men handed him a 'not so clean' kerchief. He shoved it in his mouth anyway to keep himself as quiet as possible. He thought of them risking their lives for him and the least he could do was try to do what he could. As the soldiers marched to the bottom, along the corridor to their of duty room, halfway down the corridor, the men carrying Derek circled the column so they wouldn't be seen. The others were still in the cell with the door pushed too. After the last soldier had disappeared into their room, shutting the door behind themselves, the men in the cell came running silently to them, after, of course, locking the cell door again to give themselves as much time as possible. They then made for the stairs and started running up them, two first and then him with the three carrying him, the rest bringing up the rear. Halfway up, there was what looked like bookshelves. One of the lead men pulled a loose brick, and the shelves moved, and behind them was another corridor. They entered, and when they were all in, the two men pulled the cupboard door until it clicked shut, just in time. They had heard movement, on the other side, and thinking maybe they had been seen, their guns were poised ready. One of the men at the rear was quietly pushing dust and rags around the door. Derek asked, 'Why are they doing that?'

As they moved off again, the leader said, 'So there is no draft or light coming from it to alert the Germans that there is something behind the bookcase. That way we can continue to use it for future escapes.' When they exited the corridor, the lead man pushed what looked like wooden peg, and another door opened. As they went, they came into a tiny room. They had come out from behind closet that had choir robes hanging in it. Derek guessed they were in the back of a church. The leader of the resistance he now knew as Pierre said, 'Stay very quiet. It isn't a day for services, although sometimes you get an odd German soldier praying.' He passed his weapon to one of the other men and took off his cap and grabbed a broom standing against the wall and then proceeded to walk into the church itself. While he was gone, the others placed Derek on a chair, and one gave him some water as he was running a temperature. The others closed the secret door and put dust and bits against the gap and wiped all the footprints out. There was no sign of anyone who shouldn't have been there. There was movement on the other side of the heavy curtain that they were hiding behind. The men took their places, ready for trouble. They stood in front of him, ready to give their lives for him. *It brought tears to his derelict eyes. He thought to himself, I don't even know these men who are willing to give their lives for me, and I can't even remember who I am, let alone why I'm here.* But he instinctively trusted them. What seemed like eternity had just been minutes. The curtain opened, and as it did, he heard a voice he had started to recognise. 'OK, men, it's me Pierre.' Now they knew not to shoot. 'It's all clear. Lynette is outside, in the truck, waiting, so let's get going. All in one swift movement.' They all moved rapidly, but cautiously, to the main door. As they sped through the church, Derek thought, *This church seems familiar in some ways,* but he didn't know why. Within two minutes, they were out and in the back of the truck which turned out to be a baker's truck. It was Lynette's father's work truck. Pierre travelled in front with Lynette. Derek was surprised; the others said they are married, so if the Germans saw them together, it looked less suspicious than if she was on her own at this time of day. They headed out of town. They drove for about two hours, most of which Derek slept. When the truck came to a stop, he woke with a jump, forgetting where he was for a minute. As he sat up, he could smell the sea. Pierre jumped from the cab, running around to the back of the truck, as his men jumped out of the back. Pierre, with one of his men, very gently lifted Derek down. Pierre explained what would happen from now on. They were going by fishing boat with two or three of his men. Lynette was not coming. She was to drive to a farm on the coast, near to where, after the English sub has picked Derek up, out at sea, they would fish for a bit, before bringing the fishing boat into the bay, as they would normally do to sell their catch. Now that the plan was dawn, they could only hope that they would look like they were off fishing, like every other morning. They boarded the little fishing boat and set off. You know what they say about the best-laid plans. This time was no different; they had been travelling about an hour and was just rounding the coast, when a German U-boat appeared from nowhere, just afar enough not to capsise the little fishing boat. Pierre ran over to him. 'Who the hell are you?' I knew you were important. Oh god, I hadn't realised just how much to attract a submarine.' With that, he looked at Derek, 'Look at me, he turned to Pierre, who now had Derek's attention even if he was very confused. 'Get down below. Do not show yourself for any reason or whatever happens. Do you understand, sir?' With that, he moved away. Not that he could have done much else but hide. He felt the boat rock as the Germans pulled alongside. He backed into the dark corner. He heard them talking in French, and he knew by the tone of voices that it was not going good. He remembered something the captain had showed him. When he first came aboard, he went to the bunk the captain had showed him. He managed to lift the mattress, and under the base was where the captain's personal things were kept. Among them was a gun, fully loaded. At the back of storage space was what looked like a knot of wood in a plank, making up the space. Derek pushed it, and the whole of the back panel opened up. He pulled himself up and slid himself into the space that opened up as quick as he could and, quietly as possible, closed it and it locked. There was also a release button. Derek wriggled about until he was as comfortable as possible, which wasn't easy, as the area was so small and tight. He had water and dry biscuits. He just nibbled a biscuit and had a sip of water, and then just waited. After a while, he wasn't sure how long he had been there, he started to hear very loud voices and then the boat started to rock vigorously as he could hear another engine had come alongside it. He wasn't sure if it was more soldiers or friends as he first thought heavy boots jumped aboard, answering his question, and then there was a lot of gunfire. The boats rocked violently, tossing him about, in what seemed as though could very well become his coffin, then it went very quiet, he didn't move hardly daring to breath, suddenly he could hear them searching he realised it was the Germans searching the boat from the sound he guessed they weren't leaving anything to chance. He knew they were searching the bunk as he could hear them more clearly. From on deck, the officer in charge called them back. They all ran and left the boat. As they started their engines and took off from each side of the little craft, the wash was so severe it felt like the boat was going to capsise, a thought entered his head, *What if they set it on fire . . .* That was his last thought as the wash rocked even more it knocked him unconscious. They didn't set it alight. They thought everyone was dead. In their minds, they thought what was the point. Plus it would attract unwanted attention, if another fishing boat went to see if they could help. They may get there quick enough to see the dead. They just left the boat to drift. According to their charts, it would go into the bay and end up crashing upon the shore. That turned out to be a very big mistake. They hadn't listened to the latest weather report. By the time they did, it was too late. A wind had picked up, catching the little boat's sail, also with the help of the tide and the two working together, blew the boat further out into the channel. If they went after it, it could well still be too far; it wasn't worth drawing attention of any sort to themselves, so the captain ordered them to dive. With that, the U-boat blew its tanks and then started to go down, gurgling as it went. The wash was very bad that it was a wonder why the little boat didn't sink when it swished and swashed over the deck. That was the last thing he thought about before he passed out again. All through the night, he continued to drift in and out of consciousness. Day and night it drifted. On the third morning, it was spotted by a patrol boat, an English patrol boat, just bobbing around in the shallow waters near the land. The patrol-boat crew went into action, not knowing what to expect. All guns manned, they tried hailing the boat; they could see it was French. When there was no reply to their hailing, they moved alongside, ready to board. They got a terrifying shock as they went aboard. The deck was full of dead bodies of what must have been the crew. The puzzle was, there were several dead Germans and among them an officer. The captain asked the first officer, 'Why were the Germans so interested in that little craft?'

The first officer replied, 'I don't know, sir.'

They decided not to let all men go board at once. The captain of the patrol boat just sent two men on- board just to make sure it was clear of the enemy or if there was any one just injured. After about ten minutes, the two men reappeared and called, 'All clear, sir.' It was decided to take it in tow back to port. When all was safe, they set off. All the men aboard had a speculation about what was going on. The favourite story being it's a ghost ship as a lot hadn't been told about the bodies. An hour later, they docked and tied the small fishing boat where it couldn't be seen by anyone there. It was left for the night, ready for the top men to go over in the morning. Two guards were left to watch over it. All was quiet until about three in the morning. Derek had regained consciousness and just lay quietly. He was in severe pain; he had no choice other than to climb out of his makeshift coffin. Silently, he managed to get out the gun stuffed in his uniform shirt as he had lost his jacket. He couldn't remember where. He still couldn't remember who he was, and as he had no idea where he was, his head was swimming. He fought to just stay upright and made his way to the hatch. It was open, and he could see the stars above. He started to pull himself up and the boat rocked a little as he moved. He looked up again and listened in case anyone had seen the boat move. As he was listening, something smacked him in the face; it took all his control not to cry out in shock because in the darkness, he couldn't see what had hit him. H He raised his hand to move whatever it was. As he grabbed hold of the loosely tied object, the clouds cleared and the moon shone. He was now sitting on the side of the hatch, and he could see around him. The scene that hit him was so horrific that he had to clasp a hand over his mouth as he wanted to scream out but not knowing where he was. As he looked to his left, he realised what hit him in the face was one of Pierre's comrades arm. Nausea nearly took over, and he then realised that he had tears running down his cheeks. His emotions were so mixed up that he still couldn't remember who he was. All he knew was that he was a RAF pilot. That was only because of what was left of his uniform. He did not know where he was other than the fact that he was on this boat. He was clueless as to where the boat was moored, and he struggled to climb up the deck. Even with the pain, he was in, he had to try and find out. His nightmare just doubled as he came across this carnage. He just sat there too numb to move. Where would he go if he did? He was in total shock; he couldn't fight, speak, hide, or move in any way. When the full crew of the patrol boat returned, the captain and first officer went straight to the captain's cabin; they had been there about ten minutes talking about how they spent their evening visiting their respective families. The captain's name was Dennis Dayforb and the second officer's name was Charles Froner. The captain turned and looked out over at the fishing boat moored next to them. He said, 'What do you think happened, Charles?'

He waited for Charles's reply, but suddenly something caught his eye. Without another word, he just said, 'Charles, grab your weapon and follow me quickly.' So Charles, obeying without question, followed the captain on to the deck, around to the opposite side of the boat. The captain took one almighty leap and landed on the fishing boat's deck. Charles followed, and he landed and crept over to where the captain crouched. He silently looked at where the captain was looking, and he too could see a man sitting among the dead bodies and where the sun had got to them wasn't smelling too good. He was sitting on the little craft's hatch, and they weren't sure if he was alive or dead or if he was friend or foe and where had he come from as they were pretty sure he was not there the day before. Being cautious, Dennis called, in English, at the mystery person. When there was no reply or movement, he signalled Charles to go around to one side as he crawled forward from the front and tried calling again, but there was still no reaction. He cautiously stood up and moved forward. He could see his first officer was in place, so he continued forward and they reached their target together. They realised it was a man, and he was an RAF pilot, so the guns went back into holsters. They could tell he was alive as he was shaking, and there were more tears running down his cheeks, just silently dripping on to his legs, and they guessed he had been sitting there a good while as his trouser legs were very damp. The first officer saw the gun and gently removed it from the man's hand. When the captain got in front of him, he could see what a state he was in. His eye was sealed with blood, and he couldn't believe that in this state, he was moving, let alone alive. He said aloud, 'You, my friend, must have a very strong will or incentive to live.' He went to move the pilot's head and Derek cried out in pain. Dennis said to Charles, as the officer went to look at the pilot's face, 'This man is catatonic and in very, very severe pain.' Derek jumped and crawled to the captain. 'He is scared witless,' they said together. They both went to help him up. He wouldn't let Charles anywhere near him. 'It seems you're the only one he trusts, sir, at the moment.' So the captain helped him up and then realised that he could not stand up on his own. Up to now, they had only seen his top half. As the captain got him up, though they were hardened to injuries and some horrors, they had never seen anything as bad as this. They both paled and were shocked. The captain went to pick him up. He managed to get him to his cabin. Derek was too numb to cry out. Dennis just hoped he hadn't done any more damage as they made him comfortable. The medical officer arrived and gave Derek a quick look over. 'I can make him comfortable. He needs to go to London, to the top hospital for head traumas for proper treatment. He is in such a state that I may do more damage than good. I'll patch up his leg wounds as best I can. The left leg looks infected already. Some are may be twenty-four hours plus and some are a few days old. No one has even tried to treat them. What's his name?'

The captain replied, 'We don't know as he has lost his memory. As you've guessed, he can't tell us, and his dog tags are missing. You can just see where they were ripped from his neck amongst all the other injuries.'

The medical officer said, 'We don't have time to find out before we send him. He needs to go now.' The three of them moved away, and Derek fell into a fitful sleep. They moved to the captain's desk to talk. 'How are we going to get him there fast?'

'Well,' the first Officer said, 'there is a Red Cross train leaving for London in a couple of hours.'

'Oh that's right,' the captain smiled. 'We are travelling on that train. I didn't know it was also doubling up as a Red Cross. This man has been to hell and back. He will not be travelling on his own. He is to be put in our carriage. I want the bed made up and him taken by my staff car to the station, and we will follow in another car, and I want that train ready to go in an hour or heads will roll.' The car was made as comfortable for Derek as possible, so everyone started to rush around. By now, of course, the crew knew what was going on, and everyone wanted to help the nameless pilot. They decided to wait until they get to the hospital before trying to find out who he was. The hospital was where he could get the help he needs, while they tracked down who he was. Within an hour, they had got to the station, but the staff car driver had to drive at a really slow pace because every time they hit a bump, he would cry out. After a couple of miles, he stopped the car, and the others came to a halt behind him. He got out and ran to the second car as he arrived. He stopped and saluted as the captain alighted, saying, 'Soldier, you had better have a good reason for this.'

'Yes, sir' came the reply. 'The bumps are causing the officer a lot of pain.'

'OK,' the captain said. The second officer stepped from the car, saying, 'I'll go and travel with him.'

'No, no,' the captain replied. 'I'll go. I should have been with him from the beginning. I knew we had things to talk about. I just didn't think the poor fellow would feel the pain as the medical officer had given him some painkillers before they left.' The medic had handed some to the captain to try to get him to wait at least three hours before the next dose. He had also given him something to make him sleep. With that decided, the captain climbed into the car with Derek and gently put his head on his lap. With the help of the very shocked soldier, who hadn't seen Derek before as he helped, he said, 'Sir, whatever happened to him?'

'I'm not sure, son. He has lost his memory and is in total shock.'

The soldier thought for a moment. 'Whatever it was, I'm glad it was me that had the honour to help him.' Again he thought for a while. 'Could it have been the Germans?'

'Well, it could well have been. The boat we found him on was French, although there were dead German soldiers as well as the French crew.' After they had finally got Derek into a position that he seemed most comfortable in, they climbed back in and started driving very slowly to start with. Every time they went over a bump, he cringed for the poor officer in the back. After a couple of miles, as Derek still seemed fairly comfortable, he started to drive a little faster. After about fifteen minutes, they arrived at the station. The driver went around to let the captain out. He said, 'Sir, may I, if the officer doesn't find it to uncomfortable, have the privilege of carrying him to your train carriage?'

'Yes, of course, lad, you may, if you like.'

'You said if it's not too uncomfortable for the poor fellow.'

The private climbed into the car and gently moved Derek into a position he could be picked up more easily. He seemed to be tolerating the movement without too much trouble. The private climbed out of the car and, as gently as he could, proceeded to lift Derek out.

'Good lad, now follow us,' said the captain. They slowly walked through the station towards their platform. As they were walking, a Red Cross nurse said, 'I'll get a stretcher for the patient.'

Before the captain could reply, the private said, 'No, thank you, ma'am. I'm taking him to the train.'

The captain said, 'It's OK. He seems to be tolerating it well, considering the injuries and what he has been through. He is special, and if you put him on one of your things, he won't be able to stand the pain of the movement.'

'OK, sir, I will come along with some painkiller to help him a bit if that's OK.'

'Of course, Nurse, that's fine. See you in a few moments.' He then told what compartment they would be in. They carried on through the large station, reaching the platform and walking to the front of the train until they found the captain's carriage. When they did, the captain went in first to check if all was ready. As he entered the carriage, he found yet another private with the train guard, putting the finishing touches to the bed. The private had received orders to make it as soft as possible. He had done a splendid job; he had managed to get about a dozen pillows as well. When the second officer came in, they smiled at each other and dismissed the private, thanking him. 'That's OK, sir,' he said, saluting the senior officers. 'It was orders, but it was also my pleasure.' He must have heard of Derek, and he, in turn, had told the guard, who said, 'Sir, is there anything else you, gentleman, need?'

As he said that, the private entered the cabin carrying Derek. When the guard saw his terrible state, he said, 'Oh my lord, who would do that to another person?' He turned to the captain who was talking to him. 'Yes, some water and maybe some tea for us. Thank you.'

Good to her word, the nurse was there in five minutes, and she proceeded to inject Derek with the painkiller, and then they said their goodbyes as she left. She told to the captain, 'Good luck, sir.'

'Thank you, Nurse. He will stay in my carriage.'

'Oh, OK, sir.' Then she asked, 'Do you think that is wise?' She then wished that she had kept quiet, so she quickly added, 'You will be able to find me if you need me. I'm travelling on this train with the rest of the wounded.'

'OK, Nurse, thank you.' With that, the nurse and the guard disappeared. The private, as gently and humanly as possible, laid Derek down on the bed that had been set up for him. Derek opened his eyes and looked at the private and managed, 'Thank you, Private Tannis.' The soldier looked at the captain and smiled, 'Sir, he knew my name.'

'Yes, Private, it seems he does.'

With that, they saluted each other, and the Private left to resume his duties, but not without wishing this unknown RAF pilot all the best. As he went to leave, he felt something against his leg. He looked down and saw Derek's hand. The other had seen it too; they all looked at Derek's face. He looked at them, and he tried to talk. All that came out was 'Tttttaanis, stay.' The officers looked at Tannis, and he looked at them. They said, 'Well, Private Tannis, looks like you're going for a train ride. Is that OK with you?'

'Umm, yes, sir. What about my duties and commanding officer?'

'That's OK, Private. I'll sort that out for you. With that, the captain said to his first officer, Froner, to go sort it out using the station master's phone.

'Yes, sir,' Froner replied, saluted, and went off to do as ordered.

'Right, young Tannis, do you think you are up to this?' the captain asked the young private.

'Yes, sir, well, I hope so.'

'OK, son, what is your first name?'

The young chap replied, 'Paul, sir, Private Paul Tannis.'

'OK, Paul, do you need to do anything before we set off?'

'Yes, please, sir. I think I'd better relieve myself if you know what I mean.'

'OK, son.'

'Thank you, sir. Just one problem.' Lifting Derek's arm gently, they both smiled.

'Oh yes, I see what you mean. Well, Private, the toilets are right next door. He is asleep.'

'Yes, sir, he is.'

'OK, slowly, I'll slide my hand in as you slide yours out. He may be OK for a couple of minutes.'

So that's what they did.

'Now, Private, run,' said the captain. Laughing, the private did just that. The captain just stood there, trying hard not to move. After a couple of minutes, the patient started to stir and looked straight at him and started to panic, thrashing about again. Hearing all the ruckus, Officer Froner came rushing in with the porter right on his tail.

'You OK, sir? I heard you cry out.'

'Yes, Froner, I think I'm OK. Might have a bit of a shiner in the morning though.'

Froner and the porter gave him a puzzled look, so he stepped back a bit, 'Oh dear, I see, sir,' they said together. 'Where's Tannis the Private, sir?' asked Froner.

As he said that, '*Crunch!*' the Captain again got a left bash to his head. 'Wheeerrreess Tannis?' Derek asked. Tannis came running in. 'OK, it's OK. I'm here.' Looking into his eyes, as he recognised Tannis, his grip loosened a bit, enough for them to swap their hands again, and as they did that, Tannis lifted Derek's head slowly, so as not to cause too much discomfort. He slid his hand under him, and the porter picked up a pillow and walking over to Tannis, said, 'I bought this over, thank you.' So between the two of them, they packed the patient's head, so it wouldn't move too much, in case of neck and back injuries. The porter moved down to his legs. Turning, he said, 'Sir, looking at Froner, please, sir, would you please help me.'

'Yes, of course, Porter. What would you like me to do?' replied Froner.

'Sir, I'm trying to pad his legs and back so he doesn't move.'

'Oh, OK then,' the captain walked across saying, 'let's get them both comfortable.' They finished padding Derek the best they could. 'It looks like you won't be moving from there for a while, Private. You just say when you need anything – food, drink, or toilet. You are still OK with this, Private?' Tannis looked at Derek who was holding his hand very tightly and looking into his eyes. 'That's fine, sir. I feel honoured he has chosen me.'

'OK, son, having someone very close, as I think you said, is very important for him. He doesn't know who he is, so he must be rather scared. OK, lad?'

'Sir, I'm comfortable.' As that was said, the first officer returned and entered the train car and said, 'All done, sir. We can have Private Tannis for as long as we need him.'

With that, the train whistle blew, and with a sudden jolt, the train slowly, surely started to move. As it did, three pairs of eyes were on the patient to see how he reacted to the movement. Apart from the initial jolt, he seemed to settle into an uneasy sleep. Although Derek didn't know it, he was on his way home.

Twenty

At home, the twins were now a month old; they turned out to be one of each. The little girl had now been named, as Derek had wished, Jessica Marie, and the little boy had had a very rough start for the first week or so, but now, like his sister, he was thriving. They were still at Derek's parents' place, but her parents had returned home to prepare for the homecoming of their daughter and grandchildren, making them now a very large family. Back in the country, Susan had stayed with Rosy, who was up and about with her usual optimistic outlook. Susan had another reason for staying behind. Rosy still had to be told about Gilbert and the rest of Derek's men who had returned. They had just fed the babies and decided it would be nice to take them out into the fresh air, so they wandered out into the garden to the seat were she had gone into labour. The babies were in a pram, and together they sat, looking out over the fields to the woods over the other side of one of the fields. Neither had spoken. Rosy knew Susan had something to say, but she decided not to say anything. She just said, 'Those woods are where Derek and Gilbert used to play as kids.

Susan replied, 'I didn't know that.' There was a long pause, and Susan said slowly, 'Rosy, my dear friend, I have something to tell you. After all you have been through this last few months, I'm not sure how to tell you.'

'Susan, my dear, how about looking at me and saying, "Rosy, my dear, what I have to say is . . ."' They both looked at each other, and slowly, Rosy realised what was about to be said. Anyway, Susan stood and walked to the wall and stood at the gate, looking into the fields. She stood there, and Rosy left her, knowing she was having trouble. A few minutes passed, and Susan slowly started to talk. 'Well, Rosy, while you were having the babies,' Rosy got up and quietly walked nearer to Susan. As Susan carried on, she just waited. Slowly she came to the point. 'Well, you see, Rosy, I had a phone call, well, two actually. The first was from Gilbert's parents. You see, Rosy, he and the rest of Derek's crew have been brought home safely.'

Rosy instinctively knew Susan hadn't finished, so she stayed where she was waiting. She was right as Susan carried on. 'I then had a phone call from Gilbert. He said he had broken his arm as the plane came down, so he stayed with the men while Derek and Rob went to scout about. When they didn't come back, he set off with the men as ordered and were rescued and helped to get home.'

Realising her dear friend was crying, Rosy moved forward and put her arm around her shoulder. With that, Susan broke down; she had been holding back for so long a mixture of grief and happiness. She was sorry for Rosy and at the same time also relieved that Gilbert, her love, was OK. 'It's OK, Susan. It's OK. You cry, my dear. I thank you for finally telling me what had been eating you up inside. I had already guessed that maybe it was something like this, but I knew you had to be the one to tell me. Look, I can guess that you are now feeling guilty on the inside. Please, Susan, don't feel guilty. You deserve a happy ending as much as any one else. How is your hero?' With that, Susan turned and looked at Rosy. At last they smiled and hugged, and as they hugged, Rosy looked across the fields. She saw someone; she whispered to Susan. 'I think I'll take the little ones in for a feed.'

'OK, Rosy. I'll come and help you.'

'No,' Rosy said. 'I think you'll be a little busy.'

Susan looked at Rosy with a puzzled look on her face. 'Umm, no, I have nothing else to do.'

Rosy took her friend's shoulders and said, 'My dearest, dearest friend.' With a smile on her face, Rosy turned her round and waited, until Susan saw who was coming. The penny finally dropping, she started to slowly back away. Suddenly Susan let out a scream and jumped up and down. 'Oh, sorry, Rosy, haven't woke the babies, did

I?' She turned to look at Rosy who was smiling with tears in her eyes. She was trying to hide. Rosy said, 'Go, my friend, don't just stand there. Go, go.' With that, Susan opened the gate, and with a quick glance backwards, she flew across the field into the waiting arms. Rosy watched her friend for a few seconds and then went to the babies. She slowly walked back to re-enter the house. Sitting at the door was her other best friend, Charm. As he grew up, he seemed to sense when she needed him. She wheeled the pram to the kitchen to prepare the babies their mid-morning feed. She let her mind wander to that wonderful first night with Derek, after the wedding, and how the moon was so bright. She thought of how he had taken her in his arms, how they had kissed, and that first feeling of anticipation, of what was to come, and then as they had lain there afterwards, in each other's arms, falling asleep. She was woken from her daydream by Charm, tugging at her skirt to tell her the babies were crying. At the same time, Franny walked in and Rosy said, 'This dog is more attentive to the twins than I am.' They laughed together. 'He probably doesn't like the noise,' Franny said, and they laughed even more. Franny said, 'Would you like some help, Rosy?'

'Yes,' Rosy replied. Then she asked, 'Would you take Boy up to my room?'

Franny giggled and said, 'I love you and the little ones. I can't keep calling the poor little mite Boy, Rosy.'

Rosy laughed and said, 'I know. I just can't think of a name.' Rosy grabbed the bottles, and they both made their way upstairs, just stopping long enough to pick up Jessica and Boy. When they got to the bedroom, a very large bedroom as it also had a sofa, they laid the twins on the bed together. 'OK, Auntie Franny, would you like to try feeding one of the little monkeys as Susan isn't here?'

'Oh yes, yes, please,' she said very excitedly. 'Can I please feed Jessie, Rosy?'

'OK, Franny, you may feed little Jessie, and I'll feed the Boy.' They both smiled. They picked up the said babies and sat one each end of the sofa and started feeding the twins. A few minutes passed without either speaking. Finally Franny broke the silence, saying,

'Rosy, about the name for Boy, who was the other flier that is missing with Derek? What was it? Bob?'

'No,' Rosy replied. 'It's Rob, short for Robert.'

Franny said, 'What about Robert Derek or Derek Robert?' It all went silent again. As they finished feeding the babies, Rosy replied, 'I think Robert Gilbert John sounds nicer.'

'Yes,' Franny agreed, 'so the boy has a name at last. Can I go tell Mummy and Daddy please?'

She was excited that she was the first to know, so Rosy agreed. 'Oh thank you, Rosy, I feel all grown up.' She laid Robert on the large bed and off she ran with JD hot on her heels to tell her parents the good news. Charm looked at Rosy, and she said, 'You want to go too, huh, boy?' He gave her his paw, and she said, 'Go on then, boy, go find them.' He scuttled after the other two. Rosy heard him bounding down the stairs and she let her mind wander back to the first morning of their honeymoon and after that a very wonderful first night and about what June had said as they took their breakfast tray to her. 'You two sound like you're in very good spirits. I heard you come bounding downstairs.'

'Oh, sorry, did we disturb you, June?' June had replied with a little giggle. 'No, of course not, you go out, enjoy yourselves'. She was bought back to reality of voices coming up the stairs and along the landing; she knew who it was it was Susan and Gilbert. She carried on with what she was doing and then she heard Gilbert say softly to Susan, 'I'd rather go in on my own, darling, if you don't mind.'

It was a few seconds and then Susan replied, 'No, of course not. I'll meet you downstairs later.' Rosy heard them kiss and then there was a tentative knock on the door. She called out, 'Come in. All godfathers allowed.' Gilbert strolled in and looked at her with tears in his eyes; she walked over to him and they hugged. 'Oh come here, you big softy, and meet your godchildren.' He looked at her with a puzzled look on his face now. 'What's wrong Gil?' Suddenly it dawned on her that Susan hadn't said anything about there being two and not just one baby. She had probably thought it would help to break an awkward silence. Rosy said to Gil, 'Didn't Susan tell you?'

'Tell me what, Rosy? What's going on? Is everything OK? You're worrying me.'

'Oh, Gilbert, you really are a big old softy. Come here.' She made him sit in one of the chairs in the bay window and she then said, 'OK, now shut your eyes.'

'Oh, Rosy, do I have to? I feel silly.'

'Yes, you do,' she laughed. 'Are they shut?'

'Yes,' he said. She picked the twins up one in each arm, and she walked over to him. Rosy placed little Jessica Marie in the crook of his left arm and he went to open his eyes, and she said, 'Keep them shut for just a minute more. Give me your right arm.' So as his arm opened out, she slowly placed the baby and made sure he had a hold. She looked at him with eyes itching to open and thought how peaceful he looked from when he came into the room. She finally said, 'Go on then, Godfather Airman Gilbert Somerville, meet and say hello to your godchildren as you can see we all got a surprise as well. The one in your left arm is Jessica Marie, and this little fellow up to today has just been known as Boy. Even Susan doesn't know his name. I only decided on it about half an hour ago. The only one that knows is Franny, and I would say Derek's mum and dad, if Franny found them. This dear Gilbert is Robert Gilbert Derek.'

Gilbert said he might only be tiny. 'My, wow, he has an awfully grand name to grow up with.'

'You don't think it's too much, do you, Gil?'

'No, no, I think it's great,' he said and then he looked at Jessica Marie. 'You're a very pretty little girl, and you have a very pretty name to go with those looks.' He turned and looked at Robert. 'You, my lad, are the loveliest surprise I've ever heard of. What does your mum and dad think, Rosy?'

She laughed, 'Silly question there. Still floating around about ten feet in the air. They are just so proud.'

'Where are they, Rosy? I didn't see Badger with the other two playing outside.'

'Oh, they went home to get ready for us and took Badger with them. They offered to take Zandi, with them. I don't know if Susan told you just how protective he is of not just me but also the twins.

Today is the first time he chose to go off willingly, so as you can guess, he wouldn't go. So he stayed.' As she said this, they heard what sounded like a herd of elephants coming up the stairs. 'Talking of the devil,' Rosy laughed; the door had been left open a bit and from the angle he was sitting, Gil saw a little black nose peep around the door. When he saw Gil holding his charges, his hair went up, and he flew over. Rosy said, 'Hey, Charm, it's OK. It's just Gilbert, holding the babies. He slowly crept around Gil and said, 'Should I hand them back to you?'

'No, not unless you want to, Gil. Just sit. He has to get used to other people holding them. Just let him sniff them and you, and he should be fine as long as he knows they're OK. He will recognise your scent in a minute, and he will settle down.' For the next few minutes, Charm sniffed Gil thoroughly and then, when Gil had let him sniff his charges, he went over to the window and sat looking at them. Then he lay content and went to sleep. 'Good dog,' Gil said.

'Yes, very good boy Zandi,' Rosy added. Rosy asked if he was OK holding the babies.

Gil replied, 'May I hold them a bit longer? Is that OK?' She looked at him and felt he could do with a few minutes on his own, so she asked him if he'd like a cup of tea.

'Oh, I would love one if it's not too much trouble.'

'Well,' she said, 'you watch that pair for a few minutes. I'll go and make some.'

He absent-mindedly answered, 'OK.'

She wasn't sure he knew what he was agreeing to. She smiled and looked over to Charm and said, 'Good boy, you stay and watch them for me, will you?' He gave a very low ruff so as not to disturb them. 'Thank you, boy.' With that, she headed out the door, silently shutting it behind her. After making her way slowly downstairs and into the kitchen, she moved the kettle more on to the heat of the range, and then collected a large tray and then two cups and saucers. Moving round further, she found a milk jug and she filled it up with the fresh milk from the pantry. All the time she was thinking back to somewhere else. The last time she had, they had milk straight from the cows, when Derek was right there by her side until a pushy little lamb had come between them, the memory brought a smile to her face. She hadn't smiled like that for a very long time. She re-entered the pantry and cut two slices of fruit cake and placed a piece on each side plate. She then placed them also on to the tray that was sitting on the very large farmhouse kitchen table. She walked over to a cupboard and pulled out a box. Inside was a surprise for Charm; Rosy placed what she had in her hands into the tray that now was getting very full. A small dish of water was also very carefully added. Still thinking about Lamikin's and wondered how big she must be, also wondering, if she'd had her first lamb or did she have twins too. With that thought, she gave a little laugh. She had written to everyone they had met on their honeymoon, and hopefully the replies would be waiting at home when she gets home in the next couple of days. Rosy was bought back to reality by a very angry kettle, boiling its head off. The water was poured into the pot, and the kettle was placed to one side of the range. It kept just warm for whoever needed or wanted it next. She took the tray and started for the stairs just as James was coming out of the library and offered to carry it upstairs for her. She accepted gratefully, then hesitated. She turned to James, 'Would you be OK if I take it from you at the top if that is OK?' He looked at her puzzled, and she explained about Gilbert, adding she didn't think he was ready to see anyone else just yet.

'That's OK,' James said. 'I suppose he is blaming himself.'

'Well,' Rosy replied, 'he is very much so.'

James just said, 'OK, I'll see him later at dinner if he stays.'

With that, he left her at the bedroom door. Just as Rosy went to enter, there was a sound that made her stop dead in her tracks. Gil was sobbing. Rosy was not sure whether to just enter or give a little knock of the tray on the door as if by accident. She decided she would do that so as not to embarrass her dear husband's, now also hers too, best friend. Thinking for a few moments, as the crying subsided a bit, she slowly entered as the large tray would allow. When he heard her, he was at her side in seconds to take the tray from her; he placed it on a table near where they were sitting.

He told Rosy, 'Sit, and I'll pour, if you don't mind, Rosy.'

She obeyed guessing he needed to feel busy. He poured the tea, handed hers to her, with some cake, and then he grabbed the box. Looking at the dozing Charm, he said, 'Now I wonder what's in this box and who they are for.' Slowly stretching, Charm moved to Gil to see what he had got. It looked like dog biscuits, although his doggy senses knew it wasn't. He sniffed the air, and he remembered Rosy saying he and DJ had finished them. *Well, what is in that box that smelt so good?* He sat at Gill's feet, who said, 'Good boy,' and then handed him the box. Charm carried it off, back to where he had been sitting, and there, he pulled the box apart. His work paid off; there was his prize, a lovely, juicy boiled bone. He was happy the babies were asleep. As they sat there quietly, all they could hear was the babies breathing in their sleep and, of course, Charm chewing. Gilbert broke the silence. He stood up and took two strides, and he was at the window, looking out at the wonderful scenery he had seen many times from this room as it was Derek's room. Whatever season, it was just as beautiful. Rosy sat quietly; she knew it had to be him to speak when he was ready. Finally, Gil broke the silence with what sounded like a little sob. 'Oh, Rosy, my dear Rosy, I'm so sorry. I feel awful about what's happened. If I hadn't have broken my wretched arm. I couldn't even hold my gun. I would have been the one to go with Derek. Oh, I know Rob is a great soldier.'

Rosy then realised that Gil didn't know about Rob. She thought she should tell him, so she went over to him, turned him to face her, and then gently she said, 'Gil, has no one told you that they had word.'

'What, Rosy, what? I haven't heard. I came straight here from the hospital, and I had been there as you know for three weeks.'

'Well,' Rosy carried on, 'Rob was executed over a week ago, and about the same time it seems, Derek was rescued or escaped or just disappeared. That came in the same radio message from one of our top agents posted over there. That's all the agent told the authorities before the radio went silent, so no one is sure. They haven't heard from that agent since.' Gil had wandered back over to the babies and was gently rubbing Robert's back; he seemed to be in a world of his own. She wondered if he was reliving what happened. As Robert settled down, Jessica stirred awake; she looked up at Gil and gave a little smile. She watched as he picked her up and held her close to him. He said out loud as if he was thinking out loud. 'You, sweet little mite, you are so innocent.' His face was in her hair that you even smell innocent. Rosy just sat, not wanting to disturb him, so she just listened. Gil started to speak again, cuddling Jessie as if he was never going to let her go. He said, 'That day started out as normal. The weather was right, and we were all ready. We boarded the *Hope and Glory* and started the engines and taxied on to the runway. The other crews did the same with their planes. Thirty minutes later, we were well on our way to our target. All was going well. We were all in fairly high spirits. We found the target fairly easily. Within seconds, all hell broke loose. We went to bomb the target but had to pull off. It turned out that they had POWs imprisoned at one side of the target, so we had to take another fly over, and we had to bomb and try to hit as near the target, trying not to hit the poor fellows being held there.' Again, he was crying. Gil went silent again, hugging Jessie with tears rolling down his face. 'We only knew there was POWs there because of the large white sheet that had been draped over the trees and the letters in red.' It went quiet for a few seconds then he went on. 'Derek said he thought the resistance must have put it there during the night. Thank god for them – brave men and women. Yes, Rosy, there were women too, fighting alongside their men and some children doing some of the running around. The idea being the Germans wouldn't suspect them. When the bombing had finished, we set off for home. The Germans weren't going to let us out easily. They were mad as we had got past them without too much trouble, so the guns were going full out. The explosions and flashing was rocking the plane. We thought we had just about got through unscathed, when one last shot got us, and we started to lose power. Between the two of them, Rob and Derek managed to keep us up for a while. Truth is we all knew we were going down, and that this was the end for our dear friend, *Hope and Glory*. Rob called over the radio, "We are going down. We are too low to parachute. Make sure you are all in the main part of *Hope*." Slowly, we could feel the *Hope* going down. The engines started to fail and then one completely died. We started to descend rapidly with no time to dwell, just cope, hope, and pray. Derek managed to bring her in nearly level. We skidded across the field, coming to a halt just short of the edge of some trees. As we escaped the wreck, we all made a run for it as we knew we would have been seen coming down when the poor old girl went up in flames. We found that there was a building just at the edge of the woods, well-camouflaged. That was where we stopped and where my arm was tended to. I fell asleep, and the next thing I knew when I awoke, Derek and Rob were about to set off. Now my dearest, Rosy, you know as much as I do.'

They sat in silence for what seemed like an eternity but in reality, it was only a couple of minutes. The silence was broken by Gil, who said, 'Rosy, when you go back to your parents, will you let me drive you and couple of little beautiful babies?'

Charm looked up and gave a little bark as if to say, 'Hey, don't forget me.'

They laughed, and Gil said, 'I won't forget you. You're their guardian. When their dad or I are not around, you must look after their mum too. Will you do that for me, boy?' As if to answer him, he cocked his head to one side and barked. By then, the babies had started to wake for their next feed.

Rosy said, 'Gil, do you realise we have been up here for over two hours? The others will be wondering what has become of us, and I bet there is a certain young lady waiting for you to take her out.'

They picked up a baby each and made their way downstairs Charm was following close behind; he ran straight past them through the kitchen and out into the garden. A week later, they all left the estate and headed back to town and home. There was no news of her beloved husband; at least, if there was no news, he could be still alive. At least, that's what kept her going. When she just wanted to give up, the memories of those first weeks they had, had kept her strong. Of course, the main force in her life was Derek's babies. They arrived home about mid-afternoon, and as they pulled up, her parents came running out, and you guessed it, so did half the street. Rosy, Susan, and Gil laughed. Badger had come out to looking for his friend. They found each other and ran around and then there was a bark from the car. Then out jumped JD and Franny. To no one in particular, she said, 'Shall I take them into the back garden?'

Albert said, 'Yes, please dear, if you would.'

Rosy greeted her parents; they hugged, and as they parted Susan alighted from the car with a baby in each arm. Gil went to her and took his little princess in his arms, and then he and Susan walked into Rosy's parents and handed them a baby each. The smile on their faces said it all. They looked at Rosy; Rosy said with a smile, 'Off you go now. Go show your grandbabies off.'

'Oh, Rosy, we can't introduce them as this is our Granddaughter Jessica, with our Grandson Boy.'

'It's OK. He has a name,' Gil interrupted, saying, 'oh, wow, is it ever a grand name?'

Rosy smiled, 'You ready, Mum, Dad? Here we go.' Slowly Rosy said, 'Hello, everyone,' picking little Robert up, 'I'd like to introduce to you my son, Robert Gil Derek Rook-Leigh,'

'Oh, Rosy, what a wonderful name!' When they had taken it in, they said, 'After that we are off with our precious well-named grandbabies.' They all smiled. After they had gone, the three of them went into the house to have a cup of tea before Susan, Gil, along with Franny, oh of course not for getting JD, headed back to the country.

Twenty-One

After settling in back at her parents' place, things started to get into a routine. Her mind often drifted back to the honeymoon. The only real memory of her husband was the letters that had been waiting for her when she had returned home. They were all full of congratulations on the babies and sympathy on the news of Derek. Rosy set about answering them first was June in Southend-on-Sea, explaining they had not heard any more news about Derek. Then Rosy told June the babies' names, how they were getting on, and that her parents had offered to look after them, and she had decided to go back to work as a nurse as she was needed there. In the end, she promised to keep in touch and come and visit as soon as the time was convenient. The letter to Jeff and Kathy at the Haymaker was much the same. As was the one to the farm, Jed and Grace, adding a large paragraph about the pups and about how well they were doing, how they all had at least one special thing. Charm and how he looked after the babies. When the letters were all written, she got the babies ready, and she told her parents they were off to post them, and then they would be going to feed the ducks at the park. Sensing she wanted to be on her own, they said OK. Her mother added that dinner will be ready when she got back. Off she went, and they had hardly got to the top of the road when they bumped into several people they knew, all wanting to see the twins and ask about Derek. She mailed her letters, and they made their way to the park, the same park where she had gone to feed the ducks once before. Rosy made her way to the same bench this time without twisting her ankle. She sat, leaning into the pram, and started talking to the twins, saying, 'This, my darlings, is where I met your daddy. He was in his lovely uniform. It was a lovely spring day. Your grandma had given me some bread, like today, and I was going to feed the ducks, but as I stepped off the grass onto the path, I twisted my ankle. Your daddy picked me up and got me to this bench. My ankle was very sore, so we stayed and talked for a long time. Finally, he offered to walk me home as my ankle was still sore.' The babies gurgled and cooed as Rosy sat there reminiscing. By this time, the ducks had got fed up with waiting. They had come to them loudly quacking and that bought Rosy back to reality. 'Oh, you made me jump,' she said to a very brave duck sitting by her feet, and with him was, she guessed, his wife and kids. 'Well, my wonderful feathered friend, I see you're not alone, and what a wonderful family you have. Mr Duck, would you like some bread?'

'*Quack, quack,*' he answered her.

'Well, here you are.' She scattered some crumbs right next to them. The mother duck and ducklings had first pickings and then papa had some; a few minutes later they all waddled off and slipped back into the water and they swam off. Papa turned and Rosy gave a double quack, as if to say, 'Thank you for caring about my family.' Then he turned around, and they swam to an island in the middle of the lake, where Rosy guessed their home must be. The babies were gurgling happily in their pram. Rosy just sat watching, right up until the last little duckling clambered onto the island, finally catching up with his five siblings and parents. Then they all disappeared out of sight. Rosy sat there a little longer, just thinking and reminiscing. Robbie and Jessie, as they were being called, had both fallen asleep. She covered them up a bit more and made her way home, passing the hall where the dance had been the night they met where she and Derek had gone. As she walked the rest of the way back to her parents, she daydreamed of that night and remembered how brave she had been to ask him to the dance and how very forward that had been. She smiled to herself, thinking how the thought of never seeing him again was unbearable. As she turned the corner of the road, coming towards her was Susan and Gilbert. Susan ran to her, giving her a hug, and they asked each other how they were, Susan also asked about the babies. 'Rosy, how old are they now?'

'They're four months old.' By now, Gil had caught up. They both said, 'Goodness. Look how much they have grown.' They chatted as they headed home. Susan said, 'Gill's leave is up in a week and then he gets the all clear to go back to duty.'

As they arrived, her dad was just leaving for work. He greeted his daughter with a hug and kiss as he always did. 'I won't kiss the tinkers,' he said, 'as I don't want to wake them.'

After greeting Susan and Gil and asking how he was and being told he will be returning to duty in a week, Albert said, 'Well, good luck, lad, look after yourself.'

They shook hands, and he went on his way, whistling as he went. 'He's happy,' said Gil.

'Yes, he has been ever since we got home,' Rosy said with a smile. They finally entered the house, and her mum came out of the kitchen, drying her hands on a tea towel.

'Hello, darling.' Then on seeing Susan and Gil, she said, 'Hello, you two, how are you? Well, you look happy.'

'Yes, we are,' they both said together and they all laughed. Then her mum said 'How are my grandbabies?'

'They're fine, Mum. Fast asleep.'

'So I see. Would you like me to put them to bed?'

'Oh yes, Mum, if you don't mind.'

Then Gil asked, 'Would you like me to give you a hand?'

'That would be very nice, dear.' They picked up the twins. Gil, as always, held little Jessie and her mum had little Robbie. Off they went to put them to bed. After they had gone, Rosy and Susan headed for the lounge. There they sat and started to chat. After a little while, Susan became very quiet, and then to Rosy's surprise, tears were running down her cheeks. Rosy's arm instantly went around her friend's shoulder. 'What's wrong, dear friend?'

Susan took her handkerchief from her handbag and wiped her eyes. 'Well, Rosy, you know Gill's leave is coming to an end. Now his arm is all healed and back to normal. Please don't get upset, but . . .'

Rosy interrupted, 'I think I know what you're about to say.'

Susan looked at her as Rosy said, 'You and Gil are (taking Susan's hand's in her and looking her in the eyes) getting married. Am I right?'

She didn't need an answer; the tears were there again. Rosy took the hanky, lifted her face so that their eyes met again; she was smiling as she said to Susan, 'You silly goose, why on earth should I get upset? It's the best news I've heard in a very long time, and it couldn't be happening to a nicer couple.'

With all tears wiped away, Rosy said, 'When is this happy event happening?'

Susan said, 'We are off to book it tomorrow. We knew you were back at work, Rosy. We so much want you, the twins, and your parents to be there. Please say you will, Rosy. It wouldn't be right without you. I want you to be beside me.'

Hearing a loud cough, they thought it was Gil and Eleanor coming back down. They both got a surprise when Duncan appeared at the door. He said, 'I coughed so you knew I was coming in.'

Rosy jumped up and hugged him. 'Hi, how are you, Brother?'

'I'm fine, and how are you, Sis?' She replied the same and then asked him if he had just come from upstairs. When he replied no and that he had just got home and even Mum doesn't know that he was home, she said. 'Did you know you have a niece . . .'

Before she could finish, he interrupted, 'Wow! I have a niece. That's great.' Rosy and Susan looked at each other and smiled, guessing his letters hadn't caught up to him.

'Hey, girls, what's going on?'

'Well, Brother, you had better sit,' she said just as Eleanor and Gil came in. Rosy put her fingers to her lips. She sat him down. 'As I was saying, your niece is upstairs asleep with . . .'

Again he interrupted, 'With dad.'

'Oh, Duncan, shut up a minute and let me finish talking. As I said your niece is sleeping up stairs with her brother.' Everything went silent. Duncan was sitting with his jaw nearly on the floor. He was speechless. All he could say was 'uh oh.' The others laughed, and at that, Eleanor said she would go and make tea.

Gil offered, 'Would you like a hand, Eleanor?'

Both realising the brother and sister needed some space to talk, so off they went to the kitchen, where they found a big ball of fluff under the table. It was Badger, and Charm, who now had started to relax a bit more, was being a normal dog. Eleanor said, 'Gil, would you mind feeding the fluff balls while I make the tea.' As soon as he walked into the pantry, they were up and instantly by his side. They knew what he was doing. He smiled and said, 'Well, chaps, you're quick of the mark.'

He put their bowls on the table, and they sat by his feet. As Eleanor put the kettle on, she had her back to him. She said, 'Gil, how do you think Rosy is coping really? She says she is glad to be back to work. Her father and I thought maybe it was too soon as now she is a sister. She has taken it on herself to meet the Red Cross trains every day.'

He placed the fluff balls' dinners on the floor, walked over to her, and placed his hands around her, saying, 'Your Rosy is a one in a million. She is coping, but I don't know how. She is tough. I suppose that is her way of coping.'

'OK, Gil, if you think so. We will leave it well enough alone. Please promise that if you notice anything change, you will tell us at least while you're home.'

'Yes, I will,' he promised.

Meanwhile, back in the lounge, Rosy and Duncan were still talking. 'Did you say brother?'

'Yes, I said brother.'

'How? I mean Derek's not back, is he? So how?'

Rosy had gone silent; it sounded as if he didn't even know he was missing. She managed to rally herself and said, 'No, Derek's not back.'

Again, he said, 'So how?'

'Oh, Brother, honestly, you are daft. I ended up having twins. Your niece's name is Jessica-Marie Rose Rook-Leigh, and, my dear brother, you also have a nephew. His name is Robert Gilbert Derek Rook-Leigh.'

Duncan sat for a minute and then when he spoke, all he could say was 'Blimey, Sis, poor little kids. What a mouthful their names are?' With that, everyone laughed.

Duncan said, 'If I know you, you already know that hubby of yours approves. It's as if your minds are entwined.'

Rosy said to him, 'Did you get any of our letters?'

'No,' he said, looking worried as Rosy's mood had changed dramatically. 'They either haven't caught up with me or, like sometimes, they may well have gotten lost. Why, Sis, what's wrong?'

She got up and walked to the window and looked out. It was gently snowing; big snowflakes were falling and landing, only to melt as they touched something. *Such a short lifespan*, she thought with tears silently running down her cheeks. He got up and went up behind her and put his hand on her shoulder. As she felt him touching her, she let go of the log, held back tears, and she turned and wept into his shoulder. He led her to the sofa and sat her down and let her cry herself out. He knew something must be really wrong, as there were great big sobs racking her whole body. Although she was still crying, between sobs, she told him about Derek and Rob and what had happened. Some of the talk was so mixed with the sobs, but he got the gist. He thought of what she was trying to say, but she had cried so much that she had worn herself out, and she drifted into a very disturbed sleep. He manoeuvred himself to the edge of the sofa and held her head so as not to startle her. He pulled a cushion and placed it gently under her head and then he pulled a blanket over her and got up gently so as not to wake her. He quietly moved away and out of the room. He headed to the kitchen; as he entered, he found his mum and Gil in the kitchen. He closed the door as quietly as he could. His mum started to panic. 'What's wrong, Son?' she asked, seeing the worried look on his face.

'She's asleep on the sofa after wearing herself out crying.' They both looked at Duncan; they looked puzzled. Gil was the first one to speak. 'You didn't know, did you? You didn't know Derek was missing.'

His mum inhaled sharply. Duncan replied, 'I had no idea my letters either haven't caught up to me or have got lost which happens all too often. I'm afraid I got the gist of it through the sobs. I didn't think. I saw you here, Gil, and just took it for granted that Derek was around somewhere. Oh my god, what happened?'

Eleanor said, 'Gill, take Duncan upstairs to the twins' room so as not to disturb Rosy. She has a shift in a couple of hours, so let her sleep, lads. OK, here, take your tea. You can drink while you fill Duncan in. The babies are due for a feed soon, so it doesn't matter if they wake. You can play with them for a while and get to know them. I'll go sit in lounge and watch over Rosy.'

With that, they all went their separate ways. When the boys got upstairs and reached the bedroom, they entered silently. Duncan went straight to the cot (as they both still slept in one at the moment) and just stood, knowing he was going to like what he was about to find out. As he was watching the twins sleeping or so, he thought he saw a little head turn and bright blue eyes trying to focus on him. It was little Jessie, rubbing her eyes and giving a great big ear-to-ear smile that lit up the whole room. He turned to Gil and whispered, 'What shall I do, Gil?'

He smiled at him. 'Hey,' he said, 'she's your niece.'

'Oh, right,' he said, smiling, so he bent into the cot and gently, so as not to wake her brother, he had lifted her out. He walked over to a chair and sat down.

'Hello, my little niece, you are going to be a real heart breaker when you grow up, aren't you, sweetheart?' He had forgotten for a minute that Gil was there, so when he said, 'Do you know their names?' It bought him back to reality. Suddenly it dawned on him. No, he didn't know. 'Gil, I didn't get my post still. It hasn't caught up with me.'

'Well, now,' said Gil, 'let me introduce you to Uncle Duncan. That beautiful young lady you have in your arms there is the one and only Jessica Marie, and that handsome young man down there is Jessi's younger brother who goes by the name of Robert (that's after our crew member that died, the one with Derek). His other names are Gilbert Derek.' They sat talking and holding a baby each, telling about the things they had seen and done. About fifteen minutes later, there was a tapping at the door. They both said, 'Come in at the same time.' They laughed, and the door opened slowly.

Then Eleanor poked head around the door and said, 'Thought you boys had got lost or run off with a baby each.' She entered the room and sat down next to Duncan. 'Well, Son, what do you think of your nephew and niece?'

'They make me feel there is hope and light at the end of the tunnel, and also, I feel better when I see life carrying on as near normal as possible in these dark days. Is that somewhat how you feel, Gil?'

It was silent for a while before he replied, 'Yes, I agree. Also, I look at these little ones and see the future. They are the future, weather we are in it or not. Things will carry on and get back to normal.'

'Well, boys, on that sombre note, what I came up for was to see if our little bits of the future are ready for their feed,' she said with a smile on her face, as they looked at them. They were both wide awake and smiling.

'I thought Rosy was going to come up,' Duncan said. 'She did come up, but hearing you talk, she didn't want to disturb you. She just got herself ready and left to work.'

'Oh dear, hope she wasn't upset,' Gilbert said.

'Don't be daft. She would have come in if she wanted to. She knew her babies were in good hands. Now come on, you four babies,' Eleanor said, laughing. 'Let's get you four fed.'

They made their way downstairs and into the kitchen where they found Albert smoking his pipe and reading his paper. Badger was sitting with his head on his knee and Charm was lying at his feet. Eleanor said, 'If you boys take one of these of these each,' she said as she handed them a baby bottle each, 'and one of these. Oh and these, of course, handing them a towel and a nappy.' They smiled as they left the room and went into the lounge. They got comfortable. Gil threw a cushion to Duncan. 'Oh, what was that for?'

Gil said, 'To put under your arm while you feed that little lady you have in your arms.'

'Oh, they're adorably cute, and all those things no one told me. They seem to weigh a ton when lying in your arm feeding.' That made them both laugh. The next hour was spent on feeding and burping. That had both the grown men in stitches, and then came the testing chore of nappy changing, and as they just finished, a pretty head popped at the door. It was Susan; she came to tell them dinner was ready. 'OK, my love,' Gil said and gave her a peck on the cheek. Duncan watched them with a smile on his face. Susan said, 'And just what are you grinning at?'

'Well, you two.'

'Could have given a man some warning. I didn't realise you were so close.' They both blushed. After they got over their embarrassing moment, Gil said, 'OK, darling, we will be right down as soon as we get them settled.'

'OK' came the reply as she disappeared downstairs.

'Now, Duncan, this will put you to the test,' Gil laughed.

'It can't be that hard,' Duncan replied. And looking up at Gil, he said, 'You're not joking, are you, Gil?'

'Now would I do that to you, Duncan?' They both moved over to the cot, very gently, slowly, as they were asleep, lowered them down and covered them up again gently, so as not to wake the little mites. Gil closed the curtains and said, 'OK, let's go.' They slowly walked out of the room and not a peep. When they arrived downstairs, Duncan said, 'They have gone down without any fuss. Must be my touch.'

Eleanor looked at Gil and Susan and said, 'OK, you two, what have you been up to?'

The two of them giggled and Duncan said, 'Will someone let me in on the joke?' So now they were all puzzled. Anyway Albert said, 'The question is who is taking the message to Rosy? If Duncan went, she would panic, thinking something was wrong. Well, the same as any of us, as we don't normally go to her work.' It became quiet.

Then Eleanor said, 'It wouldn't frighten her if you two turned up, arm in arm, would it, Susan? She would think you and Gil are just out.'

'Good thinking, Mum. That's a great idea,' Duncan said to his mum and got up and gave her a cuddle. 'Don't worry about the twins. We will all be here. Yes, even Dad's off this afternoon. I think, with three of us, we can tackle a couple of little monkeys,' said Albert, who had been sitting so quietly, puffing on his beloved pipe, so when he said what he said, they all started to laugh. You know those big over-exaggerated laughs when you get good news that then ends up in tears of joy. 'Now, come on, look at us, this is Rosy's news. Don't need to get hysterical over it,' said Eleanor. 'So let's get this plan into action. Oh, as Rosy was leaving, she said, I start as sister today. One of her new duties is to meet the Red Cross troop trains. There's one coming in, I think she said at four or four thirty, I'm not sure, so she was going on her way to work at the hospital. That's why she left early, but there had been an air raid going on, since about three thirty. The all clear hadn't gone yet, so she will be in an air raid shelter. I would say more than likely the one near the park as she always goes that way to work. The station is between here the park and work.' Interrupting her train of thought as the 'all clear' sounded, at the same time on the other side of the park, Rosy was jolted from her daydreams of her memories, which kept her going at the moment. She smiled, gathered her things together, and then joined the long slow-moving queue. Ten minutes later, once outside, Rosy was standing in the fresh air . . . She just stood, taking in the silence, after the siren went silent; then slowly the normal sounds returned – the birds, people going on about their business, and the babies crying for attention, and after all the loud noise, they settled down for their parents. Looking at her watch, she thought, if she hurried, maybe I'll just get to the station as the train gets in, hoping it was only going to be the one as she turned the corner; at the station, there were, lined up in front, about twenty or so ambulances. There was also something different; there was a large staff car, strange as this train was supposed to be for just injured troops . . . As she got to the station, there was an announcement coming over the Tannoy system . . .

Twenty-Two

After the initial ten minutes of severe discomfort, Derek seemed to settle into a restless and uneasy semi-conscious state. He was shouting and thrashing about and poor young Tannis got caught in the face a couple of times; after that, he managed to duck as best he could. On the whole, Derek travelled better than any of them expected. The carriage door suddenly opened, and the train guard stuck his head in the door, saying, 'We will be pulling into the station in about ten minutes, sir,' he said, addressing the captain, who replied, 'Thank you, for letting us know. When we pull in, would you please go, with my officer, to get a stretcher, also hopefully a doctor? If possible, a nurse too.'

'Yes, sir, I'll come back when we pull into the station.' He went off to finish his other duties, so he would be free to help the captain move the poor RAF pilot. As he went about his duty, his mind kept going back to the poor fellow's injuries of what he could see, of course. He kept thinking he had never seen such terrible injuries. To himself he muttered, *I'll never understand how one human being can inflict such horrific injuries on another human being.* He made his way to warn the Red Cross staff that the train would be pulling into the station very shortly. As he was turning to leave, the nurse that had spoken to the captain when the train was in the station asked him if the captain needed her. He said, 'He didn't say when I was with him.'

'OK, maybe it is for the best not to disturb the poor pilot until absolutely necessary, poor soul.'

'Yes, I know. I was just saying to myself, how does one human do that to another human being? It's such cruelty.' With that, the train guard left. About fifteen minutes, as promised, the guard returned to the captain's carriage, where he found him, with his officer, ready to leave the train. He was just in time, as the train was now pulling into the station. As it came to its final halt, the guard, with Officer Froner, said they would go together. They left the train to find a stretcher, doctor, and hopefully a nurse. As they tried, they found the station was crowded and very busy. They knew it would take a long time, like that, so the guard suggested to the officer that they go to the station master's office and ask him to put a request over the Tannoy system. 'That's a great idea,' Froner replied. Off they went to do just that. When they got there, the guard explained to the station master what was needed.

The master said, 'Well, that's not the way it works. Sorry.' Officer Froner took over, showed him his credentials, and then he went on to say, 'We do appreciate it as it's not the normal way you normally do things.'

'Well, you see, sir, this whole situation is not normal. My captain would be most grateful if you, just this once could help us. We would really be most grateful. I will leave the guard here to explain everything that's needed. Is that OK?' The station master thought for a minute or two, and then said, 'Yes, of course, sir, that will be fine. After that's done, I will join the guard to come to tell you it has been done.' All being carried out, they said, 'Thank you. We are most grateful. My captain will thank you himself when you come to the carriage.' With that, Officer Froner left, heading back to the carriage, knowing Captain Dayforb will need his help. As he boarded the train and started walking down the passage to the carriage, he could hear there was a problem. He hurried, entering the carriage; there he found Derek was fighting Tannis again, and the captain was trying to restrain his arms a bit, trying at the same time not to hurt him too much. He was so very disorientated with the pain; he also had a fever. Where he found the strength from, they could not fathom. All they could think it was fear; he must have been that scared. He was a real fighter. Officer Froner hurried over to help the others to hold him down as he was thrashing about. He was making his wounds that had stopped bleeding, open up again. There was blood all over the place.

The captain's white tunic was covered. Poor Tannis, on top of the black eye he received earlier, he was splattered. They slowly managed to calm him down, plus he had exhausted himself. Derek once again fell unconscious. About ten minutes later, the station master, with the guard as promised, arrived to say all was being done. After that they left again, saying they were returning to the office, ready to bring whoever over. 'OK,' the captain said, 'see you soon . . .'

Twenty-Three

The voice coming over the Tannoy system was asking for a doctor and also a nursing sister to report to the station master's office. Rosy could see the office from where she was standing; she thought, *That is very odd. They don't normally get called to the master's office*, so Rosy rushed over. As she did, she saw Dr Neil Tranten, top doctor, at the hospital where she worked. As he saw her, they greeted each other. Neil said, 'What's this all about?'

Rosy replied, 'I don't know, Doctor. I've only just got here myself. I think we are about to find out.' They got to the office door, knocked, and entered. There they were met by the station master, and also with him, was a train guard. They all greeted each other, introducing themselves at the same time. Dr Tranten said, 'OK, Station Master, can you tell us what all this is about? We have never been summoned to your office before.'

The station master replied, 'Just let me send a message out that we have a doctor and nursing sister that we asked for so that the other medical staff know that they can carry on. The guard can fill you in better anyway. He was there from the start.'

'OK,' Dr Tranten replied. While the master was doing that, the guard from the train started to fill them both in. As he was talking, Neil said, 'Sorry for the interruption.' It came to his mind that he needed to talk to the master. 'For a moment. Could you hold on a moment, sir?' With that, he went to the master, who had finished his announcements. 'Could you please ask for a stretcher with orderlies?'

'Yes, sir, right away.' Neil left him to it. With that done, he turned his attention back to the guard, who carried on explaining 'This poor chap ain't in the Red Cross carriages like normal, sir.'

'He isn't?' They both asked puzzled, intrigue crossing their faces. They looked at each other and shrugged their shoulders. 'Oh no, sir, miss, there was some big wig, Navy guy found him, ees a navy captain, I fink with anova Officer, sade dey did find im, next day, after towing a French fishing boat in, ie were sitting on da atch, iee all smashed up, coodn't move like iee were dead. dere swas undred of dem dead SS soldiers on the deck wiv a lot of French blokes proberly resistance.'

'Hang on,' Neil said, 'you're telling us this bloke lived, as you said everyone else was dead. Who the hell is this bloke?'

'ees pilot, RAF, iee fink. Up in rank, he flies the big guys, you know,' Looking at Neil, he said, 'zem bombers, eis somfink special too.'

Rosy said to him, 'Are you sure he is a pilot?'

'Yeah, ees uniform ins rags it is,' said the very East End of London guard. 'Oh my god, this must be bad top-brass secrecy.' The guard turned saying, 'Mum's za word,' tapping the side of his very large nose, 'in other words, I've told you too much.'

'That's OK. Mum's the word,' Neil said, tapping his nose too. 'OK, Rosy?' 'There goes a real east ender. I barely understood him, it's like a foreign language,' Rosy said to Neil, they both laughed.

'Yes,' she replied, 'just hurry. Hurry! Get us to the poor serviceman.' Neil asked Rosy if she was OK with this. 'Yes, Neil, I'll be fine.' The three went to the door as the guard opened it. Two orderlies with the stretcher came running up to them.

Neil remarked, 'That was quick, guys. Follow us. They all set off for the train, not quite knowing what they were going to find. They rushed to the carriage, passing a lot of other patients being helped. Some were walking by themselves, the others were hanging on to another, and more were on stretchers. *Just too many*, Rosy thought. Rosy looked at each and every one of them, as she always did, just in case it might just be Derek. As they arrived, they boarded the train. At the first carriage they got into, as it was easier than weaving through, all the injured and with nurses or stretchers or even porters carrying the injured men. They found that it was now empty. All the poor souls were injured or, what's worse, dead. Of course, what hit you most was the terrible smell of death, decay, blood, still wet, sticky trickling between the carriages and plank floors. There was vomit, going the same way, with dressing, gauze, and bandages all soaked in blood. Of course, Rosy was used to it to some degree, and as now she was a sister, of course, she gets to see this side too, not just the operating room, where they were asleep. A thought crossed her mind; she spent more time in the hospital than at home. This really is above and beyond what her eyes had ever seen; she prayed she would never see this again. Although hardened somewhat, you can't say used to, you can never get used to it. This amount of death, such senseless waste of good young men and then the ones who had lost their limbs. She remembered, a few moments earlier, when passing a couple of soldiers, she saw one who had lost his leg, and his left eye was covered. The second had lost his arm and his face was badly burnt. They were crying, saying they wished they had died like their mates. Nurses were trying to placate them. She couldn't believe they would rather be dead. After walking through all this, she slowly started to understand. They were lost and scared about how they will cope and they probably were thinking about being a burden to their families, wives, mothers and that their normal, athletic husband or son needs to rely on people. Neil brought her back to reality. 'Are you OK, Rosy?'

'Yes, I'm fine, Neil. Just thinking of the everlasting waste of our young men. Most of them were dragged into the forces whether it be soldier, sailor, or pilot, but for what? Just to get killed or, worse, to be maimed in some way?'

They walked along the corridor, following the guard to where the patient was. When they entered, the sight they found was pretty awful that it took both their breaths away. Neil turned to Rosy and they looked at each other. Neil started move over to the patient, who was still lying on Tannis's lap. His face was turned towards the private's chest; it was bandaged as best it could be. It had been left to Tannis; he did the best he could. As Neil approached him, he thought, *I'd better move slowly. I don't want to make him jump.* As he moved a little closer, his foot, accidentally, kicked something that had been left on the floor. It made quite a noise, disturbing poor Derek. He came around a bit, once again, and started catching Tannis in the face, although this time in the eye. Poor Tannis tried not to move so as not to make him worse. Neil quickly opened his bag to retrieve a sedative, while the captain and his officer and Tannis were gently trying to hold him to stop him hurting himself even more, let alone poor, battered Tannins. Rosy still didn't know if it was Derek, as his face was facing away from her. Neil found the sedative; the captain said, 'The poor soul needs painkiller.'

'I know,' replied Neil. 'I need to calm him down first, so I can access him, and then the painkillers, depending on what I find. Has he had any on his journey?'

'Yes,' replied the captain. 'One of the Red Cross staff gave him some. As we were settling him on the train, it wasn't strong enough up to then, he had been fighting the pain. The trouble was the sedative not being very strong. It relaxed him a bit, although not enough. Consequently, it didn't help. I know it sounds odd. To be honest, he was better, without it. He was in control of the pain before he had painkiller's he has such a strong will. When he relaxed, on the painkiller you can see the result by poor Private Tannis face and our uniforms, as it wore off, he seemed to get control. God knows how, although a bit of agitation, as you would expect, I don't think I could cope with even a bit of the pain he must be in.'

'Me neither,' Neil said. Neil looked at Rosy, who was looking at their uniforms. They had been, she guessed, lovely pristine, white uniforms when they set off, and now they were more of red than white. As for poor Tannis's, face, well it was black and very blue with blood trickling down his forehead. Neither the captain or the officer had realised it was his blood. They thought it was from the pilot. 'I'm so sorry, Tannis,' they spoke together. The officer carried on, 'If we had realised, we would have patched you up.'

'That's OK, sir. We were all more worried about this, I suppose for want of a better word, hero.'

'Yes, I agree,' the captain replied. Neil lifted Tannis's hair, and he found a wound an inch or so long. 'You need a few stitches for that, Private.'

'Can you do it now, Doctor, while we are here, as the pilot is settled for a few minutes. I know as soon as I move, there be no chance. He will get very agitated. Also it will bleed if I move without having it stitched, right, Doctor?'

'Yes, Private, it is quite deep. So as soon as you move or even lean forward, it will bleed badly, maybe enough to make you very light-headed or maybe even faint.'

'OK, Doctor, thank you. Carry on, as I will be carrying our friend here.'

'Carrying him? What do you mean?'

'We have a stretcher for him.'

'With all due respect, Doctor, I'm here in the first place because he won't let anyone, and I do mean when I say *anyone*, touch him. What you saw was only a mild episode.'

'Oh, I didn't know that.'

With that, Neil started stitching the private's wound, with Rosy's help. He looked at the pair of officers and asked, 'Why wasn't this pilot seen by a doctor before the train left on its journey down here?'

'Well, I have some medical background,' said the captain. 'I was in my last few months of training to become a doctor, as soon as I found this poor feller. I knew he couldn't wait for the next train, which was in three days. I was coming here anyway, so I had booked the carriage, as we have meeting. I took on myself to see he got the best of everything. So now, here we are.'

Twenty-Four

'I knew there was a flier missing who had flown a highly secret mission. With that also in mind, I thought rightly or wrongly that he had been like that, for god knows how long, drifting at sea. He is delirious. He may have said the wrong thing to the wrong person. He is having a bit of trouble with his breathing. There is a high risk of his ribs being broken and split. It may have entered another vital organ. He has boot marks all over his chest.'

'Did you say boot marks?'

Neil asked, looking at Rosy, 'Yes, Doctor, I did. I'd say dirty great big goose stepping boots. That's not all, Captain,' Tannis said. 'When he yanked at himself, he ripped what was left of his shirt, revealing a lot more. There are marks on his chest that look like a chair frame. Also there are a lot of, maybe, cane marks, like what an officer would carry. He also . . .' he stammered.

'What is it, Private?'

Tannis looked up at them all, not sure how to say it. Then slowly, he continued, 'Well, sir, I'm not sure about his back. I'd say it's going to be the same if not worse.'

Neil said to him, 'Please tell us what you saw.'

'I saw there were burns.'

'What? Like cigarette burns?'

'Sorry about this, with the cigarette burns, it looks like he has been . . .' He stalled and looked up and then down. He shut his eyes to hold back the tears that were threatening to spill over. He swallowed hard and then said he had what looks like a large brand. They all looked at him.

'What did you say?' the captain asked.

'He has been branded. Yes, sir, it's quite large. It looks like a swastika with two lines next to it.'

The captain looked at his officer, who said, 'Tannis, think carefully now, Private. These lines, think and tell me exactly, what did they look like?'

'Well, sir, they looked like three small straight lines attached.'

With that the officer drew a notebook, turned to the picture, and then showed Tannis. Then Tannis said, 'Yes, sir, that's them. What do they mean?'

'Well, son, they are the insignia of the worst sort of people. They're one of nastiest, cruellest regiment of soldiers that ever existed, Hitler's SS. If they had him, the mission he was on must have been the greatest threat to the Germans. When we find out who he is, we may find out what.'

Rosy said, 'Poor fellow. There are quite a few of them all down his arms. The ones on his back nearly made me sick. I've seen my fair share of injuries. This I have never seen and will never want to see again. The only way I can describe them is it looks like someone has heated a chisel-shaped tool, heated it up, and then . . .' she became silent for a few seconds, then carried on, 'then pushed it onto his back. They didn't stop there. They dragged it down across, and then they must have heated something long, as they have pushed onto his stomach and then again dragged it across after trying to write on him his execution date, time, and even the year. It seems they wanted him to read that every day. Thank God, that isn't so deep. It should heal without a scar. There was a sort of cry, like as if you had trodden on maybe a dog's foot or something. They all turned and found Rosy had fainted. They made sure she was OK.' Tannis said, 'Sir, if that's his front . . .'

The captain stopped him, saying, 'That's enough for now.'

'Sorry, sir, I wasn't thinking.'

'Well, all is OK, Private, so we will leave it at that, OK?'

'Yes, sir, OK.'

'Time being of the essence to save him, he had coped with the pain to a degree. He is a tough bloke. After he had the first sedative painkiller, it relaxed him too much, he couldn't control the pain as he had managed all that time, so I didn't get him any more. I got him here. He is still alive. I also knew there are lot of specialist surgeons here. Yes, they may have kept him alive back there till the next train. He would have been patched up and may have lost his arms and legs. Most of his face looks infected. It is not a pretty picture for a hero, wouldn't you say? Do I need to go on because that is what would have happened if we waited for a doctor back there, and then he would have been sent here anyway,' the captain replied. 'So instead of him suffering any more, God knows how long he had been drifting on that boat. I felt I can't help them all. I was in a position to help him. I feel maybe what happened to him may need reporting to higher up, so he mustn't speak to anyone except immediate medical staff attending to him. That must be limited, of course, to staff from the military.'

'OK, Captain, just from what I've seen, this poor fellow is a physical mess. Goodness knows what his mental state will be like that's if he gets his memory back.' Rosy was listening to all this, still not knowing they were talking about her beloved strong, clever, loving husband, the father to her babies whom he had never met. As Doctor Neil had to wrap a bandage around his head and face to try and stop him opening up the wounds on his face and neck from thrashing around, clawing his own body because of the pain. As most of the wounds were bad enough on their own, they found they were all very badly infected, some more than the others. Doctors felt that some were older than the others, the reckoned at the very least, three maybe four different days. He was also very thin. Before his face was covered, she could see whoever this chap was. His face was drawn; you could see his cheekbones and sunken eyes. He looked nothing like her wonderful husband. She called the orderlies in and told them to put the patient on to the stretcher. Just as before, any movement was distressing. The captain said, 'May I make a suggestion, Doctor? How far is the ambulance?'

The doctor replied, 'Just outside the entrance.'

The captain looked at Tannis, 'Well, son, do you think you can do it again?'

The doctor and nurse looked at each other puzzled and then at Tannis and the captain.

Neil asked, 'What are you talking about?'

The captain replied, 'You see, Doctor, please don't ask me why or how. It's just what it is.'

He supported Derek while Private Tannis slid out from under. As this was happening Derek got very upset, crying out for Tannnis, 'Where's Tttttanis?' Soon as the private had stretched himself. He proceeded to bend and lift the poor patient up. As he did, Derek fell silent, even though the movements must have been so very painful, he knew straight away when it wasn't the private holding him. What they witnessed was a miracle. Tannis had him in his arms and was proceeding to walk out, down the corridor to the open carriage door, where the two orderlies were waiting. They helped him down off the train. They had been told to only walk with him, just in case he needed help. He found the strength. No one knew where from. Even though Derek had lost weight, he was far from light, and Tannis wasn't a big fellow.

Rosy, Neil, Captain Dayforb, and Officer Froner all followed, admiring the private for what he was doing. It's not as if he knew any of them. He didn't have to be doing what he was doing. Neil said, 'I see it. I just don't believe it. The pilot hasn't murmured since the private picked him up.'

'No, Doctor, he won't while the private has him. It's a weird sort of trust. I think he must sense the same touch. It's been like that since Tannis first touched him. That's why we have him with us,' the captain said.

Then the officer added, 'He is on leave, Captain.'

'Why didn't tell me that, Froner?'

'No, sorry, sir, but the private didn't want me to tell you, just in case you sent him off to enjoy his leave.'

'Well, if we hadn't have met the private, when we did, well, that doesn't bear thinking about.'

Rosy said to them all, 'Those two men seem to have some sort of rapport that we won't ever understand. However long we try, it's just is, no rhyme or reason.'

After about five minutes, they reached the ambulance and the orderlies tried again to put Derek on a stretcher. Once again, he panicked, so the doctor suggested, 'Just help the private into the ambulance.' So that's what they did; holding an arm each, they managed to get him up. By this time, it was showing on Tannis's face; he looked so exhausted. His one eye bashed in so hard that it was shut tight and the other was black, but they didn't even try to separate them. They just hoisted the private up, by the elbows to keep his balance, into the ambulance. Then they helped him to sit as comfortable as possible. 'It's about ten minutes' drive. Will you be OK, mate?' one of the orderlies asked.

'Yes, thanks, mate,' he said. 'I want to see it through. I feel I owe it to him as he trusts me. I'll be fine. I have come this far.' (He would have said that whatever to get the officer's help as fast as possible). He wasn't going let this poor fellow suffer any more than he had to. A couple of minutes passed, and then the Doctor, Rosy, Captain Dayforb, and Officer Froner joined him in the ambulance. 'Sir,' said the Private, 'I forgot to say to the driver to go fairly slow.'

'OK, Tannis. I'll go tell him.' With that, Officer Froner leaned into the front, asked the driver to go slowly.

'OK, sir, will do.' They all started introducing themselves. 'I'm Dr Neil Tranten.'

Rosy said, 'I'm Sister Rosy Rook-Leigh.' After introducing themselves, they started chatting. Derek was resting quietly, but his mixed-up foggy mind started to whirr when he heard the name Rosy. He wasn't sure why. All of a sudden, he started getting very agitated. He didn't know why. When he started to thrash around, Tannis shouted, 'Doctor, Sister, quick! He is hurting himself.'

By the time Dr Tranten got to him with a small dose of sedative, Tannis said, 'Sir, please, sir please, no sedative. I'll just hold him gently.'

Neil and Rosy didn't question. He had been with the patient all the way. After a few moments, he eventually, calmed down. Again they were surprised. 'Sorry, sir, it's just that the captain and I found that giving him sedative makes him worse, as it seems when the relaxing effect weakens, he fights off the pain.'

He had managed to pull his bandages nearly off; Neil, very gently, placed them back over. He turned to Tannis, 'You must get that face of yours looked at, Tannis, as soon as possible.'

Rosy said, 'Doctor, can I try?'

'Well, of course, Sister, if you think you can help. I know I don't need to tell you how urgent it is to calm him down.'

Rosy went to him and held his hand. Instantly, Derek seemed to calm down. Rosy started to talk to him softly, telling him about herself, her family, her wonderful parents, and then all about her Hope and Glory, her babies, the whole story. She thought, *I wonder if this how, I will tell my beloved, husband, Derek.* Then she told him all about the father, with tears in her eyes, and how wonderful and gentle he is, who she loves so very much. Not sure why she was telling him, some strange RAF officer, maybe that's why she felt safe and able to open up. It felt like a weight off her mind, telling him some things she couldn't tell her parents or Susan. With his injuries, she doubted he would remember anyway. She started to talk about Susan and Gil, hers, and also her husband's, best friends. How Susan stayed with her through everything and helped with the babies, while all long, she was desperately worried about her love, Gil. 'I went on and on about my problems, still she didn't tell me. Of course, I knew obviously. They flew the same plane. It seemed she had forgotten or maybe she felt that if she said it out loud. It would become all too real, anyway. I left it like that I knew she would open up when she was ready. When she does, I will listen, and then I'll be the one to do the helping. I was right, as just after I had my babies, she opened up. She had slowly realised, I must know. The reason she told me then was that her Gil was found, and he had a broken arm. The whole crew were flown back, except Rob and Derek.' Rosy suddenly saw that something had set the patient off again. Neil saw this, and he went over, whispering in her ear. 'Repeat the last thing you said to him.'

She looked at Neil, realising why, he had asked her. She turned, softly, putting her other hand, on top of his. Starting again, going on from where she had left off. 'So you can imagine how over the moon Susan was, pausing to see if there was any reaction.' Neil whispered again, 'No reaction. Carry on please, Rosy. I know this is hard for you. I'm sorry, I overheard some of what you were saying.' Once again, Rosy turned to the patient, 'Where did I leave off? Oh yes, I was saying how over the moon Susan was to see Gil agai . . .' That's as far as she got. Jumping from the chair, Neil had to pull her away. The chair falling over as Derek went so frantic flaying around, knocking all in arms' length, kicking, and then crying as the pain hit. 'We have to stop him from hurting himself more.'

The others had been chatting a little way away, and they turned when they heard the commotion. Tannis realised what was happening and rushed over, pushing past Neil and Rosy. They moved away. He went straight to Derek, shouting, 'What in the hell did you do?' Turning back to Derek, he said, 'It's OK. It's OK. I'm here. Tannis is here, sir. Calm down, please, sir. Please calm down.' He grabbed his hands and looked into his face and said sternly, 'Sir, look at me now. Sir, look at me.' Derek turned his head; there was recognition on his face and tears were rolling down, either because of pain or frustration. As he calmed down, he tried to talk, which must have been very painful with the face injuries. Tannis leaned into listen. Very slowly the words came, very muddled and grave. Tannis listened, although it didn't make sense to him. It didn't matter; it probably will to someone. Derek fell asleep. He stayed for a few minutes to make sure the officer was asleep and then slowly, he slid his hands free; they were being held so tight that they had gone numb. Once free, he went straight over to Rosy, shaking his numb hands as he went.

Neil said, 'Are you OK, Private.'

'Yes, sir, I'm fine. I would like to apologise for my verbal outburst. I was just worried about the officer, as he seems as he has gone through so much already.'

'That's OK, Tannis,' Rosy replied.

Neil just said with a smile, 'What outburst? I'm afraid I couldn't make much out. Maybe some of it may make sense to you. It sounded like *Jill* or *gill*, then *rab*, *rib*, or *gib*. The last *shan*, *suez*, something like that. Does that make any sense to either of you?'

'Oh, he did say one other thing.' Rosy held her breath. 'Canada, panda, and then the last thing before he fell unconscious . . .'

'Oh, Tannis, stop teasing,' Rosy interrupted, giving him a friendly punch.

'OK, OK', Neil said, 'I think you had better tell her.'

'Not sure I can control her much longer.' They all smiled. With that, Tannis said, 'Well, dosey, posy.'

Rosy turned to Neil and then back to the Private. She stepped forward and gave him a great big hug. The shocked private said, 'I take it, it means something to you, Sister,' he said, smiling.

'Yes, it does,' Rosy said, smiling. She went on to explain that the rib or gib bit is Rob his friend, who hasn't come back because they executed him. Jill or gill is Gil his best friend, whom she must call.

'Don't worry, Sister, if you have a number, I'll ring for you,' Tannis offered.

'Thank you, dear Tannis.'

'Sister, may I listen to the last couple of bits before I go.'

'Of course you can. I think the shan or suez bit means my best friend and also Gil's girlfriend, Susan. Panda, Canada, is our dog Charm.' Now they all laughed.

'Then the last I would say is me.' With tears in her eyes again, she turned away.

'You OK, Sister?' The two men enquired.

'Yes, I'm fine. Thank you for caring, Tannis. While you're at the phone, you can use the one in the sisters' office. That will be OK, won't it, Neil?'

'I should think, Rosy. I'll go check.' Off he went.

Rosy turned to Tannis. 'Yes, Tannis, would you please make two more phone calls? The first to Derek's parents, telling them what's happening. Also ask them to bring Francis, his sister, to look after the babies. Then to my mum and dad. They also need to know what's going on.' Rosy took a deep breath. 'Tannis,' he looked up from his notebook, 'thanks for doing this.'

The reply was 'That's OK.'

Twenty-Five

Fifteen minutes later, they arrived at the hospital. The driver rushed around and opened the doors. They started to alight; the doctor, the captain, Froner, and then Rosy released Derek's hand and proceeded to get off the ambulance. As she was about to climb down, Tannis said quietly, 'Sister, he is getting upset again.'

Neil went to jump back in, but as he did, Tannis said, 'He is trying to say something, and I can't quite work it out, but it sounds like *dosey*.'

'No,' Neil said and moved forward. They listened, both Neil and Tannis.

Derek muttered again, 'Rooossy.'

'Oh my God,' they both said in unison; they looked at each other and then at Rosy, who had her back to them.

'Sir, what shall we do?' he said to the doctor as the realisation hit them both. Neil had heard her talk about her missing husband many times. He knew they were devoted to each other. Also he had seen pictures of him. While Neil decided what to do, Rosy turned and said, 'Well, are we going to get this poor feller inside? What she didn't say was deep inside she was feeling as if she knew him, but she didn't want to believe this poor smashed up man was her strong tall handsome husband. She tried to block it out. The memory of every one saying how well tuned they were to each other kept flashing through her mind. Anyway she turned, and they were both staring at her. 'What is it, fellers?' They were just staring silently. Few seconds passed, and the men looked at each other. Neil moved towards her and sat next to her on the step of the ambulance. They looked at each other.

Rosy said, 'Neil, you're scaring me. What's wrong? He hasn't died after all he has been through, has he?'

'Oh no, Rosy, no, no, he hasn't died.'

'Well, what then?' she asked. 'Neil, look at me, what is wrong?'

Behind them a voice said, 'Sorry, Doctor, Sister, I think we need to get this chap into the hospital.'

'OK, Tannis, bring him out. There is a team waiting for him. Tell them I'll join them in a moment.'

'Yes, Doctor.' He got up. He was tired and exhausted. He staggered a bit. The captain and Froner saw him and both rushed to help.

'No,' said Tannis, 'I've come this far. I'd like to finish this if that's OK.' Saying that, he said, 'I would like a hand down from here.'

Rosy and Neil moved away, and the captain and Froner gave him a hand down. They followed him inside the hospital. Rosy and Neil stayed outside.

Neil said, 'Rosy, my dear, I don't know if your prepared for this. Well, anyway, here it goes. Now we are not sure, but the patient tried to speak. What he said sounded very much like . . .' he took her hands in his, and she looked at him.

Then she asked, 'What did he say, Neil?'

Slowly he replied, 'Rosy, I'm not sure how to say this, so I'll just say it.'

'For goodness sake, Neil, you're scaring me. Tell me now, OK.'

'When Tannis called me over, he told me the patient had said something. He said it said something like cosy or posy, then while I was there he did it again, and I don't know if I'm sorry or happy for you.'

'What are you trying to say, Neil?'

'Rosy dear, he said your name, Rosy.' She sat there, not taking it in at first, and then her face started to change from being sad to bemused. Then she started to smile when the news finally filtered through and sank into a very confused brain. She leapt up, and all of a sudden, tears started to roll. Neil had to catch her as she nearly collapsed on the floor. He said, 'Rosy, please calm down, my dear,

I know he said your name. It may still not be your Derek. It could simply be someone who knew him or met him somewhere.'

'I know, Neil. I also know he doesn't know. He can't remember who he is. Derek and I have this thing, sixth sense, rapport, or whatever you like to call it, between us. My family thinks it's peculiar. Now how did my brother Duncan put it? Weird,' she smiled and then laughed when Neil did. 'His sister thinks it's lovely. She goes all love struck and says, "I hope Duncan and I are like that."'

Neil said, 'I didn't know they were together. They're not. It's her daydreaming.' Neil realised Rosy had calmed down.

'Rosy, do you have any feelings like that right now?'

'You didn't laugh or make fun,' said Rosy.

'I'm not saying, one way or another. If it works for you, use it.'

'Well, how about an answer to my question?'

'Well, he remembered my name even though he couldn't remember his own. I feel it's him.'

'Right. Come on, my dear. Let's go and see if this feeling of yours is working. We can also see what the doctors think,' Neil said, smiling. 'Are you ready for this?'

'Yes, ready as I'll ever be.' He helped her up, and they walked slowly to the hospital entrance, entered, went straight to the emergency room, where they met Tannis who had carried the patient all the way to the ward, then he put his charge on a bed.

'Still he wouldn't let me go, so they gave him a light sedative for now, so he would let me go. Also to make him relax some, so they could work on him, as he was in so much pain.'

Just then, there was an almighty racket as quiet obvious as a hospital trolley going over and then a panicked and frightened voice calling Tannis's name.

'Oh no,' he said, 'it's wearing off.' He turned to go to his charge.

Neil said, 'Would you mind if Rosy comes with you?'

'Of course not,' he replied. The two went off while Neil went to find the doctor in charge. As Tannis arrived at the bedside, with Rosy close behind, he said, 'Hello, Sir, now what's all the noise about?'

'You left and it hurts.' There were tears running down his very badly bleeding face.

'I was just on the other side of the curtain. Remember what I told you, so the doctors and nurses could check you over in private to see how badly you're hurt.'

The reply shocked Rosy. 'I'm so scared, Tannnnniis,' he stammered. 'You were gone.'

'It's OK, sir, I'm here now.' He turned to Rosy and whispered, 'Are you together enough?'

She stood for a couple of minutes, not sure whether she hoped it was him, with all those injuries or that it wasn't, which would mean she still wouldn't know where he was. Thinking about it for all of thirty seconds, it was no contest. This was *him*. Finally, she whispered, 'Yes, Tannis, I'm as ready as I'll ever be.' It was only a few steps, slowly she took those few agonising steps keeping hidden behind Tannis. Tannis turned to the patient and he said, 'You're OK, sir.' He sat next to him and took hold of the outstretched bandaged hand, as Derek had been given another mild sedative. He had drifted off, to sleep. Tannis put his hand out to Rosy, who took hold, 'Please don't let go, Tannis. I won't, miss, until you say so.'

There he was, one hand holding the patient and the other holding Rosy's. 'One thing, miss, the doctor said operating room will be ready soon.'

'Oh, right,' Rosy replied as she moved nearer. Finally, she had made those steps. Tannis said, 'Look, miss, please sit before you look.' Rosy did as she was told automatically without thinking about it. She seemed to be on autopilot. The doctor said, 'It will have to be quick because of risk of infection. Of course, I know you know that, dear Rosy. Just a friendly reminder as you're in shock and on the other side to what you're used to.'

'Thank you, Neil.' Gently the nurse pulled the face bandage back. Rosy slowly turned, looking, and sobbing hard. They just managed to make out what she said, 'That's my Derek, without a doubt.'

Also she could see the birthmark on the chest just below his left nipple. They had always laughed about it as it looked a bit like an anchor. They had covered his face up, and he was still asleep. While she had being looking Doctor Neil had arrived. He said quietly to Tannis, 'Well, any luck?'

He replied, laughing, 'Well, with any luck, I maybe about to get my arms back. Both my hands have gone to sleep.' Then he smiled. Neil looked up at him with a puzzled look and then he could see what Tannis meant. He laughed; there was the poor lad, being stretched in two, Rosy on one side and Derek on the other. He was about to bend down and speak to Rosy, when she suddenly looked up on seeing Neil. 'Oh, Neil, how long have you been there?'

He replied, 'I've just arrived.'

Together, they asked, 'What is it, Rosy? I'm sure it's him, Neil. Everything is right. Right down to his birthmark.' While they were talking, Derek had relaxed enough for Tannis to get his hand out. Slowly he moved forward and he held Derek's hand, slowly releasing Rosy's grip slightly, he replaced his for Derek's and then gently put the clasped hands onto the bed. The sister of the ward demanded what was going on, as they couldn't see Neil or Rosy's faces. Everybody jumped, even the patient. 'It's OK, Doctor Franks and Sister Lowly.'

'Oh, Doctor Tranten, what are you doing here?' They asked with lowered voices. 'And what is she doing, Doctor Franks?'

'It's OK. We think it could be . . .' Rosy turned and finished the sentence.

'Oh, Rosy, honey, it's you,' said the sister.

'What Neil is trying to say is, I think, this maybe my husband Derek.'

'Oh, Rosy, we're sorry.' The sister moved closer. 'Would you like me here with you?'

'Yes, Sandra, please.' Both the doctors stepped back a few paces, leaving the sisters at the bedside, although Doctor Franks whispered softly, 'Rosy, love, we must hurry a bit. The operating team is waiting.'

Sandra replied, 'OK, sir, we won't be long. Well, it's now or never. Listen, honey, there's no hurry.' She turned and gave Franks a 'don't say anything' look. Slowly Rosy's hand reached out and gently took the corner of the bandage in her fingers. Her heart was beating like a big bass drum. She was sure everyone could hear; she turned slightly, looking at Neil, who mouthed, 'Go on, Rosy' so tentatively so as not to hurt him, as the bandage was fairly stuck. Somewhere from behind, she heard Tannis say, 'He is so still. It's the first time.'

A new voice said, 'Yes, Tannis, you're right. This is the first time since we found him.' It was the captain speaking; he stopped there, realising what was going on. Officer Froner looked at the captain and Tannis just whispered that the patient maybe Sister Rosy's lost husband. 'Oh my lord!' Froner exclaimed.

'It's all right,' the captain said. 'Oh, Froner, calm down.'

They watched poor Rosy; Tannis stepped forward, and all eyes turned on him, wondering what he was going to do. He put a hand on Rosy's shoulder, bent, whispered in her ear, 'Are you sure you wouldn't rather do this alone, Sister.'

'Oh, Tannis, you are so thoughtful, but I don't have much time. I would like you to stay right there next to me, as you have bought him all this way. You deserve to know.' With that she started to pull the sticky bandage up, and when she got stuck a bit, scared to pull to hard, Tannis moved in next to her; they looked at each other, and then together, they got it up enough to see him clear enough. Then Tannis stepped back, and Rosy looked up, close; she was greeted with that wonderful smile she remembered, like the eyes, smile even when it must be hurting. She swayed as Tannis had expected; either way, he held her up. The captain also stepped forward, as Froner found a chair and placed it near. As she was saying, 'Yes, this is my husband Derek, my very own brave RAF pilot,' they all sighed.

The Captain said, 'Sister Rosy, look.' So she looked to where he was pointing. She lowered the bandage gently back down, took a step back with Tannis still behind her. He pulled the chair that was there and helped her into it, and then she saw what the captain had seen. Derek was trying to move his arm; it wouldn't move, so he was moving his fingers. Once she sat, Rosy gently, careful not to cause him any pain, lifted his hand into hers. Tears had started to roll down her very pale cheeks; she raised herself up and then kissed him on the lips. Seeing that, Froner said, 'Sir, don't you think we should all step away?'

'I know there isn't much time. Let's just give them a couple of minutes. At least till the porters arrive.'

The Captain beckoned to the others. Doctor Franks nodded and tapped Sandra on the back, and so they all left and stood several feet away. Rosy said, 'Do you know who I am, darling?'

He looked at her, in a very quite squeaky voice, making Rosy lean in closer, 'No.'

'Well, that was a very harsh reply.' Rosy looked puzzled. 'When you came in, you were calling my name.'

'Oh, I heard the doctor say your name, and for some reason, I felt I have a connection to the name, Rosy.'

She couldn't control her tears and couldn't hold them back much longer. 'Where's Tannis?' He asked, starting to panic and snatching his hand away. 'Why isn't he here?' Derek asked, panicking even more. Rosy, tears rolling freely now, turned beckoning Tannis over. He looked at her puzzled and concerned. All she could manage was 'He doesn't know me at all. Look after him.' She ran as fast as anyone could with tears gushing down their face. Rosy ran and then ran some more. When she finally stopped, she found herself among some trees, one being a very large willow. After fighting her way out of its tendrils, the tears slowed a bit. There was a wonderful river; it was very wide just where she was, and she sat on the banks and starting to sob again. Her eyes and face were both sore from rubbing. She sat till the sobs calmed a little. Her mind cleared enough for reasoning to tell her, *He will get well. Hopefully, his memory will come back.* Her emotional side doubted it, and her brain was tossing one way then the other. At that moment, she wished she wasn't a nursing sister. There was torment in knowing everything One thing was sure – if he did get well, if his memory came back or not, just as long as he gets well from all the other numerous, very life-threatening injuries She swore, if his mind came back, then she'd stay, and if it didn't, she will gather the strength, from somewhere, to let him go. Just the thought of it made her feel sick.

Twenty-Six

Five minutes passed, and then they all heard the trundle of a hospital trolley coming closer, ever closer. Tannis took it on himself as the three seemed to have a connection; he moved closer slowly, as the trolley arrived with Doctor Neil, as Tannis was trying to get his hand free. Even while sedated, Derek had a good grip. He stirred, hearing a voice. They all turned to look at Derek; he was trying to say it was so very painful. He also called for Rosy; Tannis said, 'You just saw her, sir.'

'No, I see a nurse, not my Rosy.' He looked with a puzzled and very confused look on what you could see of his face; he lost consciousness again. Tannis looked at Neil and said in a whisper, 'He didn't recognise her. He just saw the uniform. Rosy wasn't in uniform when he went away.'

Neil mouthed, 'Where is Rosy?'

He shrugged his shoulders and whispered, pointing at Derek. 'As you just heard, he didn't recognise her. I'm about to go and find her. You go with him first, as he trusts you.' Neil carried on, 'Hopefully, you will be able to keep him from harming himself on the way for his operations. He should be OK until they get him under.' With that, Neil saluted Derek, and, seeing that, the other officers saluted with him. The doctors, porters, and Sister Sandra managed without too much discomfort to manoeuvre him on to the trolley to be wheeled to the theatre. As he was very quiet and it wasn't far to the operating room, Tannis slowed down. 'What's the matter, Tannis?'

Neil asked, 'Well, sir, he is settled.'

'Quiet! You're just about in the operating room.'

'As you'll be in there, operating and doing your bit with the other specialist surgeons, I thought I'd go and look for Sister Rosy, as we got quite close.'

'Yes, Tannis, that is a good idea. I would think as you are that close, she wouldn't mind you calling her Rosy.' He smiled and continued, 'Besides, you know more about Derek at the moment.'

'OK, sir, you sure I can the sister, Rosy?'

'Yes, I'm sure. If I'm wrong, you can blame me.'

'Yes, sir, I will, oh, I mean . . .'

Neil stopped him mid-sentence. 'I know what you mean.' They both smiled again, and they saluted each other. They all stood watching. Everyone was having their own thoughts on the situation. Then Tannis left on his quest, thinking over the last four, no five days and going over and over what had happened and thinking how glad he was where he was, when he was – just happy to be there at the right place and time.

Twenty-Seven

Tannis turned and headed for the entrance and then started running around, asking everyone he met if they had seen Sister Rosy. He went back into the hospital to see if there was any sign of her in the canteen. When he arrived, he had a good look around, but saw no sign of her. By this time, he was getting really concerned. To be sure, he asked the canteen staff. 'No, sorry,' the staff behind the counter said. Just then, a fourth member of staff came over from wiping tables down. 'I heard what you were asking? Do you mean Sister Rosy Rook-Leigh?'

'Yes,' he replied, 'have you seen her?'

'Well, I saw her about ten maybe fifteen minutes ago. I nearly run her over. Looking at me, she started to run again. There was an ambulance coming the other way with its blue lights flashing and speeding. The driver, oh my, how he missed her, I'll never know.'

Tannis said, 'Oh, dear, do you know where she was heading?'

'Well,' she said, 'I just glimpsed her heading into the woods. Maybe she has gone to the lake.'

He made his way down there, and he saw her sitting by the water's edge. As he drew closer, he could hear her crying. He approached softly, and he said, 'Sister, Rosy.'

Looking up, she wiped her eyes, 'Oh, Private, how did you find me?'

Sitting next to her, he said, 'Well, I just followed the trail of destruction.' He handed her his hanky. Smiling at him, now calmer, 'Listen, Private, is it?'

'Yes, ma'am, Private Tannis.'

'Well, listen here, Private Tannis, I want you to keep in contact. I know 'the poor thing' will want to meet you.'

'That would be lovely, ma'am. I'd love to. I'm afraid it won't be for a while, as I disembark in three days, but as soon as I'm back.'

'That sounds good. We will more than likely be on his family's farming estate.'

'A real live farm?'

'Yes, of course.'

'Oh, I'm sorry. I've never seen a farm, especially a working one. Oh, I can't wait for that.' Rosy must have looked puzzled; Tannis said, 'What is it, ma'am?'

'You've never seen a farm or animals? How old are you?'

'I'm nineteen. You see, I was brought up by a very drunken father, who never thought twice about beating my mum.' There were tears now. 'Eventually, he killed her, in front of me. I was sixteen. I tried to stop him. I hit him hard with a fire poker that I pulled from the fire. He just turned around and threw me across the room. I landed at my fourteen-year-old sister's feet. Then he grabbed a curtain rope and proceeding to put it around my semi-conscious mum's neck. Then looking at me, he slurred, "You shouldn't have interfered, brat. Now you can watch what I'll do to yer mum and then yer sister, yer keep till last. I looked up into Katie-Joe's eyes, whispering for her to run to the street and find help, but that made him even madder that she had gone. With the rope tightening, he snarled at me, saying, "You're next, you rotten kid." With that, he continued to stare at me with those scary dark eyes, as he strangled my sweet mum to death, in front of me. There was absolutely nothing I could do. The only thing that helped me is the fact I got Katie-Joe out so she wouldn't see. He started to come towards me. As he did, he pulled another hot poker out of the fire and headed towards me. I had nowhere to go. I was backed into a corner, so I just put my hand over my head, crouching as best I could. I could see the poker was still white hot, and he had gotten to me. I saw his arm rise up and then the whoosh as it came down onto my back. I heard something crack. Once wasn't enough. He raised his arm again, and this time, with more power, he slammed it down onto my head. This time, I could smell my skin and hair burning. By this time, he was even madder, as I hadn't cried or yelled out. I didn't see Katie-Joe creep back in. He bought it up again, now red hot, and I was still crouched, tightly in the corner. I could feel blood running all down my back, arms, and face as it seeped off my head. Yet again, that poker whooshed down onto me. By now, with my shirt gone, burnt away, I just had my bare back. This time though, he kept it down, pushing it with all his weight, into my back. Time passed, not sure how long, but he kept pushing, as I had passed out. When I came around, I could hear shouting. My eyes were sealed shut from dry blood. I could feel a heavy weight on me. It was too heavy to be the poker, I thought. I knew what had happened. He had more than likely, passed out on me. I rubbed my eyes; it hurt to rub too much. I managed to clear half of one, enough to see a bit. I shoved as hard as I could, and he finally fell to the floor. As he fell to one side, I saw, standing just behind him, dear Katy-Joe. In her hand was a carving knife. It was clean. I pushed him right over, puzzled. My first instinct was to grab her and to get the hell out of there. "I have killed Dada?" "Why would you think that?" I asked as I took the knife away. I looked where she was looking. I was shocked. There, sticking out of my father's back was his very own axe. Where on earth a little girl found the strength to embed an axe so deep as to split his back nearly in two. The voices I'd heard were neighbours and police. When Katie-Joe heard them, she passed out, still caked in blood, only able to see just a little. I managed to pick my dear sister up, as I was carrying her through the front door, our uncle came up. Looking at me, he thought Katie-Joe was hurt, as my blood was running all over her. I managed to say, "It's not hers." I went down like a brick, and uncle caught her. The police saw the carnage. With Katie-Joe's statement taken with our uncle Stephen by her side, it turned out, I knew, I never saw him touch her or hit her. I thought I'd keep her safe by taking the beatings. Being a fairly large house, her bedroom was a long way from mine. Unbeknown to me, he was creeping into her bedroom most nights if he wasn't too drunk to move. He had been creeping into her room since she was six.' Tannis stopped talking.

Rosy, knowing that, that must have taken a lot of courage for him to open up like that, put her arm around him. 'That's why you were so traumatised by the marks on his body.'

'Yes.' He slowly got up, opened his shirt and dropped it down and turned so Rosy could see his back. He slowly moved around until he was facing her. Rosy's hand flew to her face with a great gasp.

'Rosy, that's why I wanted to help right from the start. Help where I couldn't help my poor mum. Oh I know it's not quite the same.' It was just that, not wanting Rosy to see the tears. He stood up, walked to the water's edge, picked up a handful of stones and skimmed one across the water. Rosy saw how much pain he was in and then when she held him, he calmed down. 'I felt, I truly thought that I could help him, where I couldn't help my mum or my sweet innocent little sister.' They sat, talking for what seemed like forever. Neither wanted to say the words, 'Will he be OK?'. Both prayed he will be OK for different reasons, both very obvious though. Rosy as he was her husband and also the daddy to her wonderful babies, he has never met, so he must pull through. As the thought from earlier, came back in her head of her close feeling let her down making believe he was dead, the loss of his memory properly answered that. Right then and there, a promise was made. Without realising it, the prayer came out loud. 'Dear God, as much as I wish him fully well, for his sake, as far as I'm concerned, he is my husband. If there are everlasting problems, I'll know and we will cope somehow with love for each other and the love of both our families. There are also good friends. There is one of those sitting right here with me now. Yes, we will get through. On the other side of the coin, if he really doesn't recognise me, I will walk away to let him make a new life again.' The sobs came racking through her already tired body. Tannis moved closer to be able to comfort her. They sat, talked, sobbed, then again sat and talked. Then after what seemed like a short time, although in fact, it had been well over two hours, more like three, Rosy wiped her eyes, not for the first and, more than likely, not for the last time. Tannis wondered if he really could walk away, knowing how strong Rosy was. He knew she would if that is what was needed, no doubt. As if reading his mind, she said, 'Tannis, if I did have to walk away, would you keep me updated on his progress?' It looked like tears were welling up. 'No more tears, dear Rosy, please. In answer to your question, of course, I'll keep you up to date. While back at the hospital, Captain Dayforb had been summoned by a nurse to take a phone call. He excused himself from the others. They were all waiting to see if Tannis had found Rosy. Derek was still in surgery and had been for nearly four hours. When he got to the phone, it was a soldier, passing on a message summoning him and Froner to the office of which was known as the hush-hush team. He listened to the travel arrangements that had been made. He replied, 'Got it. We will be there as soon as possible.' With that, he hung up. He stood for a few minutes to gather his thoughts. He was hoping to see Derek come out of surgery and also hoping to see Rosy back safely. He knew Froner felt the same. Before they had to leave, he smiled at the nickname hush, hush. He wondered who had thought of it; he smiled again. *Yes*, he thought, *I like it.* He turned, exiting the office and bumping straight into the sister whose office it was, causing her to drop the papers she was carrying. 'Oh, I'm so sorry, Sister. Let me help you. After all, it was me who caused you to drop them.'

As they bent to pick the papers, he said to her, 'It's all yours again now.' He smiled at her.

'Thank you, sir, are you sure, it's OK?' she said, smiling back at him.

'Say, Sister, do you have a break coming up?' Surprised, she went to stand up, and he was doing the same.

The obvious happened, and their heads collided with a great thump. They stood laughing upright, both rubbing their heads. He said, 'Ouch!' and she had a shocked look on her face, partially from the collision. She thought he just asked her out. They looked at each other, and he said, 'Well, Sister, would you like to have coffee with me during your break?'

She looked down and straightened the papers and blushed, 'Yes, sir, I would love to have a coffee with you, good Sister. When is your next break?'

'In about an hour, sir.'

'OK, Sister, I'll see you then.' They both smiled at each other. They parted, her to her office and he rushed back to find the others in the waiting room. When he arrived, he beckoned Froner over. When Froner arrived, he took him into the corridor. 'Any news, Charles?'

'No, sir, not really. Just his holding his own. I hear you got a phone call, sir.'

'Yes, the top of the top.' They both smiled. 'Wow! It's that hush, hush, is it, sir?' Again, they smiled. 'Seems like it, Charles. We have been summoned to report for debriefing.'

'But, Sir, we don't really know anything more than we told them.'

'Well, it seems if this fellow is who they think he is, then you can guess the rest.'

'OK, sir, when do we leave?'

'As soon as possible, although I'm dragging it out hopefully long enough see him out of surgery and danger, and his lovely wife next to him.'

'OK, sir, do they want Tannis too?'

'Well, I told them he was due to embark. With the fact he was never really alone with the patient, he knows no more than we can tell them. I thought the poor kid needs a few days to relax. They agreed.'

'Oh, that's good, sir. So how long can we realistically stall them, sir?' Charles asked, laughing.

'We have about five hours before we have to get the train. We'll grab a cab to the station. Hopefully, Derek will be out of surgery. Oh, by the way, I have a coffee date, in about forty minutes,' he said, looking at his watch.

'Well, lucky you.' They laughed and then headed back into the waiting room. Just in time, both sets of parents arrived. Gil was with Susan, and to everybody's surprise, there were two tiny babies.

Twenty-Eight

By now, the powers that be, those who were behind the orders, the hush, hush team that had sent Derek, with his crew, following the orders were also in the room. There was Derek's own senior officer. 'We're just starting to get wind of what was going on. About the circumstances and conditions the poor soul was found in. He was found drifting on a French fishing boat, and there were many dead. The ship's crew seemed to be the French resistance, working underground. There were many of them, but the biggest shock that there seemed to be too many SS soldiers. The real shock for all was why were there a few U-Boat crew but so many Germans all over the deck and below. There were far too many for such a little boat, and most of them had guns in their lifeless hands, although there was a good few just laying strewn over the deck, implying that there had been many other men, both Germans and Frenchmen, that had managed to get away or fallen overboard. One of the Germans found was a high-ranking German SS Officer.'

The general thoughts in the room were 'What would one of the highest ranking German soldier be doing in a place like this? Probably his own dirty work.' That was one question that may never be answered completely. 'How is our lucky pilot, if you can say that in this situation?'

'Well, sir, I have been to the hospital to see him, and he had a bullet lodged on one part of the skull that was already smashed. They couldn't fix it up yet. After making sure it was clean, they had to place a drain, in case of any clots or any other problems. Then when it is dealt with, later, they will be putting a permanent plate in his head. Part of his skull is too smashed to put back together.'

Back at the hospital, Neil was telling dear Rosy all this and also adding, 'It's a waiting game to see when or if he comes round. You do understand he may not or, if he does, may be the same or even remember you.' Rosy squeezed Tannis's hand harder, which made him grimace. Neil carried on. 'There were so many injuries that the poor nurse tried to count them the best she could. She had to be replaced halfway through. Poor girl. He will be taken to the ward, where he has a private room, in about half an hour if he stays stable enough. Well, sorry, I'd better get back.'

'Hold on a minute, Doctor,' Tannis said. 'Can we have a talk outside for a minute?'

'Yes, OK. I'll wait in the corridor.'

Rosy grabbed him, pulling him back. 'Tannis, why do you need to talk to Neil?'

'Oh, nothing for you to worry about, Rosy.'

Just then, there was a commotion coming towards the waiting room which let Tannis of the hook for now. He thought, *Oh thank goodness! This gives me breathing space.* The doors opened, and he held one open while mums, dads, brothers, a sister who was holding the peace da la resistance, two of the most-content gurgling babies you would have ever seen. He closed the door quietly, moving over to Neil, who said, 'Can we walk and talk? I have to get back to my office.'

'That's fine, Neil.' Tannis started talking. 'May I ask why you didn't tell her about the rest? The marks all over him and also the boot marks.'

Neil turned, looking at Tannis. 'Well, I thought she'd had enough to come to terms with.'

'Yes, of course, although, Neil, you do know she knows about the marks.'

'Oh, how?'

'Don't you remember, on the train, before we knew he was her husband, remember she fainted?'

'Oh, I remember now.'

Tannis said, 'Yes, I agree what you told her was enough to digest for now.'

'Well, I'd better get back to the recovery room.'

'Yes, of course, Neil. I'm about to be introduced to a real family, with the loveliest pair of babies. We'll see each other later.'

With that, they split, going their separate ways. As Neil walked away, he was struck by something Tannis had said about Rosy's family being a real family. When he returned to the recovery room, he didn't know what to expect, but what he found surprised him. It was only about an hour since the very long operation. The sister approached him, saying, 'We have had no problems, Doctor.'

Just then, the other surgeons arrived to check on him. Neil turned to them, telling them what the sister had just told him. They all approached their prized patient, and they chatted for a while and then all concurred that he was OK to go on to the ward. While the nurses got him ready to move, Neil went off to the waiting room to fill Rosy in on what was happening and also to show her to the private room he had managed to get for Derek. As he approached, Rosy must have seen him coming and she came flying out of the room. They nearly collided. 'Hi, Neil, any news?'

'Well, Rosy, he is stable. No one knows how he is as stable as he is.'

'Neil, what does that mean?'

'It means, dear Rosy . . .' He heard a trolley approaching and he turned.

'Neil, what does it mean?' Rosy asked again. He turned back to her and took hold of her hand, leading her to the side room. As they entered, Rosy turned, looking at him, ready to talk. Just then the sister, with the porters, arrived with her much-loved husband. As they transferred Derek to the bed, Rosy and Neil moved over to the window, where Neil said, 'Rosy, can I ask you something?'

'Yes, of course, Neil. What is it?'

'Well, I was talking to Tannis earlier and he said something odd.'

Rosy stopped looking out the window and turned to face Neil. 'What did he say?'

'After we chatted, he said he was now off to meet a real family.'

Looking up into his face, Rosy replied, 'I said I wouldn't say, although I don't suppose he would mind you knowing.' Rosy told him what Tannis had told to her, about his past.

'Oh, that is awful. What a load to carry around? That's going to take time to come to terms with. Poor kid. He is only what eighteen or nineteen.'

'I'm not sure, Neil. I think he is nineteen.'

They turned around to find Derek, now on the bed. 'He looks peaceful enough now. A lot different from when you bought him in.'

'Yes, Neil, he does. Neil, what are you and Tannis hiding from me? Please, Neil, whatever it is I have to know. I need to know. Nothing can be as bad as what I'm seeing now.'

He turned slowly, slowly raising his eyes to meet hers, unable able to talk. 'Neil, please, if it was a stranger, you would tell all.'

Gradually, as he still searched for the words, he looking into her eyes and grasped the edge of the crisp cotton sheet. Then slowly, he pulled it down, with the help of the nurse. They rolled Derek gently onto his side and then, while Neil held him, he told the nurse to open the gown. 'Are you sure, Doctor?'

'Yes, Nurse, please.' Gently, the nurse undid the gown as it was stuck in places. Rosy hadn't looked yet. Neil looked at her and asked, 'Are you ready, Rosy?'

'Yes, Neil, I need to do this.' Slowly she turned and lowered her eyes and saw but she could not take in what she was looking at.

'Are you OK, Sister?' The nurse could see her expression Rosy couldn't answer. She moved forward, nearer to the bed, and put a hand out as if to touch. The nurse looked at Neil as if to say, *Look, she's going to touch him.* She was about to stop her, but Neil saw and shook his head, no. He thought, *Well, there is no real harm if she needs to do that to believe it, to come to terms with it all.* Up until then, Rosy knew Derek was hurt, although she hadn't come to terms with how badly he was. Her hand moved ever closer until her hand touched his skin. She sat on the edge of the bed and her other hand moved an inch or so over the sores. Finally, realisation hit her like a sledgehammer. Her fingers followed the lines of the swastika that had been cut into his back. She turned to Neil, tears rolling down her cheeks, and said, 'Amongst all these marks is a wound that will scar. Am I right?'

'To be honest, Rosy, we're not sure. Depends on any of them getting infected.' He turned to the nurse and said, 'Nurse, will you help me lay him down.' Rosy looked, not saying anything, as they rolled him back. They were careful not to disturb attachments. Again Rosy steeped forward to the bed and looked at his chest, tummy, and legs. There were many boot marks and burns, which were hard to tell apart. There were also many that looked like cigarette burns. They were dry and healing well.

She sat there for a few minutes and looked up at the nurse. 'Thank you, Nurse, for caring for my husband.'

'That's OK, Sister.'

'No, Nurse, it's Rosy when we're in here, OK?'

'Yes, Sis . . . sorry, Rosy.'

She got up to allow the nurse to cover him up again, then grabbing Neil's hands, she led him to the window. 'Neil, thank you. For some reason, I feel better. Silly, but I think it must be the nurse in me.' Both of them laughed. After a few minutes of silence, she let go of his hands and turning to look out of the window and take in the view. 'What is it, Rosy?'

She did not turn. 'I don't understand how one human can do that to another human.'

'I know how you feel, Rosy. All I can think is they're not human. They seem to be sadistic for the sake of it, plus I understand that he was being interrogated when most of them happened.'

'Yes, that's as much as I have been told. Something about the mission being special – a top secret.'

Twenty-Nine

While all this went on, back in the waiting room, as Tannis walked in, every one had just about settled down. The waiting room was more like a high-class lounge. There were comfortable sofas and chairs. He walked over to Rosy, who had her back to him. He tapped her on the shoulder. Turning, she said, 'Oh, hi, you're back.' Then she hugged him and said, 'Now for introductions.' Walking over to a small sofa, she saw her parents. 'Now this is my mum and dad, Eleanor and Albert. Mum, Dad, this is Private Tannis. We call him Paul. He is the only one Derek would let near him. Paul held him on his lap all the way, even carrying him across the very busy train station from the ambulance, still taking the thrashing about, as you can see by the bruises.' They both smiled; he shook the hands that were being offered to him. Just as he finished, the captain with his officer came in Tannis said, 'Rosy, please, may I go meet your little ones?'

'Of course, you can. That's if the captain doesn't need you for anything.'

'They both looked at the captain. No, Private, as of now, you're back on leave. You have gone above and beyond your duty. You deserve a medal. Saluting the captain, Tannis left, heading for his goal – the babies.' After he left, the introductions carried on, and by then, Duncan had come to sit with their parents. Rosy made her excuses, leaving them in deep conversation. She looked around that room and thought to herself. *I'm so lucky to have such a great family that's happy to rally around when you need them. That would be plenty normally. On top of that, I married into the same type of family. Then there were the two best friends of mine too.* Then her thoughts went to the aunt and uncle; she couldn't remember Derek mentioning them or if he did. *I can't recall*, she thought, *they were probably at the wedding.* There were so many people there she hadn't really taken them in. There was such a sea of faces. Walking over to Derek's parents and after greeting each other, Rosy, asked them if they would see that everyone gets to Rob and Dora's. 'Of course, dear Rosy,' Looking at them, all she could say was 'Thank you so much.' She wasn't sure if she could control her tears, so she turned and headed for the door. Seeing that everyone was busy, she moved towards the door and took one more look at Paul. He was holding a baby in both arms. The look on his face was that of happiness and there were also tears of joy. It made her wonder if maybe there was a bit more to his story. She slowly slipped out the door and she thought, *I'll talk to him later.* Rosy rushed back to Derek's room and silently opened the door and then silently went over to his bed. She sat down in the chair and took a hand into hers and thought, *This is where I'm staying for as long as I am needed. I don't need to worry about my babies.*

Thirty

Several weeks later, Derek still hadn't come around. Like every day, she waited, smiling, getting up, leaning over him, kissing his cheek, and whispering in his ear while laying beside him, cuddling him, wanting him so much. 'I love you, my darling. Please don't leave us.' The *us* was very firmly said again. Then she went back to sit in the chair and chatter away. The nurse whispered, 'How do you find different things to talk about?'

'Well, Lizzie, isn't it?'

'Yes, Sister.'

'Oh, Lizzie, call me Rosy, when we are not working, OK?'

'Oh, thank you, Rosy.'

'Well, in answer to your question, I don't. A lot is just repetition.' They both giggled.

'I admire you having the patience to sit there every day, plus, most nights. I wish I had someone I loved that much, Rosy. I heard your family are all going back home.'

'That's right, Lizzie, as Derek is stable and out of immediate danger. They all have lives to get on with, you know, their jobs and all. No point in all of us sitting around, plus Paul, the young soldier, has his leave.'

'Well, please don't think I'm interfering. I wondered if you thought of keeping you babies here with you. I could go to maternity, and they will lend us one or two cots. Also we could put you a bed next to Derek. As you will be looking after the babies, you will need to sleep a bit at least. Would you like that?'

'Oh, yes, Lizzie, I would love that. I hadn't even thought about it? Do you think the matron will allow it?'

'I'm pretty sure,' Lizzie smiled.

'What are you smiling at, Nurse Lizzie?'

'Well, Rosy, you see, I've already cleared it with her.'

Rosy looked outside the door; then gently letting go of Derek's hand, she silently walked to the door. Lizzie opened it, and there, outside, was one bed fully made up and behind that were two cots. The Matron smiled. As quietly as possible, they rearranged the room to accommodate the extra things. Rosy was so overwhelmed that tears were running down her cheeks. The matron looked at her and took her hands in hers. 'Listen to me, Rosy dear. You are very strong. But you do need proper sleep and then you'll be strong when that husband of yours decides to grace us with his presence when he comes around.'

Rosy looked up, smiling, and said, 'Yes, ma'am.' Both of them laughed. Just then, there was a tap on the door. She looked at her watch and exclaimed, 'Oh my goodness, is that the time?'

Lizzie opened the door to find the two mothers there. 'Hello, dear, are you OK?' Rosy's mother asked, as she put her arms around her.

Rosy hugged her and said, 'Yes, Mum, I'm fine. How's every one?'

'Oh, Rosy, will you stop worrying about everyone else? Please concentrate on yourself for once.' Lizzie and Elizabeth both agreed with her, saying, 'Your mum's right.'

She put her hands up and said, 'OK, OK, I surrender.' Rosy laughed.

'Well, what we came for was to just let you know that we are all packed and ready to go home.'

Eleanor said, looking around the room, 'Oh, two baby cots, all made up ready, and also a proper bed.'

Turning to Elizabeth, she said with a smile, 'I have a feeling we will be going home baby-less.' Then she pretended to be upset, but Rosy got all upset. So she said, 'Oh, sweetheart, we were only teasing.'

They all hugged together, and Rosy said, 'I love you, Mum. You too, Elizabeth.' They were all huddled together, laughing and sighing with relief. There were so many different emotions all at once. Just then, Derek gave a big grunt. Suddenly, all went silent. They looked shocked. They turned to face the bed and realised that, that was the first time he had made any sort of sound. Lizzie turned towards them, smiling, 'Well, ladies, he seems to agree with you.' Then seeing the shock on Rosy's face, she said, 'Hey, don't worry. That's good.'

Slowly realisation hit Rosy; that's the first sound he has made that didn't indicate being in pain. She broke free from the hug and ran over to his bedside. 'Oh, sweetheart, you are in there somewhere. I knew you were. I knew it.' Turning to the mums, who were still stunned, she beckoned them over to say their goodbyes. Suddenly, there was a knock on the door, and Lizzie opened it. Standing on the other side was a wonderful sight. There was Paul, a different Paul to the one she met that day at the station, when he bought her one and only love, back to her. She beckoned him over with a smile and said, 'Paul, he made his first sound that wasn't a sound of pain. We were hugging and laughing, then he grunted.'

'Oh, wow Rosy.' He turned seeing the cots. With the help of Nurse Lizzie, they gently placed one little one in each, and turning back, he walked towards Rosy.

Rosy said, 'Come here, hero. Give me a hug.'

'Oh, Rosy, I'm stuck for words.' Giggling a little and laying her head on his shoulder, she cried a little, 'Oh, Paul, he is in there. All the thanks goes to you, the captain, and his second officer.' She went quiet, too quiet. Paul pushed her gently away from him, and seeing the look on her face, he said, 'What is it, Rosy?'

'I was just thinking, Paul.' She turned away from him and going towards the window, she looked out, not really seeing anything. He went over to her and put his hands on her shoulders. He did not turn her, just letting her talk. 'Those poor men, the ones on the boat and maybe others, all died to save my Derek. Oh, don't get me wrong. I'm eternally grateful, but I don't understand why so much fuss was made to get him out.'

Her mother came over. 'Oh, Rosy, I forgot I have a message for you. An army general is coming to see you, later today. I'm sorry.'

'Well,' Paul said, 'there you are, Rosy love, may be you will at least get some answers.'

The mums said, 'We really must go or we will miss our eleven o'clock train.' Rosy went to them, leaving Paul, who had gone over to Lizzie as she was about to feed the little ones, asking if he may help for the last time before he goes on his leave and then overseas. 'Of course, you can.' They chatted while feeding and tending to the babies' needs. Seeing that he was happy, Rosy carried on with her goodbyes. Elizabeth came to her and said, 'Please phone us to keep us up to date, as we are going back to the estate soon, probably in the next couple of days, OK?'

'Elizabeth, of course, I'll keep you up to date, as soon as I know anything. I'll ring everyone.'

'OK, love, I'm off now. Tell your mum, I'll wait outside.'

Rosy went over to her mum, who was still sitting with Derek and talking to him. 'You OK, Mum?'

'Yes, dear. I'm fine. Just saying we will all see him soon.'

'Oh, Mum, you old softy, I love you.' Rosy hugged her hard and then said, 'His own mother didn't even do more than a peck on the cheek.'

'Well, darling, some people are like that because of their upbringing. Others just don't like sickness. Anyway, my love, I'm going to go now.'

Rosy said to her mum. 'Please give Dad a big hug and kiss, and my other baby JD.' They laughed. 'OK, you big softy, also please tell everyone thank you for all they have done, to help. Tell Susan I'll ring her later.'

'OK, darling, I will. Now you look after yourself. You'll be no good to that hubby if you get sick. OK, Mum, I promise.'

With that, Eleanor said, 'I won't go over there. Just give them both a hug from Granddad and nanny.' She looked over to where her mum was looking. 'I'm talking about Jessica and Robert.' They both laughed. 'Tell Paul he is welcome to visit any time.' Eleanor headed for the door after one last cuddle. Rosy opened the door for her and said a final goodbye to both mums.

Thirty-One

S everal weeks, almost a month and a half, Rosy thought, re-
entering her room, after having a well-earned bath, wondering
what today would bring. She saw Lizzie and Paul were sitting with
the babies and talking. He had his arm around her, and their hands
were entwined. They looked happy and content; it was nice to see
him happy. She decided to leave them alone. Well, he was at the end
of his leave. Rosy headed over to Derek and she sat next to him. She
gently picked his hand up to hold it and lay her head down next to
him, chatting to him, and in the end, inevitably, falling asleep. When
Rosy eventually awoke, it was late afternoon. She felt something on
her back and then finding his hand missing from hers, she gently
raised herself up; his arm slid into her hand, and she thought, *How
on earth did your hand get up there, sweetheart? Oh, I bet it was
Paul and Lizzie, thinking I'd like it.* She smiled to herself. It was very
quiet in the room, so the two of them had probably settled down the
twins and then decided to go out. Rosy was thinking this and walking
towards the cots, which had been moved to the other side of Derek.
There was a note on the end of the bed, and her thinking was right.
They had gone for a walk, and not wanting to disturb her, they just
left the note, saying they would be back by the six o'clock feed. She
looked at her watch; it was five to five. *Right I think . . .* Disturbing
her thoughts, there was a knock on the door. *That will teach me to
think*, she thought again, smiling to herself and going over to the door.
She opened it quietly, and then stepped outside, Neil was standing
there in a rather mucky, surgeon's gown. 'Hi, Neil.' Derek had been
there for several months, and Rosy hadn't seen much of Neil in those

months. He was busy, and also with her looking after the babies and Derek, most of the time, there wasn't time to meet. 'I'm sorry to ask this of you, Rosy. Can you give us an hour?'

'Oh, dear, that bad, is it? What's up? We need another pair of hands in surgery. The sister who was supposed to be on duty tonight, called in sick, also it's between shifts, so I cannot find a sister to help. A nurse isn't trained for what we need. I promise if another sister comes available, I'll let you come back.'

'Well,' Rosy said after again looking at her watch, thinking what it said in the note, it was now five twenty-five, 'OK, Neil, the twins will be OK for another hour or so. Just give me a moment.' She rushed to Nurse Penny, who was on duty at the ward, asking her watch over them and telling her what was going on. 'OK, Sister. I'll be happy to watch them babies. They are so well behaved, Sister Rosy.'

'OK then, see you in about an hour.'

Lizzie and Paul should be back before then. With that, Rosy rushed off with Neil. All was quiet in Derek's room. The nurse, as promised, checked about every ten minutes, peeping in the door and didn't open the door to wide, so as not to wake them. Not hearing anything, she went back to her duties. Just as Rosy had said, Lizzie and Paul, hand in hand, returned right at six. Penny explained what had happened. 'OK,' they said. As they were just about to turn away, Paul turned back to her saying, 'I wonder if you would do it again. After we have fed them and, of course, changed them and then settled them down again, that is. Of course, if Rosy isn't back by then. Would you mind?' He suddenly became very shy. Blushing, he said, 'It's just that I have to get the last train as my leave is over. I'm off to wherever the war is right now. I would like, so very much, to have Lizzie to see me off.' Grabbing Lizzie's hand, he continued, 'Also, Lizzie, I hope you would like to come to see me off.'

She said with a smile, 'That's fine. I'll be here till late anyway. I'm not one to stand in the way of true love. There aren't many patients in the main ward. Any way Derek's room is part of the ward.'

'OK, that's settled.'

'Now go. Go or you will be late.' With that, they went their separate ways. Lizzie said, 'May I feed little Robert. This time, of course, that means I get to feed the little princess.' Lizzie looked at him. 'Oh, Paul, you daft thing,' They both laughed.

'Well, then that makes little Robert a prince.'

'Mmmm, I suppose it does. Having got to know Rosy and all, I've been told about Derek.'

'Well, I think that is exactly how they will be treated. With that, they got on with preparing the bottles and then laying the nappies out.

Paul said, 'He doesn't even know he has two babies. The twins came as a surprise to everyone. Even Rosy and even the midwife apparently. She was really caught off guard. He was so tiny. He had been hiding behind his big sister.'

Lizzie replied, 'Oh how exciting and wonderful.' They carried on chatting, while getting on with the feeding and changing, and, of course, burping them. With all that done, they sat for ten minutes or so just to make sure they were settled. Paul also checked on Derek. He saw that he had all his tubes and wires, which meant he was breathing on his own. Just then, there was a knock on the door. Paul hurriedly went to answer it before whoever it was knocked again, maybe waking the babies. As he got to the door and opened it, there was a doctor, who had come to check on Derek. As he turned to the door to close it behind him, someone in the room said, 'Shut the door.' Looking at each other, they looked back at the doctor, saying that wasn't us.

'Well, folks, if it wasn't you and it wasn't me or the babies, that leaves us with only one person in the room, if I'm not mistaken.' Smiling at them, Doctor Trent, as he had introduced himself, went over to Derek. He examined him and saw that he hadn't come round, although it was a very good sign. It meant that he had maybe as much as 80 per cent or maybe even 90 per cent chance of coming around. 'With all of his faculties, when he came in, all those months ago in such a state he was in, I, well not just me, most of the medical staff, didn't give him even 10 per cent.' Paul was standing on the other side of the bed, and excitedly tried to say something. It came out all garbled. Lizzie went to him and held her hands.

'Now look at me. OK, take it slowly. That's it. Now what's got you into this state?'

'Haven't you seen it?' He said.

'Seen what, Paul?' the doctor asked, and Lizzie gave him the same questioning look.

'Look at him and tell me what you see.' They both stared at Derek, together. They answered the same, that they couldn't see anything wrong.

'No, not that there is something wrong. Look at his hands and legs.' Once again they looked; Paul couldn't wait any longer.

'Look, his legs have moved, so have his hands,' said Paul. Lizzie looked and said to the doctor. 'He is right, sir. His legs were straight. Now one is drawn up. His arms were also straight down at his sides, now he has one across his chest.'

'Well, Nurse, that's good, but how is it you didn't notice?'

'To be honest. I was looking at you in case you had questions.'

'OK, Nurse, that's fine.'

Turning around, Doctor Trent looked at Paul. 'You seem to have quite a rapport with this man. Is he a relative of yours?'

Paul looked at him with tears in his eyes. 'I wish,' and then he turned away. He couldn't talk.

Lizzie said, 'Sir, may I have a word with you, outside?'

'OK, Nurse.' They went to the door, and he opened it for the nurse, stepping out after her. 'Right, Nurse, how can I help you?'

'Well, sir, I thought an explanation was needed.'

'Well, it would be nice. I mean he said they are not related, and then added he wished he was. That intrigued me a bit.'

'Well, sir, it's like this.' Lizzie went on to explain repeating what Paul had told her and also adding what Rosy had told her – his background, the train, and getting Derek to hospital. 'Oh, sir, you should see him with the babies. He is wonderful.'

'Well,' he replied, 'with that background, I can see why he is so close.'

'Yes, sir, he adores the babies and Rosy. Also he respects her very much for how strong she is. Well, as for Derek, I've never seen such closeness between any one, let alone two strangers. Well, at the end of the day, that's what they were.'

'Yes, Nurse, I quite agree.'

With that, he took his leave, saying, 'See you soon.' He went off to attend to his duties. Lizzie just stood, watching him walk down the corridor and then turned to re-enter the room to rejoin Paul. She shut the door quietly and then turning around, she said, 'Oh, Paul, what have you done, my darling?'

'Well,' he said, 'I thought it would be nice with their gurgling and, of course, the crying may help bring him around. With his nature being the way it is, he would feel protective even if he doesn't realise straight away that they're his babies.'

'Oh, that's very nice, dear.' He had put the twins into one cot on the side of the arm that had moved.

'Oh, but, Paul, I'm not so sure. I don't think he knows he is a daddy.'

'Well, that would make him even more eager to protect.'

'Anyway, sweetheart, he does. He was to be a daddy. The thing he doesn't know is that he had hit the jackpot, getting two for the price of one.' They both laughed.

'I just wish he had come around before I go, so we could meet properly.'

'Oh, Paul, he will be fine as will you, and then, when you return, you can get to know him. Also he can get to know what a wonderful fellow you are, but then, I am biased,' she said, giggling.

'Oh, I love you, Lizzie. Well, anyway, that's why I have put them in one cot. I hope it won't be such a shock,' he said, smiling. 'A wonderful smile is better.'

'Paul, darling, it really is time to go.'

'Could you give me a couple of minutes?' Lizzie agreed, telling him she will wait outside and off she went. Paul went closer to Derek; he started talking to him. 'Well, mate, it's been really great meeting you. I know the circumstances could have been better.' He carried on, 'You are a really lucky guy, you have a wonderful wife, not to mention your family, not forgetting your newest additions. They all need you. Rosy does more than anyone. I also hear there is a four-legged friend who can't wait. Charm, isn't it? Well, he can't wait to relinquish the harness back to you. He has had enough of being the head dog. He wants to just be the pet again.' Looking at Derek's face, he was sure he saw a slight smile. 'Now you're out of any danger. I hope your mind will let you come back to them.' With that, he shook Derek's hand. 'I'm honoured to have met you, sir.' He stepped back, raised his hand, and gave Derek a salute, respecting his rank, as he was now in his own uniform. 'Well, I'll say goodbye. I'm off to do my bit for the country. I pray to God I don't, get any treatment like you have endured, sir.'

He looked in the cot, at the little ones; Jessie was awake. She gurgled at him. 'Yes, my sweetheart, your daddy needs you.' Just then, Robbie too woke and copied his sibling. 'OK, you too, buddy. Yes, daddy needs you too. Do as much gurgling as you like.' He bend down and he gave them both a kiss. He placed a note on the bed for Rosy, explaining what he had done. He then stood back, waiting to make sure they had nodded off again. He turned, tears rolling down his face, opened the door silently, and stepped through, into Lizzie's waiting arms. After he had pulled himself together, Lizzie said, 'Have you said your goodbyes to Rosy?'

'Oh yes, darling, I did that earlier.' Walking together arm in arm, heads held high, and both knowing each other was near to tears, they headed out of the hospital, making for the railway station. Fifteen minutes later, they arrived, both silent and not daring to talk, knowing what will happen, although inevitability, it had to happen. They slowly headed for his carriage, and as they arrived at the door, Paul was the first to speak. 'Lizzie, please look after yourself. I'll write when I can. Please could I ask you to do something for me?'

Lizzie knew exactly what he was going to say, but she let him finish with out interrupting him, knowing he needed to ask. He went on, 'Can I ask you to look after dear Rosy? I think she needs it, although she won't admit it as her family have gone home. She would also need help with the babies. Last of all Derek, I know he is your patient, but I had to say it.' After he had finished, she looked straight at him, saying, 'Yes, yes, yes, and yes, my love, I'll look after them like my family.'

He looked back at her, with tears in his eyes. 'Well, Lizzie, they are my family.' With that said, they grabbed each other into a hug, neither wanting to be the first to let go. After a couple of moments, the train whistle blew and the porter shouted, 'All aboard.' With one final kiss, he jumped onto the now-moving train. Lizzie waved even after the steam from the train hid his carriage. Then it had left the station, disappearing around the corner. Now that he was gone, she could cry, although there was no choice. The tears ran down her cheeks on their own accord. There was no stopping them even if she had wanted to. Pulling a hanky from her handbag, dabbing the tears, as they flowed over her cheeks, she slowly headed back to the hospital to start her shift. Just before exiting the station, she took a look at the very large station clock. Lizzie realised there was about half an hour before it started and decided to go for a cup of tea.

Thirty-Two

Rosy and Neil had finished in the operating theatre and were just cleaning up. When they were done, Neil asked her if she had eaten. Rosy laughed, replying, 'I don't think I've eaten all day. Oh no, tell a lie, I had an apple at breakfast time.' They both laughed at that.

'Well, my dear friend, you can't live on that. I haven't eaten all day either. I would be happy for the company. No fun eating alone.'

Rosy looked at him, ready to say, no, but changing her mind a bit, she said, 'I would be happy to eat with you, but, Neil, I have to get back to the twins. How about you find some food and bring it here? We can eat there if that's OK with you. I'll understand if you say no.' After thinking for a bit, he replied, 'That's fine with me. I'll go find some food and meet you there.' With that, off he went. Rosy walked on heading for Derek's room; she passed through the main reception area and turned her head to look outside. She realised it was getting dark, and then in the distance, they were heading for the station. Two familiar people were walking away from the hospital. It was dear Tannis; she thought to herself, *Oh, dear, dear Tannis, please come back to us.* With him was sweet Lizzie. *Oh, my friends, my heart goes out to you.* She stood watching until they disappeared into the distance. Suddenly, she wanted to talk to her parents, and she realised they must have just left the room. There were a few minutes. Heading to the sisters' office, she entered asking the sister on duty if it was all right to ring her parents. 'Of course.' With that, the sister, said, 'I have my rounds to do, so I'll leave you in peace.'

'Thank you, Sister.' With that, the Sister left the room, shutting the door as she went. She also put the Do Not Disturb sign up. Rosy made her phone call and talked to her dad first and then spent a good while talking to her mum, not about anything in particular, just needing to hear her voice. After hanging up, Rosy sat for a while and pulled herself together to be strong enough to go back to see her one and only love, the way he is. *Oh, it's so hard*, she said aloud to herself. *I think I should better get to the room. I am not sure how long Neil may take.* As Rosy approached the ward, Nurse Penny came over to her and said, 'I had checked a little while back, and Derek was the same. The babies were sound asleep. Everything was quiet.'

'Thank you, Penny.'

'That's OK, Sister, oh. . . Rosy.' As Rosy was just a patient's relative, she had told everyone to call her Rosy, as her surname was quite a mouthful. They walked together to the ward and then the side room, chatting, as they got there. Neil came hurrying along the corridor. He, as promised, brought a lot of food, and also a bottle. They greeted each other. Neil said to Penny, 'I'm about to try and make Rosy eat something. I keep reminding her she will be no good to that little family of hers if she goes down sick.' He continued, 'That's right, isn't it, Nurse?'

Penny agreed. She said, 'Yes, Doctor, you're quite right.'

They both looked at Rosy, who sighed, 'OK, OK, I surrender, I give in. I don't stand a chance against you two.' They laughed. Rosy, quietly as possible, opened the door; they were still chatting, and Neil headed straight for table to place the goodies down. He went back to Rosy and Penny. Penny said, 'Goodbye. I'll pop in before I go off duty.'

Neil had wandered over near the bed; he saw the note. He took it to Rosy, who read it. 'Oh,' she said, 'it's from Paul, you know, Neil, the young lad who carried Derek in.'

'Oh, yes, what does he have to say?'

Penny interrupted to say, 'Bye for now.'

'OK, and thanks again.'

'That's fine. Only too glad to help.' Then she turned and disappeared through the door, Rosy's attention returned to the note.

'Oh,' she said almost to herself.

'What's wrong, Rosy?' Neil asked. 'That he has gone off to fight, and Lizzie has gone to the station with him to see him off. He also says it was him who put the twins in one cot. He goes on to explain why.' Rosy walked over to the cot. 'Neil, look.' He moved over to her to see what had caught her eye. 'Neil, I think you had better get Penny back here. Nothing was said about that.'

'OK, Rosy.' Off he went to find her, leaving Rosy to contemplate what was right in front of her. A couple of minutes passed and then there were hurrying feet approaching the door. There was a light knock and then in rushed Penny and, not far behind arrived, Neil. At this point, the real facts hadn't crossed Rosy or Neil. Rosy was a bit cross; Penny hadn't told her. Paul stated both babies were in the cot. Penny slowly approached Rosy, feeling she was in trouble, although not sure why. 'What's wrong?' she asked looking at Rosy and then at Neil.

'Penny, when you checked Derek and the babies earlier, did you come right in?'

'Yes, of course, Rosy. I saw they were fast asleep in one cot. There was no change with your husband. Why are you asking me this? I did tell you.'

'That's fine,' Neil said, 'although we would like you to see something.' As they walked over, Neil asked, 'Has anybody else been in this room, since Paul and Lizzie left, besides you?'

'No, sir, just me. Why, you're scaring me.' They reached the beds. Penny, a bit puzzled at what she was supposed to be looking at, saw the baby in Derek's arm. 'Oh, what a lovely thing. A good idea, putting a baby in his arm. They look so content and hap . . .' Her speaking slowly came to a stop when it dawned on her that they thought she moved the baby.

'You didn't put the baby there, did you?'

'Rosy, no.'

'We thought you did, Penny.'

'No, I promise it wasn't me.' They all looked at each other in bewilderment.

'Well, it also wasn't Paul or Lizzie. They would have said so.'

Neil asked, 'Could he have done it but just forgot to say so in the note?'

'No, Neil, he wouldn't take the risk. You saw him with the twins. He dotes on them.'

'Well, OK, then how? Paul, Lizzie, Penny, you Rosy, and me didn't move the baby.' Looking again at Rosy, he said, 'Look, Rosy.'

'What do you see, Neil?'

'Well, the baby isn't just lying there in danger of rolling off. Derek's arm is around it. I can't keep calling it baby. Which one is it, Rosy?'

'It is Robbie, Neil.'

'OK, Derek's arm is right around little Robbie.' Turning away from the beds still chatting and wondering how, Penny said, 'I'm sure nobody else entered the room, although the sister was around. I'm sure she didn't do it. I'll go find her and ask her.' Penny reached the door, then turned and said, 'What if it wasn't her? We know it's not us.'

'We will sort it out,' Rosy said. After Penny left, Jessie started to get restless. She looked at her watch and said, 'Oh, here we go. Feeding time.'

'Oh, OK. I'll help you, then we can eat. Is that a deal, Rosy?'

'Sounds like one to me,' she said, smiling back at him, and then right on cue, the little lord and master Robbie started to gurgle. 'I'll get him. If you get my little baby girl.'

'Yes, Rosy.' He turned to go pick Jessie up. He suddenly stopped.

'What's wrong, Neil?'

He whispered, 'Come here, Rosy, quick.'

She rushed over to his side. He couldn't get the words out, so he just pointed. She looked up to where he was pointing. Just then, Penny came rushing back in. 'Rosy, the sister didn't.'

'That's OK, Penny. I have realised that the sister didn't do it. I think I know who did.'

Penny was puzzled; Penny followed to where they were looking. She gasped loudly at what met her eyes. There were both babies on the bed. Robbie still in Derek's arm, and Jessie was now with them lying half on his chest and half on the bed.

'Oh my' was all Penny could say.

'I quite agree, Nurse,' said Neil, agreeing with her. 'If I hadn't of seen this, I wouldn't have believed it.'

Rosy was listening to them and, at the same time, moving towards Derek quietly as the babies had gone back to sleep. She gently took his fingers and just held them. She was perching on the edge of the bed. Following her lead, Neil sprang back into doctor mode, taking hold of his free hand to check his pulse. He was then about to use his stethoscope. Suddenly, he stopped. In a slightly slurred voice, Derek said, 'It's OK, little ones. Please don't cry.'

'Did I just hear that? Did you hear it, Rosy?'

Stumbling over her words, she said, 'Eh, yes, if you did.'

'I did, Rosy. I did.' As he was about to move closer, he saw something. 'Rosy, look.' Rosy looked, and at the end of the bed, Penny started crying, looking at Derek's face. There looking back were those wonderful eyes Rosy had fallen in love with all that time ago, while feeding the ducks. Lost for words, tears started rolling down her cheeks. All she could say was 'Hi'. Slowly the words started to come between sobs.

'I knew you were in there somewhere, my darling.'

Neil said, 'Sorry, Rosy, to interrupt. I'll examine him later. We will leave you alone for a while. I'll be around outside if you need me.' With that, he turned beckoning to Penny to follow him, and they left. They were just staring at each other, as he didn't speak. Rosy started to get worried that he didn't recognise her like back in the emergency room, when he was admitted, in July. Now it was November. She started to weep again; she let go of his hand and Rosy pulled a hanky from her pocket. Derek got agitated. Although still slurring, Rosy listened closely to what he was saying. 'Please, please, Rosy, darling, don't leave.'

'Oh God, sweetheart, you do remember me. I wasn't really sure you would, as when you were bought here, you didn't.'

Slurring again, he asked, 'Whose babies?'

'My darling Derek, whose do you think?' She smiled at him and he smiled back. She did not want him to talk too much, in case it tired him out.

'Well, my darling, let me introduce you, the little one in the crook of your arm is Master Robert Gilbert Derek Rook-Leigh and the one attached to your side is Miss Jessica Rosy Rook-Leigh.'

It seemed like forever before it sunk in. Slowly, his empty arm raised, and she looked at his face. Seeing the smile with the tears on his cheeks, Rosy rushed around to the other side of the bed and climbed into his open arm.

'How?' he asked; they both laughed.

'I didn't know until I went into labour. I gave birth to our little girl. Although she was not so little, the midwife, was checking and cleaning her up when I cried out as I had another labour pain. Bubs there was handed to the mums as the midwife turned her attention back to me. Before she had time to get a towel or anything, the lord and master slipped into the world. Everyone was shocked. He didn't cry at first. He was a lot smaller than Jessie, and the midwife worked on him. Then suddenly, he let out a lovely long scream. It then turned into crying. Well, that's the short version.'

Slowly Derek said, 'I remember meeting you, then marrying you, but I don't even remember you being pregnant.'

'Don't worry, my love, it will come,' Rosy replied, kissing him on the cheek. That's where they stayed and after a while they fell asleep.

Thirty-Three

Lizzie had been sipping the same cup of coffee for nearly an hour, and tears were slowly subsiding. She reached for her hanky in her handbag and started to dry the last of them off her cheeks. She looked at the time and then thought, *Come on, Lizzie old girl, pull yourself together. Others need you. He will be back. I know he will. He has to keep his promise, that we will marry.* While they were saying their goodbyes at the station, as Paul had climbed on to the train reluctant to let go of her, she was just as reluctant to let him go. He suddenly threw his bag aboard the train. He had turned and he had jumped down and rushed over to her. 'Paul, your train, what . . .' he shut her up with a kiss.

Then he had said, 'Shut up a minute.' When Lizzie had begun to bluster about him and his train, he had said, 'Please, I don't have long, so hush for a minute.' He had put his finger to her lips and said, 'Let me say what I want to say.' Looking into each other's eyes, he had taken her by the hands. 'Look, Lizzie, I know we haven't . . .' the train whistle blew . . . looking at the guard, he had turned back to Lizzie. 'Oh where was I? Oh yes, well, we haven't known each other that long . . .' whistle again more urgent this time.

'Paul, what is it you're trying to say?'

He had looked up and then back at her. 'OK, here it goes, Lizzie. Will you marry me?' he had blurted out. This was the last thing Lizzie had expected. Paul had moved towards the train as the last whistle blew. 'All aboard,' the guard had shouted. He got to the train, still holding her hand. 'Lizzie, Lizzie, quick.'

'Yes, yes, yes, Paul, I will marry you,' she had shouted tearfully as the train started to move. Their hands had slipping apart. Over the sound of the train engine, Paul had shouted, 'I promise when I come back.' He had ended it with 'I LOVE YOU, LIZZIE.'

Lizzie had shouted in return, 'I LOVE YOU TOO, PAUL.' Then there had been the hissing and hooting from the train. The train, with him on board, had disappeared through the smoke. In that few minutes, Lizzie's life had been totally turned upside down.

This morning I was just Lizzie. Just another single nurse who worked hard. Now she was almost Mrs Lizzie Tannis all because of those few tiny minutes, she thought. With a big smile now on her face and feeling a bit brighter, she finished her coffee, shuddering, *Oh, yuck, that's cold.* She laughed to herself as she got up and headed back towards the ward. On the way back, she thought, *This is the happiest I've ever been.* Five minutes later, arriving at the ward, she thought, *I'd better let Penny know I'm back before I head into Derek's room.* Penny was right up at the other end of the main ward. When Penny saw Lizzie, they walked towards each other and met at the nurses' station. 'Well,' Penny said, 'did he get off OK?'

'Yes, he got off OK. The train was on time, although neither of us wanted to let the other go.'

'Oh, Lizzie, I'm so sorry. He will be back, you'll see.'

Lizzie replied with a smile, 'Yes, I know, Penny. He has no choice.'

'What do you mean, Lizzie?'

'Well, he has a promise to keep.'

Penny looked very puzzled. 'Oh yes? What's that?' Penny asked.

Lizzie turned to look at her friend and then answered, 'Well, he asked me to marry him.'

Penny squealed. 'Hush,' Lizzie said, laughing. Both the girls put their hands to their faces, trying to hide the excitement and also so as not to disturb the patients.

'Oh my goodness, what did you say, Lizzie.'

'Well, what do you think I said?'

'By the look on your face, I'd say you said a great big yes.'

'You're right, Penny. I said yes.' They started walking to the doors together.

'Oh, I'm so happy for you, Lizzie.'

'Well, anyway, Penny, how have Derek and the babies been?'

'I've stuck my head in a few times. It was all quiet. There was one mystery. One of the babies was apparently in his arms when Rosy came back. I was summoned and asked if I had done it. Of course, I hadn't. They knew you or Paul hadn't, as Paul left a note, saying what he had done with the cot. I was then sent back to work. Doctor Tranten was with Rosy.'

Oh how odd, Lizzie thought. 'OK, thanks for telling me. I'd better get back in there. OK, Penny, thank you again. I'll see you later. Bye for now.'

'Bye, Lizzie. Yes, see you later.'

Lizzie heading back to the room. *Well, it seems there was quite a mystery. I wonder if it has been solved,* she thought to herself. On reaching the room, she put an ear to the door. It was silent, very quiet. *I'd better enter quietly,* she thought as she pushed the handle and entered. She turned again to close the door just as silently. It was dark, except the full moon was shining. She tried to adjust her eyes to the darkness in the room. She headed to the opposite direction of the bed and pulled a curtain across the room. Then she put a light on, knowing it wouldn't disturb Derek and the babies. Of course, she did not know what was really going on. She sat down at the small desk and then pulled Derek's notes, checking for the last time if his checks had been done. To her horror, it looked as though they hadn't been done since *I went to see Paul off. Oh dear, oh dear, I'd better do them. Let's see. Only one set of checks is missed.* The last bit she said aloud. Picking up her stethoscope and walking around the curtain, she didn't turn on the lights thinking maybe the moon will be bright enough just for his pulse and listening to his chest. As Lizzie went to walk past the door, there was a tap on it. On answering it, Penny popped her head in, saying, 'I'm off duty now. Would you like a hand with the twins?'

'Oh, that would be nice. They must or will need feeding soon.'

'I'm just going to check Derek now. Babies must still be over his side of the room.'

They both headed over to the beds were the moon was shining. When they got near, they looked at each other. Another step forward, they both gasped loudly, putting their hands over their mouths, then really taking in what they saw. 'Penny,' Lizzie whispered, 'please go get Doctor Tranten. He should still be on duty.'

Penny didn't need asking twice, she was through the door almost before Lizzie had finished. Lizzie wasn't sure what to do. Even she couldn't move to do whatever, that's how Penny found her. Five minutes later, she came rushing though the door, closely followed by Doctor Tranten who was just about to leave for home. 'What is it, Nurse?' he asked Lizzie. 'I was here earlier. Things seemed to be fine.'

'Well, sir, I'm not sure there is anything wrong in the true meaning of the word. It's just . . .'

'Oh come on, Nurse, spit it out. Why are we whispering? Also why is there no light?'

'Oh, sir, look.' Neil walked right over to where Lizzie was standing. When he got there, he was so taken aback that all he could say was 'Oh, OK, Nurse, I see your dilemma.'

'What should we do?'

'Well, Nurse, I'd say nothing. Do nothing. I think Rosy has everything under control,' he said, guessing what had happened. 'Although if the babies cry, for what ever reason, if you can, before they wake Rosy, perhaps you could see to them so they can stay asleep a bit longer.'

'Sir, do you think maybe he has come back to her after all this time?' Penny asked.

'I'm not certain, but after what happened earlier, I'd say there is a jolly good chance. Well, you two, I am going home now. I'll pop in as soon as I get here in the morning.'

'OK, sir.' He left with a great smile on his face. Short time after, Lizzie said, 'Penny, you should go home and get some sleep too.'

'OK, Lizzie, I will. You sure you will be OK?'

'Oh yes, that is one thing I'm sure of.'

'OK then, I'm off. Yes, it's so great after all these months,' Penny said, while exiting the room.

The twins started getting restless about four in the morning. Lizzie managed to get Jessie off Derek into the cot. Robbie was a bit harder as Derek's arm was more over him. Slowly she eased him out; instantly Derek's arm went to Rosy, who responded by getting closer. Lizzie just stood quietly, not sure she was seeing what she was seeing. She thought to herself, *I didn't believe in miracles until now.* She pulled the cot away, back around the curtain.

'OK, my little ones, you have met your daddy it seems. Right, who is first?' Robbie was wide awake, and Jessie was still half asleep. 'OK then, little buster, you're first.' The feeding and changing was just finishing, about the same time as the hospital was coming to life. There were lots of crashing and banging and feet rushing about, seeming louder as it echoed around the empty corridors. A while later, as promised, Neil popped in. 'Hello, Nurse, you still here?'

'I am due to go off duty at nine,' Lizzie replied, 'but I'd like to wait a while to see where everything stands. I saw to the twins without disturbing their mummy and daddy, and I also thought about waking Rosy just before you came in. I looked at them again and then decided, they looked so peaceful. I didn't have the heart.'

'That's OK, Nurse. Let's see those wonderful babies.' With that they headed behind the curtain. That's where they were, and half an hour later, they heard a voice panicking, 'Where are my babies?'

They both got up to investigate. The call came again, as they got there. Rosy had woken. 'It's OK, my love. I'm here. It's Rosy.'

'Oh, Rosy, Rosy, where are the babies?'

Just then Lizzie appeared with Neil right behind and they looked at Derek.

'This is Nurse Lizzie. You get to call her Lizzie. Behind her is Doctor Neil Tranten.'

'The babies?' he asked again.

'It's OK. I have just fed and changed them. They are just over there, behind the curtain, as I didn't want to disturb you and Rosy. Derek, would you like me to get them?' replied Lizzie.

'See, sweetheart, they are just over there. How about we leave them there for a little while? Do you think it will be OK, Derek?' Rosy realised that he was a bit disorientated. A lot had happened in just a couple of minutes. Rosy climbed off the bed, walked around to her friends and looked at them. 'This is an official introduction. Is that OK, Derek?' She looked at him and said, 'OK, Neil, Lizzie, my dear friends, this is my wonderful husband Derek.'

Neil looked at her. 'Yes, Neil, he is back. Just a bit of memory loss. He remembers meeting me and marrying me, although he doesn't remember me being pregnant. Oh I have an idea. First say hello to Derek.' They both said hello, and to their surprise in a broken crackly voice, Derek replied, 'I'm very pleased to meet you both. Thank you so much for looking after my dear Rosy.'

Neil looked at Rosy. 'You had an idea.'

'Well, it is just another question on something that happened between wedding and being pregnant, OK?'

'Rosy, give it a go.'

She walked around to be nearer to him. Then she sat on the edge of his bed and took hold of his one hand; the other hand was too sore to reach over. Neil took that in as something to check. He thought to himself, *Oh, Rosy, you are so clever, doing a certain amount of checking without him realising.* That way he doesn't get too stressed. Rosy and he swapped glances. He nodded to let her know he knew what she was up to. 'Right, here we go now, my darling,' Rosy started. 'Do you remember us getting married? Do you remember anything about our honeymoon?'

'Some I think,' he stated.

'OK, do you remember why it was different?'

'I think so. Didn't it end up as two. The first part was at the seaside. I can't remember places or names easily,' he stammered.

'That's fine, darling. You just say what you can remember.'

Neil interrupted, 'Are you sure you can carry on?' 'Don't get too tired.'

'It's OK, Doctor. I'm all right.'

'You call me Neil, Derek, OK? And I'll carry on calling you Derek.'

'OK, Doc . . . Neil.'

'Would you mind, while your thinking and talking, if I give you a short examination?'

'No, Neil, that's fine.' Neil pulled out his stethoscope and started with his pulse. He proceeded to gently prod and poke him about.

'Rosy, do you think I could have a drink?'

'Oh goodness, of course, you can.'

'I'll go and get it,' Lizzie said. 'I'll check on your babies while I'm there.' In return, Lizzie got a wonderful smile.

'Farm,' he suddenly said, and they all looked at him startled.

'Yes, Derek, a farm, yes, a farm but we didn't stay there, did we? We just visited. Yes, darling,' said Rosy, coaxing him along.

'You fed a lamb who wouldn't let you go,' he started laughing and then coughing, just as Lizzie got back with his drink. Rosy helped him have a drink. 'The babies,' he spluttered.

'They are fine, Derek. Just fine and sleeping.'

'That's right. The lamb fell asleep on you. I think we went back to that farm, basket with a bow,' he said with a deep frown on his face.

Rosy said with a laugh, 'Yes, you're right. A big bow.' They all laughed.

Neil said, 'Sorry, but I have to do the harder bits now.'

'What does he mean, Rosy? The harder bits?' Rosy began to explain, and Neil bent over, whispering in her ear. 'I don't think he knows how badly he is hurt.'

Rosy looked up at Neil and shook her head. 'He doesn't, Neil.'

'Rosy, I'm scared. What's going on?'

'It's OK, Derek. It's OK,' Rosy answered, trying hard to placate him. He was really scared; he was trembling badly, and there were tears in his eyes. All of a sudden, there was a loud noise from the corridor. A tray or something similar had dropped. Derek screamed so loud, 'No, no more, please no more, please, sir, no more.'

He started sobbing, and his hands went to his head covering as if he was being beaten. He went to get out of bed before anyone could stop him and fell to the floor, and then scrambled under the bed. This all happened so fast that all three of them – Lizzie, Rosy, and Neil – were so shocked.

'Neil, what just happened?' Rosy asked him, knowing he had been fighting in the war until he was injured enough to be sent home.

'Rosy, I'm not completely sure. Well, he seems calmer now, albeit under the bed.'

He gently pulled the covers off the bed; he didn't want to get too close. He just let them hang. Derek pulled them under on his own and then Lizzie did the same with a pillow. Neil started to back away very slowly so as not to scare him, and the two ladies did the same.

Neil looked at Lizzie, telling her to just watch that he doesn't do anything to hurt himself. When they reached the desk, OK doctor, moving over a bit, that way Derek shouldn't get any more agitated, placing herself, were he couldn't see her, Neil carried on talking to Rosy. 'I have never seen anything like your man's injury's, or knew of anyone else who has been through anything like what your poor chap has been through. What I think happened was when that noise in the corridor echoed around, it took him back. I'm going to inform all the other doctors that he is awake. They will want to check whatever injuries they are responsible for.' He picked up the phone. Rosy looked at him, silently, with unstoppable tears running down her cheeks. 'Who are you calling, Neil?'

'Well, Rosy dear,' He started dialling, Rosy look at me, 'please, please, Rosy, come here.' He finished dialling, and by then, Rosy was next to him. 'Do you trust me?' He lifted her face so they were looking eye to eye. 'Yes, Neil, you know I trust you with my life.'

'Well then, dear Rosy, please trust me now. Hold on,' he said. Whoever he was calling must have answered. She left him to his phone call. Rosy decided to check on the twins as feeding time was not far away. It felt like her autopilot had been turned on. Rosy turned. Now everything was ready for feed time, so she walked to Lizzie and said, 'It's OK, Lizzie. You're officially off duty, aren't you?'

'Yes, Rosy, I am.'

'Well, off you go.' She hugged her and said, 'Thank you, dear Lizzie, for all your help and everything you have done. We'll see you later when you're back on duty.'

'Rosy, how about I take the little ones, feed them, change them, and give them the much-needed fresh air?'

'Oh, Lizzie, I don't know. You need to sleep. I can sleep when they sleep. It will give you one less thing to worry about for a few hours.'

'I really think you need to concentrate on Derek. He needs you now more than the twins, at this particular moment in time.'

'OK, OK. I give in,' Rosy said, smiling at Lizzie. 'Thank you, my dear friend. Luckily my parents bought the pram when they came. It's in the storage cupboard, down by the sisters' room.'

'OK, Rosy I'll sort it all out. You go and look after that handsome husband of yours.'

After Lizzie happily left with the twins, all their stuff packed neatly under the pram, Rosy's attention went wholly on to Derek. Hearing Neil hang up the phone and not wanting to talk to him at the moment, Rosy quickly and quietly went to the bed. Just then, Neil started to speak. 'Rosy, the psychiatrist is . . .' Then he saw he was talking to himself. He turned around just in time to see Rosy disappear around the other side of the beds.

Oh, Rosy, he started thinking, *what are you up to? Well, you know your husband better than any of us. You really do seem to have a strong bond, like your parents told me.* He waited; it was quiet. He went behind the curtain, expecting to find Lizzie. Not only was Lizzie not there, the twins were gone. He realised what had happened. *Oh well, there is no getting her away from Derek now.* Moving over to the side, he got a drink of water and then sat at the desk. There was no way he was going to leave her alone. Even though Derek's love for her was deep, with what he had been through, well you'll never know. That's where he was when the psychiatrist arrived; he entered the room. They greeted each other. 'Thank you for sparing some of your precious time, Trevor. I know you're very busy. Would you like a cup of tea first?'

'No, I'm fine. Thank you, Neil. I would have been upset if you hadn't of called me. I heard about this case, and I was also hoping to be called in on it. 'OK now, would you like to fill me in? I take it you are his doctor.'

'Yes, I am. Well here, Trevor, are his notes.' Neil handed him the notes and then stood waiting for his reaction. When no reaction was forthcoming, he gathered from that he hadn't read the full name. Trevor took the notes and studied them thoroughly; Neil looked at him, saying, 'What do you think?'

'Well,' started Trevor, 'I take the plate in his head is permanent. Have you managed to save all his limbs? What about the burns? Is this right? Oh my God, is what it shows here, right?'

Neil looked to where he was looking. 'Oh yes, Trevor, all too real.' They had started to fester the heat had got to them and god knows what else may have entered the open wounds. 'Who knows how long the poor bloke was drifting about? He will have scars that we hope some will fade in time. Let's hope enough so the shapes can't be seen.' He looked at Trevor. There was shock on his face. 'You look like how I did when I and the Sister had first seen him.'

'Oh dear, I bet, Neil, I'm not sure I could have handled it.'

'But, Trevor, you don't know the worst of it.'

'There's worse than this? You have got to be joking. Please tell me you are kidding.'

'Oh no, Trevor. I'm sorry to say I'm not joking. You remember I said there was a sister with me.'

'Yes, Neil, I remember,' he replied, really confused. 'Well, is it your practise not to read patient names? Doesn't the patient's name ring any bells. Think our hospital staff.'

As Trevor looked again at the notes, he exclaimed, 'Oh my God!' He staggered to a chair. After sitting, he repeated himself. 'Oh my God! You mean, you're telling me about dear Rosy? Oh jeez.' Putting his hand to his head, 'was the one with you?'

'Wow! Clang the penny finally drops. While working on him with me, she didn't realise until we got him here. He got nasty with her at first. She was wearing her uniform then and he didn't know about her profession. He did keep calling her name, and no one could control him except one person.'

'Who, Neil? The porters?'

'No, the one dear soul who had carried him. It was not a deliberate choice. He just happened to be at the right place at the right time. He was just the driver who was to drop them off at the station, a very young soldier about to go on pre-embarkation leave before being shipping out to God knows where to fight. His name was Private Paul Tannis. He carried Derek to the car to take them to the railway station and to bring him here.'

'You said "them", Neil. Who else?'

'The captain and his second in command, the ones who found him.'

'Oh yes, I know that part well.'

Neil started again, 'As they were driving, he slowed down when the patient cried out. He stopped the car, and he told the captain.' When Trevor looked at Neil, with that 'I don't believe you' look, Neil laughed, 'Oh yes, he told the captain to move so the patient can lie on his lap as the bumps were putting him in a lot of pain. It didn't stop there. When they arrived at station, he wouldn't let the porters wheel him. He carried him, and he gave up his leave to travel with the patient in his arms. In the end, no one else could get near Derek. If someone tried to, he would thrash about, so every time he needed moving, for whatever reason, there was only one person. He even carried him from the train to the exit. You know how far that is. Well, this young private picked him up, walked right across, through the crowds, to the ambulance. They offered to help him in, but he refused this time. It was him when we arrived here. He again carried him in there and didn't leave his side. He tried once and that's when the bit with Rosy happened. Once he saw him into the operating room safely, he chased after Rosy. He held her together, and then when the family arrived, he held most of them together until they came to terms with what had happened. Oh, there was one joy for Paul.'

'Oh yes, what was that, Neil?'

'Well, I suppose you could say the little ones helped a lot of us – babies, Rosy's and Derek's babies. They have twins. Well, I'm going to stop for now,' Neil said. 'I think you know enough to go with.'

'I do have a couple of questions. First, how is Paul? Does he need any help?'

'I hope not. He left for fighting the other night.'

Neil replied, 'You mean Derek hasn't even met him properly?'

'That's right.'

'OK, how about, does Rosy react around him? Does her reaction worry you?'

'No, just the opposite. They really do seem to have something. A connection none of us would understand. I'll tell you what, come with me.' As they walked, Neil added, 'Rosy seems to instinctively know what he wants. He is the same with her, I have been told.' When they got to the bed, they were awake, just talking, crying, and then crying with more talking. Neil said, 'Hello, you two. How are you feeling now, Derek?'

'Oh, apart from the obvious on the outside,' he said grinning.

'Oh, Derek, you are daft,' Rosy exclaimed.

'My dear Rosy, that's fine. It's good to hear him being jocular. This is a friend of mine Trevor. He is a doctor too.' He looked at Trevor who was shaking his head.

Neil guessed he didn't want them to know he was a psychiatrist, at least for now. 'I'm very pleased to meet you both. You, sir, are a very brave man.'

'Also very lucky to be here right, Neil?' Derek added.

'Yes, Derek, very,' he said as they chatted. What even Neil didn't know was Trevor had asked someone to make a loud noise outside in the corridor. Going by what Neil told him, he wanted to see just what Derek's reaction was, just as Trevor had arranged right on time was an even louder noise. Derek sat bolt upright, the fear showing on his face. He went to get out of bed. Neil moved to go to him. Trevor put his hand across him to stop him. He turned, saying, 'Why, Trevor?'

'Something you said about them having this connection. If I remember correctly by now, last time he was huddled under the bed.' Angry now, Neil looked at his friend. 'No, I meant why, why the noise in the first place? I don't know about poor Derek running for cover. Half the hospital has probably taken cover, thinking we are being attacked. It was stupid and thoughtless.'

'My dear friend, Neil, have you finished blustering?' Pointing he said, 'Look.'

Turning, Neil, looked where he was pointing. His jaw nearly hit the floor. 'I am not sure I believe what I see,' he carried on. 'This is so wonderful.' There, on the bed, was Derek still sitting, and Rosy had cupped her hands around his face, making him look into her eyes.

She was staring into his and very quietly whispering, 'Derek darling, I know you can hear me. It's your Rosy. Do you trust me?'

'Yes, Rosy. I trust you.'

'With your life?'

'Yes' came fast.

'OK then. Now listen to what I say. Try and take it in for me, sweetheart.'

'Yes, Rosy,' he said in child-like voice.

'Right. Here we go. You are OK. With me, you're safe. No one, or anything, will ever, ever hurt you again. You're back with us. That is where you belong and also were you are going to stay.' This slowly slipped into his poor head. *I'm safe with my Rosy.* Then tears started. 'No one is going to hurt me ever, ever again.'

'That's right, Derek.' She slowly gave him a kiss, and then her hands released his face. She half expected him to bolt under the bed; he didn't. He just shuddered and then looked at Neil, who was speechless. He shook himself saying, 'Yes, Derek, how can I help you?'

He realised Derek was asking him something. 'Is it true, Doctor, I'm going to be OK? Please tell me whatever I need to know. I'm ready to hear it.'

'Eh, hmmm,' Neil started to splutter. 'OK, Derek.' Before he started, Rosy got up and said, 'I'm going to get us all a drink.'

'Not for me,' Trevor said. 'I'll take my leave. We will speak later, Neil, OK? Bye for now. Bye, every one,' he said as he exited the door.

'OK then. Just us three. Hot or cold first, Neil? What would you like?'

'Oh, I'll have whatever you two are having.' Just as she went to move, Derek grabbed her hand. She calmly turned to look at him. 'Now listen, my love, I'm just going to get us a nice drink. Neil will be here, is that OK?' she said, trying to reassure him. *How on earth do you reassure someone who is so scared?* thought Neil. To his surprise, Rosy had done it just in those few words. Slowly pulling her hand free, she said, 'You OK, Derek? You understand where and what I'm doing?'

'Yes, Rosy, you're going to . . . umm oh. . . I know, get a drink,' he said, proving his short-term memory was back. Then Rosy moved to the door, waving as she left. 'Right, Derek, let's have a bit of a chat. Is that OK?'

'Of course, Neil. How long have I been here?'

'Oh, OK, let me see.' He looked at the notes. 'From the date you came in, it's been about sixteen plus weeks.'

Derek looked at Neil. 'That's over four months. Oh God, that's a long time.'

'Yes, it is, but the good thing about that is, it allowed you to heal fully. Have you been told about your wounds?'

'No, Neil, I haven't. I know this arm is painful.'

'Well, Derek, you had a very bad head injury. We have had to put a plate in it. That's just about healed. It did have to have a drain in as it had so much muck in it. Not surprising considering what you went through. Then being at sea all that time.'

Though he was hesitant to ask, Derek finally plucked up the courage to ask, 'OK, that's my head. What about my legs?'

'First of all, Derek, can you remember your chest and back?'

'No, I don't remember. Rosy made me look. They will hopefully fade what's left of the scar. I'll just have to come to terms with them. My legs, Neil, please tell me. OK, your right leg was very badly crushed, by being. . .' Neil hesitated.

'How, Neil, tell me.'

'. . . Stomped on over and over. It looks like a whole troop of soldiers continually marching over it. Although we did manage to fixed the inside bones, the open wound was another problem altogether. The skin had died a lot around the two open wounds. That had to be cut away and then what we did was we patched them. Once they were sewn up and bandaged, it was down to prayers. With a lot of luck, now they are just about healed, and stitches came out a while ago.'

'OK, that's my right leg, what about my left?'

'Just one more thing, the right will probably give you a fair bit of pain. Now on the left leg, every toe on that foot had been smashed. Toes have to heal best they can on their own. There are some scratches and bruising, a couple of burns, nothing too serious.'

Derek was quite for a long time.

'Are you OK, Derek?' Neil asked concerned. 'Who else from my crew came home?'

Not sure he was ready for the complete truth, Neil then thought again, *I want him to trust me. I'll have to.* Slowly Neil went on first to tell him about Gill and the rest of the crew. It was only Gill that got hurt really; the others had a few cuts and bruises. 'All in all, you did well to get the aeroplane down as well as you did. Oh yes, your bosses said to tell you when you woke up, your mission was a success.' And then what he was hoping wouldn't happen did.

'That's good, Neil, isn't it?'

'Yes, very good.' Then suddenly Derek said, 'There's a name missing. Yes, a name . . .' Slowly something slipped back into his mind. 'My babies' names.' That's when Neil knew he was remembering Rob but left him to work it out. 'My little princess is Jessica and my son is Robert. Why does that sound familiar?' He became silent again. 'Oh my God, they shot him. They really and truly shot him. Executed him.' He burst into tears. 'Oh God, I think I saw it. They tied him to a pole and just shot him. Seven soldiers just shot him. He fell to the ground, and they just left him there.' Neil moved nearer to him to comfort him a bit. 'It's OK, Derek. You're not to blame, they are.'

'But I should have done something.'

'What could you have done? Chances are you would have been shot too. Have any other memories come back?'

Derek looked at him with a 'what do you mean' look on his tear-stained face. 'Of you and Rosy. You said you remember meeting her.'

They hadn't heard Rosy come silently. She stood at the listening. 'Yes, I can remember the wonderful wedding we had, with a horse-drawn carriage too. What about the honeymoon? I think I remember walking and being in an old farm kitchen. A bird I think called Corky. That's right Corky.' They both laughed.

'Oh yes, there was also a beautiful baby lamb. Yes, it sat on Rosy if I remember it right. Rosy fed it. Oh how could I forget those three.' Neil looked puzzled, while Rosy, behind the curtain, smiled. 'Three,

three, what, Derek, let me think. There was JD, Badger, and then the other one had a funny name. Rosy named it.'

'Oh, that's lovely. Derek, what are JD and Badger?'

Derek suddenly said, 'I think it starts with a Z. Oh, they're puppies. I know it begins with Z or Za.'

Rosy came out of hiding. 'Yes, darling, you got the names right. The third you're trying to remember is Charm.'

'Oh yes, I remember now. Well, Rosy, how is he doing?'

'He is doing very well. It sounds as though you heard some of it.'

'Yes, I did. Sorry, Derek. Would you like to tell Rosy that other thing you remembered or would you like me to while you have a rest?'

'Yes, I'd like a rest if you don't mind, Neil.'

'No, that's OK. Is there anything you want before you rest? I'd love my cup of tea.' They all laughed. Rosy went to get it as she handed it to him. He grabbed her free arm and kissed her.

'OK, darling, you have a rest. Please don't leave me.'

'I won't. I'll be just over there.'

'OK, sweetheart.' He watched her every step, till she pulled a chair, so he could see her. He relaxed, drank his tea, and then lay back. After pulling one of the babies' blankets out of the cot, Rosy and Neil spent the next hour talking. He told her what Derek had remembered about Rob, even about what happened to him. As they finished, a voice called, 'Hey, Neil, can I get up?'

'Yes, of course, you can, but Derek, you have got to learn to walk again. Also you legs will be very weak. You will need help and aid, and then when you're more confident, a walking stick. That I'm afraid, you may have to use always.'

'No way.' Then realising he sounded harsh, he made a joke of it. 'I'm not having my babies grow up, saying "Oh, Dad, I'll take your walking stick away."' All of them laughed. Both Rosy and Neil knew as soon and the way he said it, he will never use a stick if he can help it. They both went to him. He had somehow managed to get up, and turned to sit on the side of the bed, Neil went to the side with the worse leg and placed an arm under both of his arms; Rosy asked him if he felt OK. 'Not dizzy or anything?'

The reply was a very strong 'No'.

Rosy and Neil looked at each other, both thinking, *Would he tell us if he did?*

'Oh well, here we go,' they said together, lifting Derek into the standing position.

'OK,' Neil said, 'get your balance. Tell us if you feel dizzy or there's a lot of pain.'

'I'm OK. Let's get on with it,' Derek said, smiling.

'Remember, put your better leg forward first.' He managed a few steps around to the other side of the bed.

'That's enough for today.'

'Oh, I wanted to walk properly.'

'Listen, Derek,' Neil started as he and Rosy lowered him on to the bed, 'you must think. You haven't been on your legs for a long time, let alone walking on them. You may feel OK right now, but later on, it may be a different story.'

'What do you mean, Neil?'

'You may have some pain.'

'OK, OK. You know best. Anyway, I'm off to do my rounds. I'll leave you to it. I'll try and come by in the morning.'

'That's great.' Neil walked to the door with him.

'Bye, Derek.'

'Bye, Neil.'

Rosy opened the door. Neil asked, 'Will you be OK, Rosy? What about food, if he won't let you leave him?'

'Oh well, we will just have to starve.' He looked at her concerned. 'I'm joking, Neil. I bought some food earlier, when I got the tea.'

'OK then. I'll see you in the morning.'

'All right,' she said and then kissed him on the cheek, saying, 'Thank you. Oh, Neil, will he need to go to Trevor's clinic?'

'No, Rosy, not unless Derek feels he needs to.'

'Thanks, Neil. You know we have family living just around the corner. I know we can't go home yet as he still needs to see you.' He stopped her.

'I know what you're going to say. Well, by what I saw today, maybe the weekend. No promises. What you must understand is he must come in every day for physiotherapy. I also insist he uses a wheelchair between here and there and no stairs.'

'OK, Neil. Thank you again. Can I tell him, maybe give him his first step to aim for. Yes, you can tell him with everything else I said.'

Rosy said with a laugh, 'I don't relish the wheelchair bit.'

He laughed back, giving her a look that said, 'No wheelchair, no getting out.'

'That's fine. I guess we will see you in the morning.' With that, he headed off down the corridor. Rosy closed the door and went straight back to Derek's.

'Are you hungry, darling?'

'Hmm, I am a bit.'

'OK, I'll get you some food.' He started to panic, although Rosy knew why. She had to make him tell her. 'What's wrong?'

'Please don't go out of the room.'

'It's OK. I bought some food earlier. OK now, I'm just going over there.'

'Can you pull the curtain back?'

'Yes, OK, I will, but, sweetheart, keep telling yourself you're safe. You do know you're truly safe, don't you?'

In a 'not quite convinced voice', he said, 'Yes, Rosy. I know.' After they had eaten, they lay together in each other's arms, kissing, and then gradually, they fell asleep, although not before they told each other, 'I love you.'

Thirty-Four

After just over eight weeks, Rosy, Derek, and the babies, went home, as now he had been discharged from hospital. Derek was now an outpatient, reporting every other day for plenty of physiotherapy for his legs to help him to walk. He also had the same for his arm. He had to give in and agree to use a stick for a while, as Rosy exclaimed to him, 'At least, you're alive. A few months back, well, you nearly weren't.' Turning away as tears threatened, she said, 'I think, sweetheart, a stick, for a little while is a small price to pay.' He came up behind her and putting both arms around her.

'OK, my darling, I surrender,' he said, laughing and turning to face him, Rosy slapped him on his chest with nappy she was holding. 'Derek, it's not a joke.' Nearly crying, he pulled her towards him, kissing her. Up till now, there was no inclination to go further than kissing. Rosy turned, carrying on with her clothes folding. He went to sit down. 'Well, how did the hospital visit go?'

'Oh, OK. I now have my stick, my new little friend.' He wasn't really thinking about hospital, what he was thinking was something entirely different. In fact something he hadn't thought of since the honeymoon. When they kissed, he felt urges, a very urgent need. 'Rosy, where are the babies?'

'Out with your auntie and uncle for the day. Why?'

'Oh, so, the house is empty then.'

'Yes, darling, why?' She turned and walked over to where he was sitting with a pile of nicely folded washing that she was about to put away.

'Oh, I just wondered,' he said, rising from the seat. He stood blocking her way.

'Hey, you, could I please come past sir?'

'You cheeky monkey,' he said as he grabbed the washing and chucking it on to the chair.

'Oh, Derek, it's just taken me half an hour to fold that lot.'

'Stop moaning.' He laughed as he said it, pulling her towards him. He started kissing her gently on the lips, slowly moving to her neck, his hands wandering. When Rosy could get free to breathe, she said, 'Oh, Derek, are you sure you're ready?'

'Oh yes, Rosy. I'm ready, OK. You don't know how much I've missed you. It hurts.' He held her close feeling her and leading her to the bed. He sat her gently down on the edge of the bed. Rosy pulled him down as he was still standing between her legs, kissing the top of her head while pulling her blouse off over her head. While undoing his trousers and putting her arms around his waist, she said, 'I love you so much, Derek. I really thought I had lost you as my sense of you stopped.'

He buried his face in her hair as he replied, 'That must have been when I lost my memory.'

'Oh God, Derek, we came so close to losing each other.' He now urgently pulled his trousers and underwear down. Quickly he stepped out of them and she held him in her arms, kissing and caressing his fast-growing manhood. Suddenly, Derek cried out, 'Ahh, oh, Rosy, I'm sorry.' He lost himself into her skirt.

'That's fine, darling.'

'Ooh, Rosy, that feels good.' As he finished, his pushed her back on the bed and took her soiled skirt off, throwing it on the floor. He did the same with her underwear, and he lay next to her, running his hands over her soft skin, until he found the part he was looking for. Her back arched as his hands played. Rosy lay there, eyes shut, moaning; her hand found him again and she turned to face him. They kissed softly to start and got more and more urgently. Before he could do anything, Rosy had pushed him on to his back; she lay on him, still kissing, and slowly, he entered her. Halfway through, he rolled her over, as they were coming to an end. They started crying with the relief. They were relieved he was safe and the fact they were back together. When they had finished, they stayed in same position, just rolling on to their sides, still holding each other tight. Sighing with the fulfilment they felt, they kissed each other. 'Rosy, how long before the hoard comes home?' He laughed.

'Not for at least two, maybe three, hours.'

'Good!' With that, he fell into a relaxed sleep for the first time, since he came home. Rosy, seeing him in a calm sleep, followed him. About an hour and a half later, Derek started to wake. Seeing Rosy lying next to him, he just watched her sleep, slowly just running his hand down her arm. He pulled back the covers and his hand went further down. Rosy stirred a bit, turning over so her back was to him. He cuddled into her. Her hand came back, pulling him closer. He lay there, enjoying the smell of her hair. While doing that, he could feel himself getting aroused. As he didn't want to wake her fully, he turned over the other way, and as he tried to move, her hand got tighter. Having no choice, he stayed. They dozed off for a while and then Rosy shuffled once again. He got aroused, and he moved closer and gently he entered her from behind. As he did so, Rosy let out a cry, 'Oh, that feels nice.' As he was able to go slower this time, he could bring her to a gentle climax. He carried on to his climax; he also managed to make her climax again. Exhausted again, they fell asleep. An hour later, they suddenly awoke when they heard voices and the shutting of a car door. Feeling like a couple of kids, they shot out of bed, laughing, 'Stop it, Derek. Just get dressed.' She was laughing just as hard.

They dressed just in time, as they were being called from downstairs. Just as they were finishing making the very rumpled bed, giggling, they grabbed each other's hands and then proceeded to run downstairs, where they were welcomed by their uncle, who had just made some fresh tea. Once all were sitting, Derek suddenly stood up and Rosy looked at him, wondering what on earth he was doing. 'Well, everyone together, including my beautiful wife and my wonderful pair of trouble in my daughter and my son, anyway, I have something to say that not even Rosy knows yet. I have a piece of paper here, well, two really. This one has given me freedom from the hospital.'

Rosy jumped up, hugging him tight. 'Well, now I wonder what this one is. He was showing the top it was from the air force.'

Rosy jumped back, exclaiming, 'No, no! They can't have you again.'

'Hey, sweetheart, please sit. I can then read it out.'

'Well,' his aunt said, 'tell us.'

'I'm also free from the air force. I have to report, sign some forms, and so on.' Rosy just sat there, not quite being able to believe it. Suddenly, after all these months, never knowing what was going to happen next, even if there was a future for the two of them, things finally seem to be working out. First Derek had managed to make love to her, and hen in just two letters, the future was there. She could see it; tears were rolling down, first silently and then with great big sobs. 'Oh, I'm sorry. What a birthday present! I have you back 100 per cent.'

'Your birthday?' Uncle asked.

'Oh yes, it's my birthday today.'

'Really, why didn't you tell us?'

'Oh, I didn't want a fuss.'

'Oh OK.' About an hour later, they had tea and had cleaned up, Rosy appeared back in the lounge to feed the babies. The other three were whispering. Pretending not to notice, she just walked straight to the twins. By the time she turned to go back to the sofa, they had sat down.

'Derek, sweetheart, who do you want to feed?'

'Me?' He was all emotional now as he hadn't fed them yet. 'You sure that I can do it, Rosy?'

'We all have to learn, Derek.'

'I know. I also know they're my babies, but I'm terrified of them.'

'Why?' his aunt asked.

'I'm so scared of hurting them as they are so small and fragile.'

'Oh, mate,' his uncle started, 'agreed they don't bounce, but then again, on the other hand, they don't break easily. Give it a go. You have to sometime. Rosy can't always do it. I'll tell you what, you pick who you want to feed. I'll feed the other one so Rosy can go have a bath.'

Rosy looked at them. 'That would be nice,' Derek said. 'Auntie, you could go too. Leave us men to it, OK?'

'You two, who wants whom?' They both moved to sit on the sofa. 'Well, guys?' Rosy asked.

'Rosy, why doesn't Derek start with baby Jessica, as the little lady is just a little bit bigger than Robbie?'

'Auntie, that's a good idea,' agreed Rosy. The decision was made, and Rosy picked up little Jessie and moved over to the sofa. She looked at her husband, trying to read his thoughts. He was scared. Anyway, firmly but gently, Rosy went ahead lay her into his arms. He really was overwhelmed, then she handed him the feed. While she had being doing that, Auntie had been doing the same with the little man and uncle. Then off the ladies went to have their time. As they were leaving, Auntie tapped Rosy, saying, 'Look.' Rosy looked, and there was her dear Derek. He had gotten Jessie to take her bottle. While feeding, he was talking to her, 'Well, my little girl.' Looking next to him, 'I include you too, little man. I'm home now forever. I'm yours. I've had surprises before, but I think you two were far, far the best than anything else.'

'Do you know, lad, that you are the luckiest bloke? I know you have a beautiful wife, two gorgeous kids.' Uncle was saying to Derek.

Rosy and Auntie headed for the stairs. As they climbed them, Auntie asked her, 'Well, young lady, how old are you today?'

'I'm twenty-one, Auntie.'

'What would you wish for if you could have anything?'

'To be honest, everything I wished for over the year I have. I have my wonderful husband back from the dead, the icing on the cake is that he is not just back, he is fit. I know he will always have that plate in his head and maybe a limp, and he still has bad dreams at night and sometimes, flashbacks after hearing something or smelling something. I am able to cope with them, with him. It's the connection we have sometimes. I know before he does.' They both laughed.

'Well, all I can say my dear Rosy is thank god for that connection however it works. I know this sounds selfish and maybe unpatriotic, but I don't care. It got him out of the RAF. He gave it everything. Look what it cost him. That's not selfish. You also have been to hell and back, dear Rosy. What are you going to wear?'

'Oh, the only dress I've got with me is a bit worky.'

'Well, I think I have just the thing. Your mum left it for you when she was here, knowing you weren't ready to think ahead.'

'Look in your wardrobe's top shelf. There is a box, OK. I'll see you later dear.'

Rosy gave her a cuddle and a peck on the cheek. Two hours later, after bathing and doing her hair, nails, and a touch of make-up, she went to retrieve the box she had laid on the bed. On opening it, she found Derek's favourite pale blue dress inside that her mother had packed. Now Rosy realised there was new pretty underwear, stocking, and even a lovely pair of shoes. At the bottom of the box was an envelope with her name on it. Taking it out and then sitting on the bed was a beautiful birthday card with a message from her mum. It said, 'Dear Rosy, if you are reading this, I guess all is well. I do hope you like what has been put with it. I had help choosing this as young Francis helped me. Well, I couldn't really take your dad or brothers.' Rosy giggled at that, and the note went on 'You will find another envelope in one of the shoes. Take it out.' It was just as if her mum was there, sitting next to her.

'OK, I take it you found it. Well, open it.' Inside, Rosy found a little felt bag. On opening it, she found a key. The top of the key was a slightly funny shape. Also, it was very old. Placing it back in the pretty little bag, she returned to the letter, hoping it might explain the key. 'Now, Rosy, as you can see, there is one more package. Go ahead and open it.' She did as she was told. There, inside, was money, quite a lot. Then she back to the letter. 'That, darling, is from everyone as everyone chipped in – your brothers, Derek's family, even Francis oh, and also Susan and Gil, who are now married and expecting their first baby. Francis and Duncan are engaged. Anyway, back to you two. Go downstairs and look in the pot on the hall table. It goes with your present from dad and me.' Rosy said to herself, *Mum, you have done more than enough.* 'I know what you're thinking. *Mum you've done enough.* Well, darling daughter, please just humour me for a bit longer. Oh by the way, please don't unfold the bottom when you find what's in the hall, it is your present, but I need you to get Derek to walk to front door and open it. That's very important, OK? Don't forget.'

OK, Mum, I won't forget. Odd, she thought, *my mother is very odd.* Anyway, smiling to herself, Rosy stood up and got herself dressed. When she was ready, she picked everything up and slipped everything but the letter into her handbag. As she reached the top of the stairs, to her surprise, Derek was there. 'Oh my darling, you look . . .'

'Well, spit it out, lad.' Uncle spoke from the bottom of the stairs.

'Oh, well, I'll say it. You look fantastic. Yes, Uncle is right. You look gorgeous. May I escort you downstairs?'

'Yes, my darling, you may.'

As they walked down the stairs, he whispered, 'What's that?' he asked, referring to the letter.

'It's from my mum. I have a lot more bits in my bag, a bit of news. Well, two bits really. First, Gil and Susan are married now with a baby on the way.'

'Why so quick?' Then it suddenly it dawned on them both.

'Oh dear,' they giggled, and they looked at each other. 'Oh, what a naughty pair!' they whispered to each other so auntie and uncle couldn't hear.

'Go on. What's the other bit of news? Well, your little sister is not so little anymore.' He looked at her frowning just as they reached the bottom. They turned to face each other. 'What does that mean, honey?'

'It means your Franny is without doubt Francis.'

'Oh God, you don't mean, she is like Susan.'

'Oh God, no, my love, but she is engaged.'

'What? Who?'

'To my brother Duncan. Do you remember him?'

'Yes, he is the younger one, yes?'

'Yes, my love, he is.' She stepped over to the hall table.

'What are you up to, Rosy?' He turned to look at his aunt and uncle, who were holding a baby each, so they wouldn't miss out.

'Well, you're a lot of good,' he said. They were just standing there with big grins on their faces; they knew all Rosy knew plus one other thing that even she didn't know. Looking at the table, all it had on it was a vase with a little card placed in front of it, saying 'Tip me up to see what's up.' Rosy did as it said; Derek repeated what the card said, 'I didn't think I could get any more confused. Please, Rosy, my love, what on earth is going on?'

'You know, just about all I do, Derek, sweetheart,' she said, giving him a kiss. Out dropped a key with a card attached. 'Another key? What do mean another key?'

'Hmmm, I'll explain in a moment.' On the card was written, 'Pass me to Derek.' Rosy passed it to him. It read, 'I belong to Rosy, but the surprise on the on other side of door is for you both. It is mainly for our dear son in-law. Go on and open the door.'

He looked at Rosy. 'Well, darling, you have been told to go on and open the door.' Rosy remembered the folded bit of letter. She decided not to unfold it yet, wanting to share with Derek. Walking to him, she said, 'Tell you what, you open that side, while I pull open this side.'

Looking back, she asked, 'Is that OK, Aunt and Uncle?'

They said, 'Yes, go ahead.'

'On three, Derek, OK?'

'All right, Rosy. Here it goes. One, two . . .,' said Rosy.

Then Derek said, 'Three' and they pulled opened the door wide.

Rosy screamed and ran straight into Paul Tannis's arms. Derek just stood for a moment with a puzzled look on his face. 'I know that voice. I'm sorry I can't place your face. You see I was hurt. I remember some things.' Rosy was about to introduce them, but Paul looked at her and then whispered, 'Is it OK if I do it? Let him just think I'm a friend of the family, doing them a favour.'

'That's OK, mate. We will chat in a minute. First of all, though . . . that', turning and pointing, 'is what that key in your hand belongs to, my dear. I played chauffeur,' he said laughing. 'I'm the rest of the letter, but in a moment OK, Rosy? I have something very important to do.'

Derek was still standing there, looking a bit confused and trying so hard to remember. He then got cross with himself when he still couldn't remember. Paul moved over to be closer to Derek, away from Rosy. Derek looked at him, and Paul smiled and winked. 'Watch this,' he whispered to Derek. 'You'll realise why I moved back.' Derek looked at him saying, 'It's not going to hurt Rosy, is it?'

'No, not in the way you mean. I wouldn't hurt anyone. You could go be with her if you would like,' Paul replied. They looked at each other. 'No, it's Rosy's day. Let her enjoy whatever you have up your sleeve, OK?'

'Paul, carry on,' a smiling Derek told Paul.

'OK, here we go. Rosy, could you get me something from the car?'

Rosy went to open the car door, calling over, 'What is it you want, Paul?' He pretended as though he didn't hear. While waiting for a reply, Rosy grabbed the door handle and tugged at it, not fully opening it. Then turning to look at Paul, who still hadn't replied, she asked, 'Well, chauffeur, what exactly is it that you would like out of th . . .' That's as far as she got. She still had her back to the car. There was an almighty shove, nearly knocking her off her feet. She just managed to keep her balance. One mass of fur and paws came bursting out like a cork out of a champagne bottle. In one great explosion, 'Oh my God! Hi, guys,' There, in front of Derek, they sat themselves, but Derek was a bit confused. 'Oh, you poor thing,' she said, as she walked up to him, smiling. 'I think introductions are needed. OK, guys, you three. Stay seated. Now, my love, this wonderful handsome canine here is Charm.' He sat right by Derek with his head leaning on his leg. Derek was smiling. 'Well, he must be ours. With a name like that, you must have named him,' Derek said grinning. Rosy grinned back and said, 'Hold your hand out like this.' He bent over and Charm placed a paw in his open hand and gave him a kiss on his cheek. 'Now this daft thing is Badger.'

'Yes, Rosy, doesn't he belong to your mum and dad? Then if I remember right, this must be JG, no JE.'

'Oh no, it's JD. He belongs to my side of the family. If I remember, we allowed Francis to take him on with his everyday care and to properly look after. That's fantastic, my love. Now why don't you two go into study?'

Paul started to speak, 'Dear Rosy, these are yours.' He picked up her left hand and gently placed the car keys into the palm.

'What do you mean?' Rosy looked up from the keys.

'Well, this message is for you both to listen to, OK? Shall I join you both in the study?'

'Yes,' Derek answered, 'please come.' He found Rosy's hand and held it tight. Although enjoying the fun, he was feeling a bit overwhelmed. Rosy picked up on this, and when he grabbed her hand so tight, she said, 'OK I'll come. Let's go I'm all excited.'

On the way, they passed by the babies being fed by Rob and Dora on their sofa. Paul saw them, went over, and said hi to Rob and Dora, and then he crouched down, taking a little hand into each of his, as if no one else was in the room, or he just didn't care who heard his such soft gentle voice, and started to talk them. 'Hello, you sweet little ones, Have you been good for your mummy and daddy?' He looked at Derek and then said, 'You're a lucky man, Derek.' Derek thought he was going to say being married to Rosy. No, he went on sort of into a world of his own. Rosy mouthed silently so that Derek, Rob, and Dora knew not to worry. 'It's a memory. I'll explain later.'

'I bet you were surprised when you found you had not just got your beautiful little princess Jessica, but you had the prince too. Such a lovely little guy Robbie is. What a wonderful thing to wake up to.' Derek went into proud daddy mode, still staying quite though he felt Paul didn't need his comment just now, Paul sighed pleased he hadn't confused Derek any further, forgetting Derek wouldn't know, how well he knew the babies and Rosy as he got up gave them both babies a kiss on their hands, then their heads. 'Well, I'm sorry, little ones. I have to go right now,' he whispered. As he was doing this, he remembered that Rosy wouldn't have told them his story yet. They reached the study and closed the door behind them. 'Would you like some tea, coffee, or anything?'

'No, thank you, Derek. I'm fine.'

'Have a seat, Paul. It is Paul, isn't it?' There was a long silence, while Rosy and Paul looked at each other and then at Derek's back as he wasn't facing them.

'Yes, Derek, Paul Tan . . .' that's as far as he got, then Derek turned to face him.

'Paul Tannis. Private Paul Tannis.'

'That's right, Derek. Do you remember how we met?'

'I'm not sure. I can't remember very much till I came to in hospital. The state I was in, I think I must have gone through my own war.' They both laughed. 'I think, Paul, there is one thing. I think you were supposed to . . .', he went silent for a few seconds, 'have been going on leave before going overseas. Was that right?'

'Yes, Derek, that was right.' Paul took the chance hoping it wasn't too soon. Although, as he had been worried, he had gone to the hospital first, as he wasn't sure if Derek was out yet, he quickly found out he was not an inpatient anymore from the main reception. He thanked the receptionist for her help, and as he started to walk away, trying to think what to do next, he heard a voice coming from behind him. He turned to look, and he suddenly saw Doctor Neil as had all started to call him, while Derek had been in. He was rushing down the stairs. They greeted each other. 'Oh, it is you, Paul. Are you hurt?' he asked, looking him up and down, with a worried look on his face.

'No, Neil, I'm fine. I came to see Rosy, Derek, and their babies. Oh also, of course, to see my Lizzie.'

'Oh yes, a little birdy told me that the lovely Lizzie has agreed to marry you,' Neil said. 'There really is no accounting for taste.'

'Oh, thanks very much, Doctor,' he said, smiling. 'Well, at least, I'm getting married,' Paul replied.

'Touché nice. Come back, Paul, but seriously, let me fill you in on your favourite little family.' They both smiled, he went on to tell him as much as he could, without breaking doctor/patient confidentiality.

'Anyway how come you're home?'

'I was sent home on army business. I'm hoping to stay with the war seeming to be coming to an end, I'm keeping fingers, well, everything crossed,' he said laughing. 'I won't go back. I guess you by now when I left I had asked Lizzie to marry me. I feel so lucky with her accepting.'

'That's fantastic, Paul. When will the wedding be?'

'Oh now that I'm not sure, as Lizzie has agreed to wait, until a certain person remembers me as I would like him to be my best man.'

'Oh well, good for you. That's great, Paul. Congratulations to you both. Most of all, be happy.'

'Thank you.'

'Oh look at the time. I'd better go. I'll see you soon, Neil. Oh by the way, Neil, where are they were staying?'

'It would help, wouldn't it, Paul?' They both laughed. 'They're staying at his Aunt's place around the corner. Remember where you all stayed before?'

'Oh right. Thank you for your help, Neil.' They shook hands and then went their separate ways. As that went through his head, he looked at Rosy. 'Just as she said, that is great, darling. Another memory back where it belongs.'

'Yes, yes, Rosy,' he said absent-mindedly. Again Paul and Rosy looked at each other. He said quietly, 'Shall I carry on, Rosy?'

'Yes, Paul, please do.' Before he could, Derek suddenly started to mutter to himself. Gradually he got louder. His muttering started to become words, not any sort of order. 'Pain, car, lorry, and then a couple of names Lynette, Pierre, pain, fishing boat, bullets flying every where, so much pain, box no a trunk thing. Oh God, I was in it. This trunk thing. Noise so much noise. Shouting, stamping, the bullets passing through just missing me. Navy boat, a captain and lots of dead bodies, train, car, Tannis.' He was getting agitated. Rosy went to go to him. Paul pulled her back. Looking at Paul, who said, 'You could, Rosy, although I think it maybe better to leave him for now. If it gets worse, I'll go to him. If he stops now, he may hide the memories never being able to bring them back to talk about them. Not doing this now could then affect him for life. I know you're right, Paul. It's just so hard to sit when the one you love is in so much distress.'

Rosy just stood staring. 'Paul, I think maybe if I left the room, he might open up and let go a bit more. I think he is holding back so as not to scare me.'

'OK, Rosy, we will do the rest a bit of the letter later.'

With that, Rosy left the room. A few hours later, Paul found her sitting at the kitchen table with a cup of tea.

'Oh,' he said, 'anymore in the pot?'

'Oh yes, of course, Paul. I'll get you some.'

'Hey, that's OK. I'm a big boy now. I think I can manage.' That made them both laugh. He sat opposite her, taking her free hand. 'Is he OK, Paul? I was scared to ask.'

'Yes, Rosy, I think he got most of it out. That will help him hopefully. Now he remembers he can start to slowly come to terms with it. I filled him from where I came into it. He does have a psychiatrist, doesn't he?'

'Oh yes, of course. He sees him most days. Although when I spoke to Neil the other day, he gets in there, he ceases up. It's not that he won't talk. It's that he just can't. He tries so hard that he ends up in tears every time. Consequently, he gets angry and frustrated with himself. He doesn't mean to. He has started to take it out on me.' Rosy told him.

'Has he hit you, Rosy?' Paul asked, sounding very concerned and grabbing her other hand. He looked into her eyes.

'Oh, Paul, no nothing like that. He rushes off and then goes for a walk. I leave him. He then comes back later. To be honest, Paul, even if he did, I wouldn't leave or retaliate. He doesn't need any more stress. Also it's not his fault. Sometimes I find him on our bed either asleep with a baby on either side, or he would be talking to them. I just walk away as he often looks a lot calmer afterwards. By the way, where is he, Paul?'

'He is OK. He is sleeping peacefully. I stayed a few minutes to make sure he looked so much more at ease and more comfortable and at peace with himself. Well, let's take this opportunity to sort this other thing out,' he said, smiling.

She grinned, 'Yes, let's do that.'

'Where are the babies? It's awfully quiet.'

Rosy replied, 'They are probably at the shops by now with their great auntie and great uncle and the dogs too.'

'OK then, let's get busy. You should have two keys by now.'

'Yes.' With that, Rosy laid them on the table in front of her. 'This one you gave me, and this one was in a present I opened earlier just before you arrived.'

'OK,' Paul started, 'that one I gave you with this one.' He placed it on the table. 'They both belong to the car outside.' Rosy looked up at him with tears in her eyes.

'Yes, it's yours. It's from your mum and dad and Duncan and Susan. Bert helped too.'

Hearing the name, Rosy butted in, 'Is Bert home too?'

'Yes, Rosy, he came home about three weeks ago. He is OK. About the car, I helped too. I asked if I could be the one to bring it. I'm glad you did, dear Paul. Look at what you have accomplished.'

'So am I, dear Rosy. Anyway about the other key. Again there are two keys. At the moment, your in-laws have one. Well, are you up to a two-hour drive tomorrow as it's Sunday? More to the point. Do you think Derek would be?'

'Yes, of course, I will be OK,' said a voice from behind them.

She asked, 'Oh darling, are you OK? Would you like a cup of tea?'

'Oh yes, Rosy, I would love one.' Rosy went to get up before she could. Paul beat her to it.

'You OK, mate?'

Derek nodded, saying, 'Yes, Paul, I'm very OK.'

'Thank you, Rosy. Why don't you fill him in, while I make a fresh cuppa? One thing though, will your aunt and uncle be OK looking after the twins tomorrow or will you be bringing them? Oh and what about the hounds?' They all laughed.

'What do you think, my darling Derek? You would know better than me.'

'Oh come on, Rosy my darling, you'll have trouble trying to take them.'

'Oh, I think we can ask them one more time.'

As that was said, they entered the room. 'Did we hear our names being taken in vain?' Everybody laughed.

'Oh no,' Derek started and then Rosy took over. 'We were just wondering if you would mind looking after the twins again tomorrow?'Rosy had barely finished when the pair said together,

'No, no, we don't mind.' Then uncle said, 'I have two more days off. It's also off season. It will be no trouble. Why? What are you doing?'

Rosy replied, 'We have to go for a drive in our new car.'

'Lucky you,' said Auntie. 'A ride? Where to?'

'Oh, Derek and I don't know where. I have this key. I have no idea what it's for.' Auntie looked at Paul who winked.

'Oh well, you all enjoy. The kiddies will be fine as will the trio.'

Paul asked, 'Where are the dogs?' It was Auntie's turn to wink, telling him to come with her with her. She put her finger to her lips. He looked around the door, and there he saw a wonderful sight. The sleeping twins between two pillows, and on one side, there was Charm and on the other was JD. At their feet was a curled up, Badger. Everyone joined them to have a look. As they moved, Derek noticed Paul had tears in his eyes, just like him. Wondering why, he recalled the story Rosy had told him. Rosy went on telling what was happening, and as much as she knew. Only Paul knew that the two of them already knew. With that, Auntie and Uncle excused themselves and then went off to bed, with the three of them following, not long after. Rosy, Paul, and Derek woke early, eager to get going. Well, Rosy maybe a bit earlier. They crept out, not wanting to wake anyone. The three of them couldn't stop giggling, feeling like naughty children creeping out when they had been told not to. As they knew where they were going, Paul drove on, and two hours later, they pulled up outside a beautiful large thatched cottage. They got out of the car and stood staring. Derek held Rosy's hand and looked at her, whispering, 'Why are we here?' A few seconds, maybe a minute, passed, and suddenly Derek started to speak. 'Hold on a moment. Hold your horses.'

Paul was waiting for the penny to drop. Paul said, 'OK, we are holding our horses.'

Rosy laughed, 'Yes, darling, we are holding our horses. I recognise this. I fell in love with it when I was a toddler.'

'Oh, Derek, is this the place you told me about?'

'It feels like a lifetime ago. A memory, a very, very large memory from his childhood. It's on my parents' land, but it's in the middle of a wood.'

'Oh, Derek, these trees you can see from the farmhouse lounge?'

'Yes, my love, they are.' He was still not sure why they were there; they both turned to Paul who was about to say sorry for interrupting. They asked him why they were there. 'OK, the reason . . .' trying to stretch it out.

'Oh, Paul, come on,' he said, slapping his arm playfully, 'tell us. Oh, oh, I give up. Two against one is not fair.'

'I agree,' said a voice behind them. They turned, and there was Lizzie.

'Go on, Paul, you tell them before they burst or attack you,' Lizzie said, laughing contagiously.

After a few seconds, they were still laughing. 'OK, OK, quieten down,' Paul said. They turned back to Paul, wondering what he was about to say.

'Well, we are here today . . .'

'PAUL,' they all shouted.

'All right, enough! It's all yours.'

'What? What do you mean it's ours? I mean exactly what I said. It's yours – lock, stock, and barrel.' Looking at each other, Derek and Rosy slowly moved to the door. Before entering, they both turned to Paul who was now arm in arm with Lizzie.

'But how, Paul?' Derek asked.

'It apparently has always been yours for when you got married. Do you remember it being built, Derek?'

'Yes, sort of. I was very young. Do you remember your parents asking you if you would like to name it?'

Slowly Derek said, 'Yes, I think so.'

'Well, do you remember what you said?'

'Not really.'

'Well, you said, ROSY'S cottage.'

When they said, you mean Rosy, you said, 'No, there's not just one Rosy, there are loads. A child's logic.'

'Is that true?' Rosy asked.

'Yes, Rosy, it's very true,' said a voice, appearing from the trees. It was Derek's mum and dad well.

'Son,' his father said, 'it's all yours. With you lovely little family, we don't know what to say. Thank you doesn't seem to cover it.'

'Oh stop it, you have us all blabbering in a moment,' his mum said, holding one of his hands and one of hers. 'Look at me. You have both been through enough. Now go and enjoy.'

Off they went, hand in hand, to explore and make plans.

Thirty-Five

Well, there are the memories. It's been three months since Derek had been discharged from the hospital, but with orders, from Neil, to go for his therapy at the nearest hospital to where he lives. Neil had become a great friend as had a lot of the dear staff. They had left his aunt and uncle's place, packed the dogs, babies, and all their luggage into her wonderful car. They had let Paul drive for now until Derek was ready. Then they had also moved into their little cottage on their bit of land. Paul and Lizzie are married, and Susan and Gil had a baby girl (no surprises for them). Everyone else is getting on with their lives. Paul, Susan, Gil and Duncan, who is engaged to Franny, have become godparents to Jessica-Marie Rosy Rook-Leigh and her lovely baby brother Robert Gilbert Derek Rook-Leigh, although he is known affectionately as Robbie. He and his sister Jessie are growing up fast as they do and they are almost a year old now.

The End?

Lightning Source UK Ltd.
Milton Keynes UK
UKOW03f0016141014

240060UK00002B/79/P